Flirting at the Funeral

Chris Keil

Cillian Press |

First published in Great Britain in 2012
by Cillian Press Limited. 83 Duice Street, Manchester M1 2JQ
www.cillianpress.co.uk

ISBN: 978-0-9573155-0-1

Cover Design: Roshana Rubin-Mayhew

Published by
Cillian Press – Manchester - 2012
info@cillianpress.co.uk
www.cillianpress.co.uk

Love and thanks to:

Ruth, Tom and Elin; Martha Caute, Edward Bates, John Gibbs and Peter Mitchell; John and Nicky Moxham for their beautiful house in rue Jean Riboult, and Catherine and David Devons for theirs in IPR; the brilliant team at Cillian Press; João David Nunes for expert knowledge of the music scene and wonderful hospitality; Karen Ardouin for master-classes in film-making; Ceri and Gaabi at Americymru; London and Lisbon: places and people that breathe fire into life.

Best wishes
Chris Kerr

Chapter One

. . .

Something was coming down the river, a bulging, asymmetric mass, dark, with a streak of white across it. The object had snagged a broken branch and a long trail of green weed, and was keeping pace with Howard as he ran, the flow of the river quickening, heading towards open water as the tide ebbed out of the estuary. The thing was rotating slowly in the current, and he glanced sideways at it, concentrating on his stride, the metronomic smack of his running shoes on the tow-path, the steady rasp and catch of breath, the stretch and flexion of the muscles. He pictured his footfalls as a series of visible impacts, exchanges of energy that flared and faded in pools of momentary light behind him as he ran. *I am the Running Man.*

The floating island had completed a half-turn in the current, becoming elongated, narrowing towards the downstream end. As it continued to rotate, its surfaces and textures shifted and rearranged themselves, contour sliding over contour, revealing the gas-bloated belly of a dead cow. He lengthened his stride. To his right, the path opened out into the car-park and he cut across the bottom corner, the scratch of his footsteps on the cindery surface as sharp as the scrape of a struck match. Breath, pace, heartbeat, the rhythm of the muscles working, sheathed, beneath the skin. *I am the Running Man.*

One of the LLanfrychan College mini-buses was parked ahead of him, a group of students from Film Studies moving around it, setting up equipment. Howard took in the stilted, leggy pose of a movie-camera tripod, and the furred snout of a microphone dipping and swaying on a long boom over their heads. A girl in a red dress stood away from the others on the edge of the tow-path, her back to the water. She brushed a lock of hair out of her eyes with an impatient gesture, the breeze fretting at it. She was standing very straight, her legs planted squarely, feet apart and slightly turned out, a posture that was open, balanced, like a ballet dancer waiting for the music to begin. She was calling out to the boys around the camera, and her voice carried to Howard as he approached.

"Should I be here? Where do you want me?" Behind her back, unnoticed, the dead cow slid past, low in the water.

She gave him a quick smile as he passed, recognising him, and he nodded back, his breath jolting between his teeth. His back-pack had ridden loose and was nudging and bumping at each footfall. He gripped the straps and pulled the weight closer to his body: ten kilos of breeze-block, a solid square of ashy concrete, crumbling at its edges. An hour ago he had brushed gritty dust off the footplate of the bathroom scales as the calibrated dial spun back to zero, then taped the thing up in bubble-wrap and strapped it into the back-pack, like a bomb. Ten kilos; he squared his shoulders, feeling the solid mass of the block against his back.

The boys by the minibus grinned and waved, someone calling out: "Go Howard! Go Dr. Lockhart!" He raised his arm in a brief salute, then leaned into the stride, upping the pace. The cow was out of sight, under the glistening lee of the emerging mud-banks. He imagined its amorphous bulk, captured unseen in the camera's eye, resurfacing suddenly in the film rushes, in the flickering darkness of the editing suite, an eruption of the anomalous, the return of the repressed, like something glimpsed in a mirror, spinning you round to confront it. The wind was getting up. Glancing back, he saw that the girl in the red dress had draped a coat around her shoulders; she ducked her head into a flare of brightness, lighting a cigarette. Howard straightened up, watching his feet, following the jarring slap of the embankment as it unrolled in front of him. *I am the Running Man. There is no Howard; there is no Dr. Lockhart. I am the Running Man.*

He turned away from the river, crossed a strip of worn and balding grass, and jogged through the lane that opened into Water Street. From here it was a mile to Llanfrychan Hospital, a long shallow rise between lines of attenuated trees, terraced houses leaning narrow-shouldered up the slope. Howard began his sprint. His heart was banging at the cage of his ribs, a hundred and twenty beats per minute, orgasm speed, acid breath burning in his throat, tasting of rust and blood.

After a couple of hundred metres the dull impact of his feet on the ground had numbed his ankles and his knees, as though the joints were fusing into undifferentiated knots of bone and cartilage. The cement block barged him at every stride; he could feel its broken edges through the bubble-wrap, jabbing and grinding at his spine, the straps of the back-pack sawing into his shoulders, abrading the skin. About half way up, someone had tied a card to a lamp-post *Happy Birthday Ivor 80 today!* - and a pair of deflated yellow balloons, shrunk to the size of a scrotum, bobbing flaccidly in the breeze as he passed. He clenched his eyes shut, trying to squeeze out the stinging sweat from under the lids. At the crest of the hill he broke joltingly out of his stride, walking splay-legged, barely able to bend his knees, feeling the concussion of every footfall working through his bones, through the ball and socket of the hips, the sacrum, the base of the skull, where it sits balanced like a basket-ball on the index finger of the spine.

In the hospital car-park he unslung the back-pack and sat on a bench for a few minutes, his heart slowing, the sweat cooling under his running-clothes. In the corridor, Rhiannon nodded and smiled at him, backing through the swing doors of the kitchen, a tray in her hands.

"Go on in," she said. "She's just had a bite to eat."

Anne was sitting up in bed, framed in a heap of pillows, the laptop on her knees. She smiled at him absent-mindedly, as though he'd only been out of the room for a moment.

"Listen to this," she said, reading from the screen. "*If you suffer from Motor Neuron Disease, Motibol is the product for you!*" She pursed her lips, swallowing, her throat working. "*Motibol has been shown in clinical trials to provide a complete Motor Neuron Disease cure in 90% of subjects. Absolutely No Side Effects!*"

She gulped, a sound that was not quite laughter. "Who puts this sort of stuff out? It's just ghoulish, isn't it, with their 'clinical trials'. It's just so debased and cynical."

Howard found himself watching the movement of her arms as she poked at the keyboard. The bones of her wrists and forearms were painfully visible, her elbows knobbed, like nuts and bolts, like the joints of an angled desklamp. Her right hand began to tap fretfully at the laptop in an involuntary spasm, a broken run of tiny clicks like Morse code, the radio operator on the stricken ship. She looked down at it. "It's so cynical. They'd sell herbal remedies to a corpse."

Howard sat down in the chair under the window. His knees felt hot, and he was aware of raised weals across his shoulders where the straps of the pack had cut him. The calf muscles in his right leg were cramping painfully.

"There was a dead cow in the river," he said. "Floating down the river, just now, on my way here." The wall above the bed brightened in yellow sunlight for a moment, then dimmed again as ponderous clouds arranged themselves above the town. "Don't you think that's strange?" he said. "It was black and white, a milking cow. It must have come from one of those farms the other side of town, on the flood-plain."

"Neutered Moron Disease," Anne said. "Don't you think that's a better name?" She closed the laptop, her hands resting on the lid. "Look how loose it's got," she said. She raised her left hand a little, looking at her wedding ring. "It's far too big, it just hangs there. It won't go over the knuckle though, so at least I won't lose it." She rotated her hand slowly, watching the movement with a look of mild surprise, as if it was unwilled. "So that's good," she said. "It won't just drop off."

"You'd think somebody would be looking for it," Howard said. "They're worth two or three thousand pounds, those cows, and there it was, dead, nobody taking any notice." The room brightened again as cloud convoys manoeuvred across the sky. "They're all tagged with a number," he said. "They keep computer records. Every cow has a unique identity, a life-history."

"Cut short in this case," Anne said. "Tragically, in her prime." She started to laugh. "Poor cow!" she said, leaning back into the pillows. "Poor cow."

"She must be almost past the sand-bar by now," Howard said, picturing the sea far out beyond the headland, receding through indeterminate swathes of beige and grey, drawing back to a line of light along the horizon. "I wonder if she'll come back with the next tide."

"The Running Man," Anne said into the silence. "Did you know that's what your students call you? The Running Man?"

"I know," Howard said. "Suggests a rather depleted personality, doesn't it? I'm reduced to a single characteristic: I run. Is that how they think of me?"

"No, it's affectionate. It's like you're one of those super-heroes. Your special power is running. What do you weigh now, by the way, eleven stone? Ten and a half?" Howard shrugged. "Are you trying to compete with me?" Anne asked him. "It's not a race, you know," she said. "Not one you can win, anyway. We're going in different directions."

Howard reached down for the back-pack and unzipped the outer flap. "I brought you a book," he said, holding it up. On the glossy front-cover a naked woman was leaning over the severed head of a man, held out for her inspection on a blue plate. *"Salomé's Tits,"* he said. "Janice Martin, she's doing some lectures on the Creative Writing course, do you remember?"

"What on earth have you got in the bag?" Anne asked him.

"Just stuff," Howard said. "It won the Lovecraft Prize."

"Leave it on the table there," Anne said.

"I thought it might kill some time."

Anne closed her eyes.

"I'm sure it will," she said.

"I had an email from Morgan," Howard said. "He's in France somewhere; he's coming down here when they get back, sorting out his mother's house, or something."

"That'll be nice. Morgan's a tonic. I'm glad you two met up again. That was the best thing about you getting this job." She struggled to sit up, dragging at the sheets. Howard rearranged the pillows behind her. "He makes me laugh," she said. "He's a lot better than herbal remedies. Is he still with that Italian girl, what was her name?"

"Gabriella," Howard said. "As far as I know." He shifted the back-pack, pushing it with his foot.

"What have you got in that thing?" Anne asked him. "Bricks?"

"I found something rather amazing for him," he said. "In that book-shop I told you about." He reached into the back-pack, straightened up. "I must have left it in college. It's a play, set in Portugal, in 1974." Anne shook her head.

"Why is that amazing?"

"You know - the revolution - guns and flowers!"

"I'm not with you. What's it got to do with Morgan?"

"He was there!" Howard said excitedly. "Don't you remember? He went with his girl-friend, a year later. I was going to go with him, the three of us, but I never did. It's called *Red Hammer.*"

"Before my time," Anne said. "That was years before my time."

"What was her name?" Howard said. "What was she called, Morgan's girlfriend? They were so crazy about each other."

"I never met her," Anne said. "I've no idea."

Closing his eyes, Howard saw the girl in the red dress, her dancer's walk, the river behind her, rain blurring on the camera lens.

"Matty," he said. "Matty James."

"It doesn't mean a thing," Anne said, subsiding into the pillows. "I never met her."

"Matty James," Howard said again. "I wonder what happened to her."

Chapter Two

. . .

Ahead of them, *Nationale 141* unrolled through meadows and woodland towards Limoges.

"I want you to imagine," Morgan said into the microphone, "that it's the morning of the 10th of June." He swivelled himself round in the jump seat as the bus rolled and slowed, swinging left off the main road. Some of the kids had stretched a banner across the back windows of the coach. *"Jefferson High,"* Morgan read, *"European Tour - The Big One!"*

"Think back more than sixty five years," he said, watching them, waiting until the silence had drawn all thirty of them in. He was aware of Tito glancing at him, murmuring something to himself as he worked the wheel round, setting the bus up on the narrow country lane. "The 10th of June, 1944."

Across the aisle, Leana and Billy closed their eyes, leaning back into their seats.

"We're imagining," Leana said. "We're thinking back. We're there already."

"It was four days after D-Day," Morgan said. "Five hundred kilometres north of here the Allies had already landed three hundred and fifty thousand troops, and the Americans had broken out of the beach-heads and were beginning to drive into Normandy."

Halfway down the bus, Tucker, or was it Trevor Ingrams, leaned out into the aisle.

"101st Airborne," he called out. "Band of Brothers. We got the box-set." Morgan nodded.

"Down here though, it all seemed very far away. People listened to the radio - in secret of course - and the news sounded good. They were beginning to think they'd soon be free." He turned back to Tito. "*On peut s'arrêter au poteau un instant*"

The driver glanced in his mirrors and nodded. From behind a hedge at the roadside a cow raised a heavy, red-blonde head and gazed at them placidly. "But in the early afternoon of the 10th," Morgan said, "a column of German armoured vehicles came down this road." He gestured at the lane. "This road we're on now."

The cow belched, breathing out a long, damp sigh, blinking mildly at them. Some of the kids were taking photographs of her. "It was a Saturday," Morgan said. "The weather was hot, hotter than today."

The bus shuddered and rattled as Tito reached forward and shut the motor off. Morgan lowered his voice, speaking into the silence of the deep lane. "The Germans drove right through the village," he said. "They stopped at the far end of the main street, and the troopers started piling out of the vehicles. They were SS, from the First Regiment of the *Das Reich* Panzer Division. Some of the half-tracks drove off, spreading out, surrounding the village, setting up road blocks and machine-gun posts. Within a few minutes they'd thrown a cordon of armed men around the village. No one could get in or out."

"What's a cordon?" Shelley-Louise asked him, breaking short the ominous pause he'd planned. "Also, what's a half-track?"

"What's a half-track?" Tucker called out, imitating her. "What's a tank, what's a gun, what's a soldier?"

"Shut up, Tucker."

"You shut up."

"Let's move on," Morgan said. "*On va au parking.*"

There were already half a dozen coaches in the bus-park. A group of drivers had gathered under the flag-posts in the snapping breeze, stamping and tapping their feet, natty in blazers and sharp slacks, the click of cigarette lighters flicking in cupped hands.

Morgan and the two teachers set off down the broad flight of steps that led down to the *Centre de la Mémoire*, down into an underground atrium of glass and sheet-steel as thick as armour-plate, dimly lit. Marie-Elaine turned and clapped her hands softly.

"Keep together kids," she called, as the last of the students clicked through the turnstiles and joined the group. "Follow us." She turned to Morgan. "That was a fine introduction you did. Very evocative."

"Thank you," Morgan said. He led the group down the corridor towards glass doors at the far end, where daylight fell in a solid shaft, as though seen from the bottom of a well. The walls were lined with black-and-white photographs, moments from the former life of the village: a horse pulling a wagon piled high with straw, a café with chairs and tables set out in the shade, a row of shop-fronts; the haunted faces of the past.

He waited until all the students had emerged from the underground chamber. Ahead of them, tramlines curved away down the main street between the broken house-fronts, the smashed and blinded facades like rows of skulls in a mausoleum. In the middle distance a group of tourists, elderly couples in brightly-coloured beach clothes, flip-flopped slowly past the empty sockets of doorways and window openings.

"The SS started herding everyone they could find towards the *Champ de Foire*," Morgan said. "The fair-ground, ahead of us there."

A little motorised road-sweeper rattled past them, brushes spinning, the driver bouncing in his seat as the machine bucked across the cobbles.

"Look, Shelley-Louise," Tucker called out, "a half-track."

"Shut up Tucker."

"The village was full of people that day," Morgan said. "Families from Limoges would often come here for a day out. The hotel had done a roaring trade at lunch-time. There was a group of teenagers on a cycling trip who'd stopped here for lunch. Kids your age."

They were passing the gaping, rusted carcase of a burnt-out car. "It belonged to the village Doctor," Morgan told them as the students crowded round. "He was coming back from making house-calls, and the Germans ordered him out and told him to join everyone else. There were several hundred people in the square by now. It was very hot. Even though it was a Saturday, the children had all been in school because there was going to be a medical inspection, so children from other villages in the neighbourhood were here as well. The SS emptied the classrooms and marched the kids and their teachers down to the square to join their parents and the other adults. There were two hundred schoolchildren here."

"Did you look inside that car?" James Aprillo asked. "Did you see how tiny it was? How would you fit in that car?"

"No way you'd fit, Aprillo," someone said, and a rustle of suppressed laughter ran through the group. "Not even if they lowered you in through the sun-roof."

"The SS were standing around in little groups," Morgan said. "They were in full combat gear: camouflage tunics, grenades hung on their belts. They were carrying sub-machine guns slung on shoulder-straps, the short muzzles swinging in casual arcs as they moved. They looked bored."

He glanced at his watch: another half hour in the ruins; an hour for lunch in the new village; forty minutes free time for shopping. "Then suddenly the mood changed," he said, picking up the pace. "The SS moved into the crowd and started separating the men from the women and children. There was a lot of shouting, the troopers pushing and shoving, waving their guns."

He could feel the group's attention focus on him again, and set off across the fair-ground, knowing they'd follow. "They forced the women and children into the church," Morgan said. "Over four hundred of them." He lowered his voice, and the kids drew closer. "Then the SS started shooting; they threw incendiary grenades into the crowd. There was smoke everywhere, screaming. The hanging tapestries burst into flames, then the rows of wooden pews. The troopers backed away down the nave, still shooting; they got out and locked the doors behind them. The whole building was on fire." He pointed up at the open shaft of the bell-tower. "That became a chimney," he said. "Everything went up in smoke. The heat was so intense that the church bells melted."

"I feel sick," Rosalyn Eikhardt said. "Mrs McCollough, I feel sick. I need to drink something, I need a Coke."

Camper vans manoeuvred ponderously round *Place Charles de Gaulle* as Morgan led the group across the square to the hotel, the bells in the tower of the new church tolling lugubriously, the breeze rattling the bright umbrellas of the pavement cafés. As he glanced back over his shoulder down the southerly slope of *Rue 10 Juin*, the ruins stared back up at him, the skull beneath the skin, hung round the neck of the new village like a dead twin.

After lunch, Jennifer Wexler sat next to him at the front of the bus.

"I'll give some commentary when we get nearer Chinon," Morgan said. He glanced back at the rows of sprawled and dozing students. "I think they could do with some down-time for now."

"That'll be fine, Morgan. We'll leave it to you."

They watched the drowsy, wooded slopes and valleys of the Limousin unrolling past them, the trees just coming into leaf, vast stands of beech and ash framing sheltered pastures of languorous blonde cattle. "How long have you been a tour manager, Morgan?" Jennifer asked him, and he came

14

awake all at once, getting control of the thought "*Too long*" on the very edge of vocalisation.

"Ten years," he said. "No, more like fifteen, off and on."

"And when you're off, what do you do? Are you married?" Morgan shook his head. Jennifer looked at him. "Not ever?"

"Twice; but not currently."

"OK, so what do you do when you're not on tour? Where do you live?"

"I have a flat in London," Morgan said. "In Paddington."

"So what do you do in Paddington? Do you have stuff to do there, work stuff?"

"I'm an actor," he said.

"My lord," she said. "An actor. Have I heard of you?"

Morgan smiled. "Not if you have to ask," he said.

"I mean, should I have heard of you?"

"No," he said. "No, you shouldn't."

"Did you see that? What was that? Was that a Ferrari?"

"How fast was that thing going?"

"There's another car you wouldn't fit in, Aprillo."

"Damn you, french fries!"

"They're coming back to life," Marie-Elaine said. "I was beginning to worry about them."

"What have you done?" Jennifer asked him. "What will I get if I google you?"

"Not much; not recently. Soaps, from time to time, nothing very exciting. *The Bill; Doctors.* You won't have heard of them."

"*Doctors* sounds familiar," Jennifer said. "Maybe I've seen that."

Morgan shook his head, smiling. "I don't think so," he said. "It never went transatlantic. Ads, of course, voice-overs. I was *Mr. Magic* for a couple of years. The longest run I ever had."

"Who's Mr Magic? Is he a super-hero?"

"An oven-cleaner," Morgan said. "*Magic that burnt-on grime!* They dumped me last year."

"I've never met an actor before," Jennifer said.

"Are you sure?" Morgan said. "How would you know?"

"Are you acting now? Is that what you're saying?"

"Listen up!" Morgan said into the microphone. "Tonight we're in Chinon,

15

and then tomorrow - are you ready for this? - Paris!" He raised both arms in a gesture of expansive, theatrical delight.

At the hotel, the boy on reception remembered Morgan from the last trip, and the two of them worked together on the rooming list. "Early start tomorrow," Morgan said. "Breakfast at eight. On the bus at nine."

Most of the students were bunched at the foot of the stairs, waiting for the lifts, sitting on their suitcases, half asleep. "Are you ready for tomorrow, guys?" he called out. "Next stop Paris, the City of Light! The Eiffel Tower, the Champs Elysées! Notre Dame! Are you ready for tomorrow?"

At the end of the evening, in the pale onset of night, Morgan crossed the Place de la Fontaine and found a pavement table at a café that was still open on the corner of rue Voltaire, the ragged outline of the Chateau dissolving beyond the rooftops in the fading sky. He ordered a pastis, and lit a long-denied cigarette.

The unpurged images of day recede;
The Emperor's drunken soldiery are abed.

***

Rosalyn Eikhardt had a panic attack near the top of the Eiffel Tower, the last visit of the last night of the trip. She'd been missing when they'd counted heads back on the ground, gathering as agreed in the centre of the vast square cornered by the four gargantuan legs of the structure, sweeping parabolas of cast-iron girders rising above their heads, so bright and flickering with golden lights that it seemed about to lift and float away into the night: this is what metal looks like when it dreams. Morgan left the others dickering with North African hucksters over plastic souvenirs and took the stairs, two at a time at first, rapidly slowing. His shirt was sticking to him by the time he found her.

"What if it all melted?" she said, gripping the stair-rail. "All this metal, like those bells you told us."

"It won't," Morgan told her, wishing he'd brought one of the teachers. "I'll tell you a story about it. Let's start down."

He wondered whether to take her arm, decided not to.

"You know Guy de Maupassant?" he asked. "A French writer, short stories mainly." Rosalyn didn't answer, but she started down the stairs with him. "Maupassant hated the Eiffel Tower," he said. "But he often used to have lunch in the restaurant here. He said: *It's the only place in Paris where I don't have to see it.*"

"I know what he means," Rosalyn said.

Across the river, James Aprillo and Trevor had found a hot-dog stand at the top of the Trocadero steps, the Eiffel Tower lifting off into the night over the Champ de Mars as they dripped mustard and relish and shreds of fried onion on to the esplanade where, in 1940, Hitler had posed with Albert Speer and some unnamed flunkey in a leather coat, the three of them leaning complacently on the granite balustrade as though they'd just been shopping, the Tower reduced to a souvenir postcard behind them, Hitler staring into the middle distance, his gaze blank and dull beneath his bus-conductor's cap. Rosalyn ate two hot-dogs without pausing between them, as though the wieners, limp, pink and slinky, were restoring some vital balance in her.

Back at the hotel, the kids were reluctant to break it up and go to their rooms. Morgan bought them internet access while he and the teachers had coffee in the little bar across the lobby.

"What's next for you?" Jennifer asked him. "What's your next role?"

He ordered last-night-of-the-tour cognacs, and the three of them perched on the high bar-stools, watching the little bulbs of bright liquid winking at them on the marble counter. Behind them they could hear the rise and fall of the students' voices as they crowded round the computer.

"I'm going back to Wales for a couple of days," Morgan said. "Playing the part of a lonely bachelor."

"Any acting jobs coming up?"

"Just that one."

***

At Charles de Gaulle, Marie-Elaine hugged him, patting his back. Her eyes were glistening as she pulled away.

"We'll have to do this again," she said. Morgan watched as the last of the group filed through to departures, Jennifer raising her hand in a brief, inexpressive gesture. He took the *RER* back into the centre of town to collect his bags.

In the rush of traffic round Etoile, the radiating spokes of the grand avenues revolved slowly around him, the sense of Paris like a great wheel, poised, rotating on the spindle of the Tower. The city rotates in a map of the universe, in a vast orrery, a mechanism from Antikythera, its purpose inexplicable, its intricate movements jewelled by Cartier and Hermès.

The cab broke out of orbit round the Arc de Triomphe in a slingshot down

Avenue de Wagram. Away to the north-east, high over their heads, airliners were beating their way ponderously across the sky, flight-paths intersecting over the sullen streets of the suburbs and the *cités*, over the ice-cold compound of Drancy where the loudspeakers had boomed and screeched for three and a half terrible years, calling out lists of names for the transports to the East, convoy after convoy. *The dead brood over Europe...*

The cab-driver lowered his window, letting in a rush of sweet April air.

Chapter Three

. . .

Morgan shuffled through the stacks of books.
"Are you sure about this?" he asked. Howard nodded without turning from the window, watching the rain.

"It's bloody cold," he said.

"I know. In Paris we were sitting outside."

"Just three or four at a time," Howard said. "You'll choke it otherwise."
Morgan made his selection: *Nancy Reagan – The Authorised Biography; On the Road* and *The Dharma Bums; Sociology – An Introductory Course.* "Good choice," Howard said. "I always hated Kerouac."

One at a time, Morgan put the paperbacks into the fireplace, watching the glossy covers curl and darken as they touched the hot coals, the pages fanning open as the heat riffled through them. Smoke bled out of the bindings as the paper turned sepia, print-black, then broke into bright flame.

"Bloody middle of April," Howard said, "and we still got to have a fire. How's your whiskey?"

Outside the window, the dull evening faded into darkness. They added *Modern Poets on Modern Poetry* and *The Sitwells - A Life.* "Are you free lunchtime tomorrow?" Howard asked him. "Come round to the Faculty Office; we'll go over and see Anne. I use that path along the river; it's a good place to run."

"Free as a bird," Morgan said.

"How's Gabriella?"

Morgan poked at the smouldering books with the tongs. Edith Sitwell's long, brooding face, like an African mask, the Wyndham Lewis portrait, looked at him out of the flames for a moment before decomposing into the heat.

"I bought her a car for her birthday," he said. "A little Fiat Cinquecento, beautiful." He shook his head, smiling. "It was pure Piazza Navona, three-strip Technicolor: cream body, lipstick-red interior. Getting into that car was like going to bed with Marilyn Monroe: ice cream, strawberries, perfect sex."

Howard poured more whiskey. A licking flare of green flame hissed sibilantly in the rustling ashes.

"You'd think they'd give out more heat," he said. "All that mental effort, it ought to release a lot of energy. Still, it's free." He threw on *The Bookseller of Kabul, Harry Potter and the Deathly Hallows,* and *The Closing of the Western Mind.*

"I drove it round from the showroom and parked it outside her office," Morgan said. "Rang her up, and told her to look out of the window."

"She must have loved that," Howard said.

"She did," Morgan told him. "She loved it so much she took the car with her when she moved back to Milan. That was two months ago."

Howard crossed the room and closed the curtains.

"Still raining," he said.

"I really miss that car," Morgan said. He picked out more books: *Big Weather: What Climate Change Really Means; The Boy in the Blue Striped Pyjamas,* and *Night of Flames - a novel of World War II.* "Can't get away from those Nazis," he said.

"How was the tour?" Howard asked him. Morgan shrugged.

"Good; ridiculously well-paid. I don't know what to do with the stuff."

"You'll find a way; you're a grasshopper, money doesn't stick to you. Where are you going next?"

"Poland," Morgan said. He shivered. "The camps."

"You've got the play I gave you?" Howard asked him. "*Red Hammer?* Don't burn that."

"I won't," Morgan said. He patted his jacket pocket. "It's right here. I'll look at it now when I get back to the house."

"Nice jacket," Howard said.

Morgan let himself in, still half-expecting his mother to appear in the hallway. Rhodri the lodger was in the kitchen, leaning over the big table which was almost entirely taken up by the part-constructed skeleton of a match-stick cathedral, an intricate, bone-coloured armature of arches and columns, buttresses, turrets, mullions, vaults and pilasters. The whole thing must have been nearly six foot long and two or three feet high. Rhodri was snipping the ends off a pile of matchsticks with a pair of nail-clippers; beside him he had a plastic cup full of phosphorous heads, like tiny cannon-balls. There was a strong smell of glue.

"Trying to think when you last saw it," he said to Morgan. "I don't think I'd started on the south transept, had I? Twenty one thousand matches so far."

"How are you ever going to move this thing?" Morgan asked him.

"I had a break-through," Rhodri said. "I was having trouble with some of the curves, those ogives, very difficult with matchsticks." He adjusted the angle of a pillar with a pair of tweezers, stepping back to assess the effect. "Then I thought: I can use balsa-wood, cut it into thin strips, do it like that." He looked up at Morgan. "I don't think that's cheating, do you?"

"I may be putting this place on the market at some point," Morgan said. "You know that, don't you?"

"Do you see the way the whole cathedral slopes?" Rhodri said. "There's quite a fall from the altar to the west doors. It meant they could sluice the nave out, all those muddy footprints, all those pilgrims."

The radiator was off upstairs, and his mother's bedroom was cold. He looked around the plain little room, thinking about his mother's life. The whole house was like that, cramped, impoverished. The book Howard had given him was a thin paperback, bound in bright red. It was scuffed and soft and the pages were spotted with damp, but the intense red of the title still glowed with a kind of heat. *Red Hammer,* Morgan read, *A play by Dave Leaper. Barricades Press, 1976.* Many of the pages were annotated in faded pencil; there were little diagrams in the margins that could have been stage directions. He turned back to the beginning.

"As the lights come up on a stretch of dusty road, we hear the sounds of a bus pulling away from a stop - the roar of the motor shifting up through the gears, quickly fading. Loud buzzing of crickets. TESSA and CHRIS are standing stage right, looking around as though trying to work out where they are. They are dressed in jeans and combat jackets; both have heavy back-packs which they now heft up on to their shoulders."

Morgan leaned back in the armchair and closed his eyes for a moment, letting in the smell of wild garlic, and cicadas singing; a flight of egrets, floating and falling like the feathers of a single bird; down in the valley, the crash and rumble of the stone-breaking machines building the new road, and a plume of yellow dust rising. The years, locked up in the rock, stored away in dry spirals, latent, unexamined, are suddenly released, uncoiled, like the snake Tito ran over in the car-park, its back broken, twisting and tumbling as though caught in the surf, rolling in breakers of pain. Time arcs across the gap.

There was music in the bars at night,
and revolution everywhere.

***

Howard's office was cramped, windowless, crowded with filing cabinets.

"I know," he said. "Find somewhere to sit; move those boxes. Do you want a coffee?" Morgan shook his head. "What did you think of *Red Hammer?*" Howard asked him. "As soon as I saw it I thought of you and Matty."

"It was like looking into a mirror," Morgan said. He took the book out of his pocket and riffled through the pages. "Then suddenly you realise that you're looking right through the glass; you're looking at something on the other side." Howard looked at his watch.

"We should get going," he said.

They took the flight of steps behind the Library down to the river-side. Howard had changed into a track suit and was bouncing on his toes, dancing forward a few steps then jogging on the spot, waiting for Morgan to catch up. He had a black nylon pack on his back, bumping heavily up and down as he moved.

"Reading that play was like seeing someone in a crowd," Morgan said. "They catch your eye for some reason or other and then, a moment later, you recognise them: it's someone you know quite well."

"I'm going to run to the end of the railings there," Howard said, "and then back again. Hold that thought."

Morgan watched as Howard set off down the path, head lowered, elbows working, the pack riding up and down at each stride. On his left, the river slid by with the oily fullness of high tide, just on the turn. After a couple of hundred metres, Howard turned and jogged back.

"And the slogans!" Morgan said. Howard glanced sideways at him, jogging on the spot, lifting his knees to waist height. "*The people, united, will never be defeated!* I haven't heard those words for thirty years. They come at you out of some deep fold in the brain."

"Socialist revolution," Howard said. "Whatever happened to that?" He nodded, smiling to himself. "I'll just go to where the river bends," he said. "By the bench there, do you see, by the litter-bins?"

"What have you got in the bag, Howard?" Morgan called after him. "Why do you run with all that weight on your back?"

The breeze rattled a shower of yesterday's rain out of a tree as he passed under it.

"In order to overcome it," Howard said on his way back, his breath coming in short gasps. "It's part of the journey of running - inner goals and outer obstacles. The weight is inside and outside, it's the same thing." He tugged at the straps of the pack, shifting the pressure.

They rounded the curve of the river. Above their heads, a pair of crows were winching themselves laboriously across the sky on creaking wings. Howard trotted on the spot for a few strides and then set off again. Beyond him, in the middle distance, a group of figures were moving around a mini-bus parked at the edge of the tow-path. Morgan watched as Howard jogged past them, turned and started back, bustling his way through. Voices, a run of bright laughter, carried across the water. "After a while you discover an inner space," Howard said. "And that's what you run through."

"You're like taking a dog for a walk," Morgan said. "Shall I throw a stick for you?"

"The whole thing between thinking and moving, between mind and body, disappears. The mind runs, and the body thinks." He jogged a few steps, shadow-boxing.

As they drew nearer, the figures on the path resolved themselves into a group of students: three boys and two girls. They were setting up equipment, a camera on a tripod, microphones; smiling and waving as the two men passed. Turning back, Morgan watched as one of the boys panned the camera round, following them, and for a moment he saw himself reflected in its dark and glittering eye.

"I still don't understand why you run with a weight on your back," he said. "What have you got in that thing? It's just masochism, isn't it?"

"I'm trying to get through to the other side," Howard said. "I'm trying to use the wisdom of the body. If you run hard enough, the mind goes quiet." He sighed. "The other day she told me I was trying to compete with her."

23

"Run, Dr. Lockhart!" one of the girls called out, her voice high and clear, and the others laughed and cheered. "Why aren't you running?"

"You'll see a change in Anne," Howard said.

In a narrow creek on the further river-bank, where glistening domes of mud were starting to emerge below the waving rushes, the bones of a little rowing boat lay half-submerged, its belly full of water.

"I want to sprint this last bit," Howard said. "I'll meet you at the hospital; I'll wait for you by the gate."

In Anne's room, Morgan sat on the edge of the bed; he took her hands between his.

***

A pheasant ran across the lane in front of them with idiot enthusiasm, his eager, leaning-forward stride arriving at the other side in triumph, like the punch-line of a joke.

"I haven't been up here for years," Morgan said. Far below them, the college mini-bus was still parked by the tow-path, the sunken river draining between mud-banks towards a line of silver on the horizon, where the sands ran out into the bay.

"The other day she told me I was trying to compete with her," Howard said. "I already told you that, didn't I? She said it was like I was trying to win a race."

Morgan watched the group of figures moving round the van, busy flecks of grey and green and denim-blue, a single pixel of bright red standing a little apart from the others.

"It's not your fault," he said.

"I don't know. You wonder."

"Don't punish yourself."

"I have to find something to punish."

They reached the top of the hill, the flood-plains laid out in quilts below them, fringed with wooded hillsides to the west, the cluttered roof-tops of Llanfrychan crowded into a broad bend of the river on their left. "You can get used to anything if it stays the same," Howard said. "No matter how bad, you get the measure of it in the end. But this changes all the time. Always for the worse, of course, loss after loss. Little by little, everything is taken away. The Stations of the Cross."

Above them, a buzzard scudded sideways through the wind, looking down on them with angry eyes. "Anyway, there's only one direction of travel," Howard said. "Down hill." He cleared his throat. "It's going to rain. Let's go to the pub."

At the traffic lights an old lady crossed the road in front of them, papery, dignified, imprecise, blurring in the rain; so much effort just to keep moving forward, shuffling one foot in front of the other, her hand spasmodically clenching and unclenching on the handle of her cane, as though manually working her heart. The wipers thumped across the windscreen, erasing her.

They sat at a table under the big window, the street outside fragmented through lozenges of stained-glass – green and yellow and orange, squares and sunbursts, movement broken up and enigmatic. Whenever the pub doors pushed open, a segment of the real world swung in, bright with rain, momentarily lucid.

"She's handling it so well," Morgan said. "And so are you. You're both amazing."

"Will you sell your mother's house?" Howard asked.

"Maybe. Never mind about that." He dipped his head to drink. "You're both so brave. Do you remember that thing Hemingway said: *Nothing bad ever happens to the brave.*"

Howard shrugged. "Evidently not brave enough, on that theory."

"Listen," Morgan said. "Listen Howard, let me do something. Let me send you and Anne on holiday, somewhere beautiful and warm, some fabulous hotel by the sea. Somewhere you can hear the waves rolling in at night. I'd really like to do that."

"Tell me about *Red Hammer*," Howard said. "I only read the first couple of pages."

"Are you listening to me?"

"I can't do that."

"Why not? Talk to Anne at least."

Howard nodded, his eyes following some movement in the street beyond the coloured glass.

"There was a dead cow in the river the other day," he said. "Such a strange sight. Do you remember that line in Four Quartets? *'The river, with its cargo of dead men, cows and chicken coops...'* It was like something had come through from the other side. I can't seem to get it out of my mind."

"Promise me you'll talk to Anne. It would do you so much good."

25

"I will," he said. "Let's talk about something else. I want to hear about *Red Hammer*. The moment I saw it I thought of you and Matty."

"So did I," Morgan said.

"You two were such an item."

"Yes, we were."

"What happened?" Howard asked. "We were all going to Portugal together, but then I didn't, I can't remember why not. It's funny when you come across these gaps, these holes in your memory."

"I feel like I fell down one," Morgan said. "I haven't hit the bottom yet."

"I can see Matty now," Howard said. "That way she walked, like a ballet dancer."

"So can I," Morgan said. "It's a bit like your dead cow."

"I remember looking for student flights with you and Matty, but I don't know why I didn't go with you. Why didn't the three of us go?" Morgan shook his head.

"I don't remember," he said.

"That's not all," Howard said. "It goes deeper than that. I have no memory of her after you two went to Portugal. I can't remember if I ever saw her again."

"You probably didn't," Morgan said.

"Why don't I remember her after university? Did she go on with acting? Why don't I remember?"

"She never came back," Morgan said. "Just a couple of weeks, to sort things out, then she was gone for good. Not a good couple of weeks for me."

"What happened?" Howard asked him. "Something must have happened?"

"Read the play," Morgan said. "It's all there."

"Tell me what happened. And why did you and I lose touch? You two went off to join the revolution, and I didn't. What happened then? You were going to do agit-prop theatre for the masses. You were going to bury capitalism. You were digging its grave."

"She met someone," Morgan said. "How revolutionary is that? In the play, he's called Pedro."

"And now capitalism is burying itself," Howard said. "We're all invited to the funeral. What do you mean, in the play?"

Morgan took a deep breath, aware of Howard watching him.

"It's so long since I've thought about any of this," he said. "He was called José Afonso, he was some sort of student activist, he was working on the commune we went to. He was very charismatic; or Matty thought so anyway. She went to live with him in Lisbon, just like that. They got married a year or so later."

"So she never became an actor," Howard said. "I always thought she'd do that. I always thought she'd be famous."

Morgan found the page he was looking for.

"It's not a bad play. Listen to this," he said. "Just a read-through, I'll spare you the theatricals: *You have no idea how bad this feels. -- Don't feel bad. -- What am I supposed to feel? You dump me, in public. -- I haven't dumped you. Things happen. -- You don't talk to me about it, you just go off with someone else.*" He looked up at Howard. "They're called Tessa and Chris. They go to Portugal to be part of the revolution. They join a commune, it's called *Red Hammer*. It all feels quite authentic; the writer must have been there at the time. Anyway, at the commune Tessa meets Pedro and splits up with Chris. Change the names, and it's me and Matty." He pushed his chair back. "I need another drink," he said.

Setting the beers down, he nudged against the table so that the brimming glasses clinked and shivered, drooling saucers of foam. He lifted the book out of the way. "Things go really wrong for poor old Chris after that," he said. "So our stories diverge a little towards the end." Howard nodded, watching him.

"I didn't know any of this," he said.

"You can see why it was such a dead cow moment," Morgan said. "Reading this last night was like seeing my life on a screen. I never thought it was a performance; I didn't know there was an audience."

Howard picked the book up, turning it over in his hands.

"*A play by Dave Leaper,*" he read. "Look at that colour - Soviet crimson; it looks like it was printed yesterday. I wonder who Dave Leaper is, or was. Anyway, go on, what happened then?"

"To Tessa and Chris?"

"To you and Matty. What happened to Matty?"

"She and José Afonso left the commune - ours was called *Red Star,* by the way. They got married. They lived in Lisbon; I suppose they still do. They had a baby at some point, a daughter. I sent her a christening spoon."

"So she never got famous? She was never a star?" Morgan smiled.

"She was always a star," he said.

"You know what I mean, a film-star. I always thought I'd see her name in lights."

"You could have," Morgan said. "She became a singer. She was quite successful, in a Euro-pop sort of way. She never made it here, but in Portugal she was famous for a while."

"I never knew," Howard said.

"She had a big hit sometime in the late 80s. It was in the top ten all over Europe, one of those songs you hear in every beach-café all summer, and then never hear again. I can almost remember how it went. What was it called?"

"And then what?" Howard asked him.

"*Flirting at the Funeral,*" Morgan said. "It was called *Flirting at the Funeral.* Good title.*"

"But then what? Did you ever see her again?"

"Then nothing," Morgan said. "We wrote to each other for a while, but, you know how it used to be - no Facebook, no email - people slip away, you lose them. At some point I stopped knowing what was happening to her; she just drifted off the radar."

He opened the book. "*Listen Chris, we're friends,*" he read. "*Who? -- You and me! -- Are we? -- Yes! Best friends, life-long friends!*" Morgan leaned back in his chair. "It didn't work out like that," he said. "Things happen, time goes by. I got married. I got divorced. I woke up one morning and realised I didn't know where she was, or what she was doing."

The girl came round from behind the bar, collecting empty glasses, wiping up spilt beer.

***

Morgan had a carriage to himself in First Class, drinking a glass of Rioja and eating peanuts in a comfortable litter of newspapers and magazines, the laptop open on the table in front of him as the Intercity ran through curtains of rain and out into broad and placid landscapes, sunlight dropping down in slanting columns through the clouds. He found Dave Leaper on the first search page, scrolling past Professor Dave Leaper of Stockport Institute of Nanotechnology, Dave Leaper Pet Accessories, and the newly signed scrum-half for the Huddersfield Hustlers. "*This is Dave Leaper's blog,* Morgan read, *at letskillallthelawyers.com*"

As sections of ploughland and pasture swung slowly by like lines of longitude, he clicked on the latest blog entry: "*Gangster-capitalism and the banking system - an anarchist analysis.*" He ate the last of the peanuts, nodding to himself as he read. There were no biographical details, and no mention of *Red Hammer*, but it had to be him.

Morgan moved the cursor into the google slot, paused for a moment, and then quickly typed: *Matty James*. The train was passing through a landscape of gravel-pits and reservoirs, silvery stretches of water away towards the airport where the motorways merge, airliners hanging heavily below the clouds. They ran into another squall, trails of raindrops driven wriggling across the window like urgent sperm. He pictured Paddington, not far up the line, its echoing loudspeakers in the teeming concourse, the buses in the rain in Praed Street, the displaced crowds of travellers converging and dispersing.

Chapter Four

. . .

In 1904, the artist Eric Gill was living at No 13, Battersea Bridge Buildings, and some time during the summer of that year he painted a view across the Thames, a pen and watercolour study of Lots Road Power Station. It's a strange little picture, only eight inches by five, but lit with an extraordinary intensity, somehow dark and lurid at the same time. The foreground is taken up with rooftops and red-brick chimneys, almost close enough to reach out and touch, as though seen from an upstairs window. Then a glimpse of the river, where a tug and a barge sit motionless on the flat, opaque surface of the water. On the far side of the Thames the power station rises up, gleaming with a dim radiance, heated from within but softened and obscured by fog, or distance, or river-mist. The sky, framing and filling half the picture, is a swirling wash of nearly-solid black, as black as the coal which fired the station's boilers.

Lots Road was pink with newness, flesh-coloured, when Gill painted it - a triumphant product of industrialism, numinous with *the living sense that beauty is power made visible*. But the picture is haunted, chthonic; Gill's celebration of the age of iron and steel is deeply troubled and ambiguous. The scene is empty of movement or activity; no smoke rises from the power station's chimneys, nor from the funnel of the tug. The river is flat and still, without tide or flow, the colour of a bone; the colour of a lake in Hell. As you stand in the upstairs window you are the only human presence there, but something is looking back at you; something William Blake, who was married at St Mary's Battersea, almost directly opposite Lots Road across the river, would have recognised.

Now, a hundred years later, the power station is a hulk, partly dismasted, a prison ship beached on the shore, sinking into dereliction. It has lost two of its chimneys, and a section of the turbine-hall has been sliced off and removed, like a supertanker reduced to scrap in a Bangladeshi breaking-yard; a gaping, severed gable-end exposing ruptured conduits and passageways.

The building's relationship to its surroundings has been inverted: from being the biggest and brightest object in the landscape, it's become residual, shabby, half-demolished, overshadowed. Across the river, the water chopping brightly in the breeze, ziggurats, step-pyramids, towers and wedges of super-luxury apartment-blocks rise to twice the height of the power station chimneys, floor after floor of stainless steel and armoured glass.

But the power station is still vast, and on its own side of the river, in the little narrow streets of red-brick terraced housing, it rears up round every corner, filling half the sky. In Lots Road itself it blocks out the light; the street is a sunless alley, punctuated by stunted trees, the south side formed entirely by a towering, endless, empty colonnade of blackened glass and brick, the side wall of the turbine hall.

Luisa paid the cab off just before Battersea Bridge, dodged through the traffic and set off down Cheyne Walk. A breeze was coming off the Thames, the house-boats restless, the lap and slop of water on the hulls, the rigging musical. She found the road she was looking for, a little street like a canyon, shadowed by the enormous bulk of some derelict industrial building. High up in the dark facade a window stood open, a pigeon patrolling the ledge.

She counted house-numbers on the other side of the street, arriving at a yellow-brick archway in a blank wall, under a rusting metal sign: *909 Jazz Club*. A flight of concrete steps led steeply down into a basement. A boy behind the bar looked up as she pushed the door open.

"I'm looking for my mother," Luisa said. "Matty James? She's singing here tonight?"

The band doodled for half an hour or so, warming up - piano, bass and drums. The place wasn't full, but there were people at most of the tables, and the bar was busy all evening. Matty slid on, leaning over the piano-player, whispering in his ear. She took the mike off its stand and slipped into the golden column of the spotlight as though standing under a shower, sparks and embers flashing on her dress. She did *Autumn in New York,* and *Broken Telephone,* and *The Dark End of the Street.* Luisa sat at a table to the left of the stage, under a publicity shot that must have been done in the 90s: sunset on the beach, the light exploding through the golden halo of her hair. A sticker cut diagonally across the image: *Matty James - For One Night Only.*

Watching her mother, she could see a sort of animating spirit enter and leave, from one song to another, even within a song. This is what soul is; it comes to you and lights you up, and then it goes away, leaving a flatness, an absence of resonance, an emptiness. People began to talk over the music then, or went up to the bar. Once or twice, though, she really connected. She did *Perfect Ten*, duetting with the bass-player, her voice full of laughter. When she sang the lines: *and if he's kinda big, well you know I dig, every little move he makes,* something travelled right around the room, translucent, like a movement in water, drawing a ripple of applause behind it, like a fin.

She took a break half-way through the set and came to sit with Luisa, calling one of the barmen over to the table.

"Sweetheart," she said. "Be an angel, get me some herb tea, camomile if you have it. How did you get here baby?"

"Cabbed it from college."

"Bad girl, what's wrong with a bus?"

"I like your dress," Luisa said.

"You don't think it's too tight?"

"I love it. Is it Chinese? How do you walk in those heels though, mother?"

The boy set the tea down carefully, smiling, glancing back at them as he walked away. Luisa patted her mother's hand. "Look, he's fallen in love with you," she said.

"Don't be silly. He was looking at you, not an old has-been like me."

"You know he wasn't. When we're out together men look at you, not at me. I ought to mind that, but I don't."

"That's ridiculous. You're beautiful."

"I know, that's why I don't mind. Anyway, I'm proud of you."

Matty breathed into the microphone.

"I'm back," she said. "Hello again." The piano player ran a scuttling riff up the keyboard, watching her. "This next song has been very good to me," she said, her voice dropping to a whisper. "I'll try and return the favour."

At the end of the set the owner of the club bounced on to the stage, big-ging it up: "Matty *James*, ladies and gentlemen! Matty *James*!" He got a burst of noise out of the audience, whistles and whoops rising briefly above the returning buzz and clatter of the crowd: laughter, the scrape of chairs pushed back, someone's phone ringing shrilly. They didn't call for an encore.

"I shouldn't have done *Flirting at the Funeral,*" Matty said, as the taxi rattled and shook, turning into Kings Road. "It doesn't mean anything to people here, and the band didn't get it either. Did you see how they were struggling?"

"Mum, they loved you," Luisa said.

"And Jack never sent the CDs round, they should have been on sale, the idiot. Can you believe that?""

"People will get it on iTunes," Luisa said.

"And fine, lay on champagne in the dressing-room, but you'd think they could have chilled it properly."

"It's so exciting, seeing you here in London."

"This gig, and one next week - it's not exactly: *Matty James - The UK Tour.*"

The cab pulled up outside the hotel, the driver twisting round to say something into the grille.

"This is pretty smart," Luisa said, looking up at floodlights, marble, polished brass.

"Baby, I'm shattered, and we haven't had a chance to talk. We've got so much catching up to do. I want to hear about your course, I want to hear about everything. Call me tomorrow, promise, first thing. We'll have lunch, we'll do everything together, just the two of us."

Luisa watched her mother tripping up the flight of steps, pausing to say something to the doorman, who waved her in with an expansive gesture. She paid the taxi, and walked around the corner to the tube station.

It turned out Matty needed to spend most of the morning with her agent. Luisa had a coffee with Sam, typed up her lecture notes, and walked from the Film School to Hungerford Bridge. At Charing Cross, she heard a girl's voice quite clearly as she passed, a slight figure talking with an older man, noticing the two of them as they stood close together, the crowds eddying around them.

"Dad," the girl was saying. "Wait, Dad, please." She was fourteen or fifteen. The two of them leaned into each other as he took their photo on his phone with an outstretched arm, then showed it to her. They looked so sad. Then he brushed her shoulder with a goodbye gesture and walked away up the Strand while she stood by herself in the hurrying, indifferent street, watching and watching until he had disappeared.

She saw her mother from halfway across Trafalgar Square, framed between the columns of the National Gallery in a bright red coat, knowing it was her before she could see any details: sunglasses, a mop of blonde hair. There was some sort of demonstration beginning to form - red banners, black Anarchist flags, disconnected groups of people gathering and dispersing, standing on the edges of the fountains or chatting between the paws of the lions, amiably rearranging themselves as though waiting for some orchestrating purpose to reveal itself.

Luisa worked her way through the murmurous, shuffling crowds and trotted up the steps. Someone handed her a leaflet: *Smash Capitalism Now!* She and her mother exchanged a series of quick kisses, bobbing their heads left and right, brushing cold cheeks in the bright air.

"I'd love to be filming this," Luisa said. "Look at the red of that banner there - with the hammer and sickle - isn't that beautiful?"

"This takes me back," Matty said. "All those red flags. A hundred thousand people marching down the Avenida de Liberdade. You can't imagine how exciting it all was."

"So many stories," Luisa said. "You could zoom in on anyone, and start to follow them, and you'd realise that they're in the middle of a narrative. They're falling in love, or getting dumped, or they've lost their job, or they've just heard from someone they thought they'd never see again."

"You're such a romantic, baby. It all looks rather aimless to me. What are they demonstrating about?"

"I have to make a short film this summer," Luisa said. "Did I tell you that? For my final-year project. I want to do something political."

"What's happening down there?" Matty said, pointing. "Something's going on down there."

"It won't be a documentary," Luisa said. "I want to make a feature-film, but with a political focus. I thought: terrorism, nothing cheesy like al-Quaida, but maybe Baader-Meinhof, something like that. What do you think?"

"Down there," Matty said. "Look."

Below South Africa House, a section of the crowd had become congested, bunching into a dense mass, pushed and swaying. They heard the whoop of a siren, abruptly cut off, and the metallic braying of a loud-hailer. As they watched, a squad of ten or twelve police in black and yellow riot gear, bulbous with body armour, appeared from behind the building and ran around the edge of the crowd in a furious, concentrated rush, shoulder to shoulder, boots hammering down on the pavement.

At an unseen signal they turned in a single, yelling phalanx and drove into the centre of the crowd. A palpable, collective gasp rose up out of the mass of bodies, as if a bubble of air had been forced out of them. Matty and Luisa could see the crowd swell and break open as though some lethal embolism was forcing its way through the flinching blood. The surge of sound that blew out across the square was scored with individual notes: screams, the dead thud of stamping boots, the sharper crack of the police batons.

Under the attack, the crowd were hacked and pushed towards the top of the square. As the main group were herded on they left broken pieces of themselves behind, bits of clothing, trampled banners, injured bodies lying on the pavement. They watched as one of these figures, crouched on hands and knees, was set on by three of the riot police; they danced around him, batons rising and falling.

Matty and Luisa found themselves backing away along the pavement. The crowd was starting to thicken around them, coagulating into an organism with a beating heart, fed by a spreading web of capillaries, forming a nervous system as synapses of rage and fear fired wordlessly between them. You could feel the shouts and screams from the base of the steps, where the riot police were tearing into the crowd, converted into physical signals, shocks and tremors that ran through the bodies around them.

"Come on, Mum," Luisa said. "I think we should get off the street."

"Who are those people?" Matty said.

"Tactical Support Group," Luisa said. "It's the latest thing: recruit violent criminals into the police - how can you lose?" Someone bumped her heavily from behind as a group of boys ran past, heads low and hooded, dodging through the crowd. One of them tripped and nearly fell as they passed a pavement artist, his foot catching a box of coloured chalks-stubs and sending them scattering into the air like fragments of mosaic rainbow. Luisa took her mother's arm. "Let's go in here," she said, and they stepped out of the crowd and into the cool recesses of the Sainsbury Wing.

At the top of the stairs, room after room opened out in front of them through tall archways, pale and airy, dove-grey, lit from above by high rooflights. On the walls, the long and melancholy faces of angels, saints, madonnas, martyrs, bishops, hermits, framed in radiant settings of blue and gold, watched them as they passed.

"I wish I'd had a film-crew out there," Luisa said.

"This country is changing," Matty said. "I've never seen anything like that before."

"All the more reason to film it."

Above them, under an arc of gilded wood, a Duccio Madonna looked down at her baby, blue-robed, surrounded by angels, her haloed head tilted in sadness or premonition.

"I want to hear about film-school," Matty said. "And your new flat; and Sam, tell me about him. Is he nice?" Luisa shrugged.

"He's a boy," she said. "He's an actor; he might be in our final-year project." Under their feet, pools of pale afternoon light glowed on the blonde oak of the floorboards. John the Baptist watched them pass, dark-eyed, emaciated and intense, his right hand held out towards them, pointing with an enigmatic gesture. A little further on, a Filippo Lippi angel of the Annunciation, delicate, peacock-winged, carrying white lilies, was kneeling before Mary in a walled garden, the symbol of perpetual virginity, the two of them as beautiful as lovers.

"That Jack has got a nerve," Matty said. "I'm really thinking about sacking him. Never mind forgetting to send the CDs last night, do you know what he suggested today?" Luisa shook her head. "A gig in a pub in Oxford; not a club, baby, a pub. *Always full of students,* he said. Can you imagine?" She glanced back at the golden-haired angel, kneeling in the garden. "We should have one of those audio-guides," she said. "Tell us what all these paintings are."

"My film is going to be about people," Luisa said. "About what happens when things start changing too fast, like out there."

"There's something I need to talk to you about," Matty said.

"I'm going to need some money," Luisa said. "Quite a bit, actually."

"Sweetheart, listen to me a minute. You need to hear this." Luisa looked at her. "I'm selling the flat."

"I don't understand, mother. What flat?"

"Don't be silly, baby. The flat on Conde de Redondo, I've decided to sell it."

"*Our* flat," Luisa said. "Where we live. Our *home*. Is that the flat you're

36

talking about?" Two burly, half-naked men were stooped over, bent double, muscles bulging as they reloaded their crossbows. Around them, three or four other archers were firing arrows at point-blank range into St Sebastian's white flesh. Matty walked on into the next gallery.

"Don't be like that," she said. Luisa turned away from the painting and caught up with her mother.

"Are you serious? What, so we don't live in Lisbon any more? Just like that?"

"Of course we do. Perhaps we'll get a smaller place or something."

"How can you do this to me?"

"Sweetheart, you're never there any more."

"It's my home," Luisa said.

"All that time in New York, and now here."

"It's where I come back to," Luisa said. "I need to know it's there."

"We have to be more careful," Matty said. "I have debts to pay, I have obligations. *Debts and obligations* - it sounds like the chorus-line of a song."

"I can't believe I'm hearing this," Luisa said.

"I didn't want to do it," Matty said. "I really didn't have a choice."

"So when is this going to happen? When am I going to be made homeless?"

"It's done, baby," Matty said. "It's already done."

"And where's my stuff? What have you done with all my stuff?"

"It's in store, sweetheart. You can get it any time you want."

Luisa turned away and walked through to the next room. Ahead of her a group of grotesque old men were crowding around the figure of Christ, tormenting him. One of them raised the crown of thorns over his head while another was tearing at his clothes.

"Where am I going to live?" she asked, as her mother caught up with her. "Where will I put my stuff? Where are *you* living?"

"Here and there," Matty said. "In the Algarve, quite a bit. I might line up a couple of gigs in the golf-hotels. All a bit naff, but they pay. I really want to get into the Lisbon clubs."

"Are you living with Arno?"

"I'm living at Arno's place."

"Is there a difference?"

"Don't be rude, baby. That's not fair." Luisa sighed.

"And how is Arno?"

"How do you manage to get so much disapproval into that question?"

"Dr. Bendt, then. How is Dr. Bendt? Is that better?" Both women started to laugh. "It's not, is it?"

"He can't help being German, sweetheart!" Matty said.

In the Bosch painting, a hideous old man is pawing at Christ's robe. Age has reduced his profile to a reptilian beak, his neck to strings of wattle. His lipless mouth is fringed with wisps of beard as white and wet as spittle, but his eyes are intensely, lasciviously bright.

"Mother, he's so old."

"He's a friend," Matty said. "He's been a good friend. There are times in your life when that's what you need, when that's the only thing that matters."

"And so creepy."

"We owe him a lot."

"*We* owe him?"

"More than you know, sweetheart."

"I don't even want to know what you mean by that."

"I want the two of you to get on," Matty said. "That's what I mean."

From within the circle of brutal faces and grasping hands, Christ looked back at her, his eyes untroubled, mild, benign and faraway.

***

"And if that isn't romance," Matty sang, *"it'll have to do, until the next one comes along."* She bobbed at the audience, her little-girl ballet-school curtsey, getting it just right, drawing out a rustle of amused applause. The crowd at Jimmy's Place was livelier than at the 909, younger, noisier, not so knowledgeable, but more fun. She picked out Luisa and Sam sitting together near the bar and gave them a smile, thinking how darkly elegant the two of them looked. The band were quick and attentive, the piano player bouncing with energy, watching her across the top of a little dusty-pink upright, his style abrupt, percussive, heavy on the left pedal.

Matty found herself going deeper into the music; jazz will look after you, so long as you treat it right. She did *Every Time We Say Goodbye*, drawing out the changes, bending the notes until she could sense a sort of hunger in the audience. She did *Lovin' Arms*, and *I Can't Stand the Rain*, the drummer hitting rim-shots off the beat, and *Where or When*. She did *The Dark End of the Street*, her voice cracking on the high notes - *They'll never find us, they'll never find us* - and felt that shiver in the room, the thing that singing is for.

In the break she took a quick decision, and showed *Flirting at the Funeral* to the piano player, tapping her feet and humming a couple of bars. He doodled a few notes, nodding, getting the bass-player's attention, and they started in. She'd been working on it, and they took it in waltz-time, a kind of lilting, melancholy swing. She glanced at the piano-player and he smiled back, dropping his shoulders, leaning into the music. *"Am I still here when you shut your eyes? Am I still here, are you still in me?"*

Deep in the audience she saw Luisa blow an extravagant kiss at her, and Sam raise his glass. Beyond them, a man was standing in a pool of light at the bar, and something made her falter, skipping a beat. She picked it back up, scatting through the hesitation, pulling a face at the piano player.

"*I'm looking through your eyes,*" she sang.

"Am I still in you, are you still in me?"

Chapter Five

...

Warsaw was cold and ugly, bitter with wind from the East and grey with lying snow. Morgan herded his group of elderly New Yorkers across a freezing sweep of tarmac and on to the tour-bus. They drove through suburbs of low-rise blocks, four or five stories high, balconies draped with limp washing that hung damply in the grey air, satellite-dishes gazing forlornly at the horizon, tuned, Morgan told them, to thirteen separate German shopping-channels. The road, pot-holed, led them out into tracts of weedy trees and marshland, scattered with rubbish, empty oil-drums and burned-out cars, a landscape of sandy soil, dead sedge, pine and birch, neither town nor country - a populated middle of nowhere.

Everyone hated Łodz. Ankle-deep in snow, too cold to take photographs, they followed Morgan around the Jewish cemetery, the largest in Europe: 180,000 tombstones walled into forty hectares of land. Blackened, tilted, fallen or sprawling amongst thin stands of birch and strangling in ivy, the graves spread out down pathways into endless suburbs, a frozen necropolis, its city centre grouped around the mausolea of the great capitalist families of pre-war Łodz - the Posnanskis, the Silbersteins. These dynasties had memorialised themselves in tormented palaces of white stone: a towering architecture of elongated domes and columns, fanged and horned; horror-Gothic, frozen marble, death-cold.

"This cemetery only survived because it was inside the Litzmannstadt Ghetto," Morgan told the group, everyone silent, gathered closely round him. He lowered his voice, his breath condensing in the chill air. "But it's a place of death twice over. When the ghetto was liquidated in 1944, there was no one left to tend the graves."

They were glad to go south. In Krakow, it was spring-time. They sat at café tables in the Rynek, under the bell towers of the Mariaçki Basilica, writing postcards, reading guide-books, sipping coffee; they bought souvenirs, and nibbled poppy-seed bread-sticks as they followed Morgan through the alleys of the old Jewish Quarter in Kazimierz and the elegant arcades of the University District. When he stopped to explain points of interest they gathered around him, courteous, attentive, dignified. They visited synagogues and art galleries and museums. The hotel was warm and comfortable, the food heavy and rich. After two days in the city, Morgan assembled them in the hotel lobby for an early morning start.

"As you know from the itinerary," he said, "today we're going to Auschwitz."

They arrived at Birkenau on the edge of a thunderstorm, the sky bruised and black, pressing down on them. Raising umbrellas and turning up collars, the group followed Morgan under the gaping, mephitic arch of the watch-tower.

"This is the mouth of Hell," he said. He pointed up at the vaulted brick-work above them. "That black stuff is soot, from the steam-engines that dragged the cattle-trucks through here to the gas-chambers. Smoke, and soot, and ashes, wherever you look." Through the archway, the death-camp lay spread out in front of them in straight lines that ran away to infinity: railway track, electrified barbed wire, rows of low huts receding to vanishing points; brick chimneys, guard-towers, desolation upon desolation. Far away, in a haze of distance, beyond the tumbled ruins of the crematoria, a fringe of silver birch and poplars swayed in the thundery air.

Late in the evening, finishing up his paperwork on the last night of the tour, Morgan sent an email to Angie at the office:

To the airport first thing tomorrow, and the city is lit with the glamour of some-where you are about to leave. There's a band playing jazz at a café in the square, and the town drunks are dancing sadly on the flagstones. He didn't get her reply until he turned his phone back on at Gatwick the next morning: *Very poetic message Morgan. You need a girlfriend.*

Someone had left an empty bottle of wine and two plastic cups on his front doorstep. He dropped them into the bin in the lobby, and collected a handful of bills and circulars from his mailbox. Opening his door released a breath of warm, stale air from the flat; he'd left the heating turned up too high. There was a bad smell in the kitchen, and he raised the window a couple of inches, where it jammed, as usual.

At South Kensington he stopped in front of the Fiat showroom across the road from the office, next door to the sushi bar. There were two Cinquecentos in the window, pink and buttercup-yellow, the colour of baby-clothes. Morgan leaned his forehead against the glass, smiling to himself. The salesman stepped out from behind his desk.

"Beautiful, aren't they?" he said. "The pink one's a soft-top." He opened the car door. "Have a poke about; climb right in." He looked up at Morgan. "Of course!" he said. "You had the cream one, didn't you, with the bright red fittings, just into the New Year. What a beauty! How's she going?"

"She's gone, as a matter of fact" Morgan said. "But you're right, she was a beauty."

They were getting ready for the training-weekend at ASOS. Bob told him they'd had a hundred job applications.

"No hope for most of them," he said. "Bookings are down forty percent, did you know that? There's barely enough work to go round as it is."

Angie's hair had changed from red to orange in the week he'd been away.

"Like a traffic light," Morgan said. She nodded at him, making sit-down gestures, talking into the phone. He slid the folder of paperwork onto her desk.

"You don't have to do this all by yourself," she was saying. "You could see someone. There's help out there; at any rate there are tablets out there." She put the phone down. "I know," she said to Morgan. "Traffic lights. You're not the first. Green next time. How was the trip?" Morgan shrugged.

"The usual," he said.

"You're a bundle of joy. At least they haven't roped you into this training thing. You got exciting plans for the weekend?"

"I'm going out tonight," Morgan told her. "I'm going to listen to some jazz."

***

"He drowned," Matty said. "It's ten years ago now; in October."

"I'm so sorry," Morgan said. "I didn't know."

"I say drowned," Matty said. "He disappeared. We never really knew what happened. He'd been fishing off the rocks. People said it must have been a freak wave."

"I'm so sorry," Morgan said again. "That's terrible."

"We never found his body. He must have been swept away. It's the Atlantic; you get some big waves." She was speaking quietly, and he had to lean forward across the little table to hear her voice against the soft roar of the crowd around them. She ran a finger round the rim of her glass, watching the ceaseless effervescence of the wine, looking up as Luisa and Sam joined them. "That's enough of that!" she said brightly. "Baby, this is Morgan. This is my beautiful daughter, my finest achievement!"

"They've sold almost all the CDs," Luisa said. "They absolutely loved you."

"You were wonderful," Morgan said, and she looked up at him, her eyes shining.

"Was I? Was I really?"

"I love that song *Flirting at the Funeral*. I remember it so well."

"Did it work tonight? Do you think it worked in waltz-time?"

"Such a good title. What does it mean, though?"

"You know, darling: it's like *Singing in the Rain*, or whistling in the dark. It's about making the best of things."

"I'm going to buy a CD for Howard," Morgan said. "We were talking about you the last time I was in Wales. Do you remember Howard Lockhart?"

"It's been good for me, that song," Matty said. "At the time I wasn't sure, when they chose it as the single off *Reasons Not To Kill Yourself*. That was my top-selling album, you know; dear old *Reasons*." She took a sip of wine. "I had more of them in those days."

The MC paused at their table.

"You were great," he said. "We'll have to have you back."

"Thank you darling," Matty said. "I'll get my agent to call you." Sam and Luisa were murmuring to each other, heads close together. Matty looked around the room; the bar was still busy, but a girl was clearing empty glasses from the tables. On the stage a couple of boys were pulling plugs and flipping switches, shutting down the amps, looping up ropes of cable. "Once upon a time they would have been queuing for autographs," she said.

"Sam and I are going on somewhere," Luisa said. What are your plans, mother?"

"You go on, baby," Matty said. She looked across at Morgan. "You can escort me back to my hotel if you like," she said. "We can have a drink, catch up properly." When they stood up to go, he saw he was a head taller than her; he hadn't remembered that.

They had the hotel bar to themselves, a dim, muted space of black mirrors and pale marble. "He was in his prime," Matty said. "He was happy; he loved his work, he was doing so well. He was a wonderful father." She lifted herself onto the bar-stool. "Get me a dry martini, sweetheart," she said. "I'm in the mood to drink gin tonight."

"Did he stay in politics?" Morgan asked. "I remember him at those meetings at the commune, at the demonstrations."

"He loved fishing," Matty said. "We'd take the boat out sometimes, the three of us, when Luisa was little. But I think he loved it best on his own, perched on a rock somewhere, like a heron." The barman gave the shaker a final flourish and poured their drinks, the thin triangles of glass misting instantly.

"And you're still living in Lisbon?" Morgan asked.

"He went into radio," Matty said. "A bit of everything at first: current affairs, then music. That's how I got started, I suppose." She looked up at him. "I was quite famous for a while, you know." She caught the barman's eye. "We need a couple more of these, darling."

"I know," Morgan said.

"But it gets harder," Matty said. "It doesn't get any easier." She speared the olive out of her drink with a cocktail stick. "On the boat we used to catch octopus sometimes. He had this little thin knife, very sharp; he'd stab them between the eyes." She shuddered. "Horrible, really." They looked at each other in silence for a moment. "It'll be ten years in October," she said. "They never found his body, I told you that, didn't I?"

"I'm so sorry," Morgan said.

"You haven't changed at all," Matty said. "I recognised you straight away."

"Nor have you."

"Don't be silly." The barman refilled their glasses from the shaker and moved away silently. "I think he's on wheels," Matty said, watching him for a moment. "What have you been up to, Morgan? Are you married?" Morgan shook his head.

"Not any more," he said. "I take it a day at a time. Not many acting jobs these days, but there's enough tour-guiding work. I've hung on to the flat all this time; I'm proud of that."

"I didn't know you had a flat," she said. "Have you got a girlfriend? Have you got a *p'tite amie?*"

"Just a flat."

"And children?"

"Just a flat."

"I haven't had a song in the top ten for years," Matty said. "You wake up one morning and you realise it's not there any more."

"Luisa's a beautiful girl," Morgan said.

"I thought she'd never get over it," Matty said. "She was such a daddy's girl."

"She's lovely," Morgan said. "You must be very proud of her."

"She's all I've got left of José, talking of flats. It hasn't been easy." She sighed, stirring her drink. "I wish she could get on better with Arno."

"Arno?"

"Sorry, why would you know? Arno Bendt, he's a friend. Actually you might have heard of him. He's a - what do you call them - a guru: self-help, spirituality. He's written about ten best-sellers. Dr. Arno Bendt." Morgan shook his head.

"I don't think so."

"Anyway, he's a friend. Luisa thinks it's disloyal or something, but when you need help, you need help."

"Of course."

"He has this place in the Algarve, his clinic; he lives there now. It's huge, swimming pools, everything. I spend quite a bit of time there. He's been kind. He helped me when I needed it." Morgan nodded. In the silence he heard the sharp ping of the bell on the reception desk in the lobby.

"Go on," he said.

"I work," Matty said. "I haven't given up. Gigs like tonight. But how much do you think they pay?" She lowered her voice, gesturing vaguely at the dull gleam of glass and marble around them. "This is all on Arno's account," she said. "Luisa doesn't know that, but what can you do?" She slipped off the bar-stool, smoothing down her dress. "I'm shattered," she said. "I've got to go to bed. And I've been talking too much. You've got me drunk, you bad person."

"Listen," Morgan said. "Let's spend some time together tomorrow. Are you free? Let me take you out. We'll have a really good lunch somewhere, go to a gallery or something." She stood on tip-toe to kiss him, her cheek brushing against his, a quick bob of the head, left and right.

45

"I'd like that," she said.

***

Luisa leaned against the steel railings of the footbridge, waiting for her mother to catch up, watching her slip through the crowds of tourists, ducking under upheld cameras, a quick smile for an elderly couple as she brushed past them. Beneath their feet a police launch pushed upstream, white water bubbling and grumbling behind it. They stood together for a moment at the rail, watching the river as it curved away under Waterloo Bridge. Far beyond, the domes and towers of the City rose in a blue haze of distance.

"So, he's an old flame is he, mother?"

"It's a long time ago, baby," Matty said, smiling. "It's more like a warm glow now."

"Tell me about him."

"He's nice," Matty said. "I'd forgotten how nice he was."

"He's the right sort of age, at least."

They clattered down the steps at the far end of the bridge, the South Bank bright and bustling below them, the pavement cafés crowded under multi-coloured awnings, banners snapping in the breeze. "He must be half Arno's age."

"Don't start all that again, sweetheart. Where's your College from here?"

"Not far. The other side of the National Theatre. So what have you been up to, the two of you?"

"It's been nice," Matty said. "We've been to a couple of galleries, had lunch, walked in the park; the usual sort of thing."

"I'm glad," Luisa said. "You look happy."

"Actually, not the usual sort of thing," Matty said. "Not the usual sort of thing at all. How's Sam? How was your weekend in the country?"

"Very weekend-in-the-country," Luisa said. "Very English." In cavernous spaces under concrete arcades and walkways, splashed with hip-hop graffiti and loud with the rumble and grind of skateboards, kids clattered and back-flipped and wheelied their bikes and yelled echoing insults at each other. She took her mother's arm. "This is one of the best film-schools in Europe, you know," she said.

"I know," Matty said.

"And one of the most expensive; I really appreciate what you're doing for me, mother."

"You're worth it, baby," Matty said, drawing in a quick breath. "You're worth every bit of it."

They turned under a foot-bridge between concrete ramps and multi-storey terraces, an architecture of car-park brutalism, the low dome of the Imax crouching malevolently ahead of them. Luisa steered her mother towards a set of glass doors which slid open on steel runners as they approached, hissing shut behind them.

"Editing suite through there," Luisa said, waving to the girl behind the desk. "Ciao, Annie!" She trotted up a short flight of steps. "Up here, couple of lecture rooms; little sound stage in there." She put her head round the door, saying something Matty didn't catch, getting a short burst of laughter from whoever was in there.

"This place suits you," Matty said. "You look so at home here."

"I know I can do something amazing with my film this summer," Luisa said. "I just need to find the right subject. I want to show the anger in people. I want to show the rage and pain they feel when their lives are wrecked by some bastard in Wall Street." She pushed through a pair of swing doors, holding them open for her mother. "I also need to put some extra cash into it," she said. "About ten thousand, maybe fifteen? This place is great, but I need locations, I need to give it a big look. Do you know what I mean? I need to put the dollars on the screen." Matty nodded, stepping aside as a boy came down the corridor carrying a cardboard cut-out figure, life-size, a blonde in a low-cut dress.

"I know what you mean," she said. "Do you know, I think that was Diana Dors, can you imagine?"

"The canteen's down there," Luisa said. "But it's crap, to be honest. We could get lunch at the BFI or somewhere."

"She was so pretty when she was young," Matty said. "You think of her as that over-blown bottle-blonde, but there was something really sweet about her once upon a time."

"I want to show people turning to violence because they've got no choice," Luisa said. "But I don't want Moslems or al Quaida, that's too corny." She pointed at a door on their left. "In there's the screening room," she said. "They screened my short in there, I sent you the DVD."

"Of course you did sweetheart, it was brilliant. Arno thought so too. He said you had real talent."

47

They found a table on the terrace in front of the National Theatre. "Are we going to be warm enough?" Matty asked.

"I keep thinking about the flat," Luisa said. "I can't believe it's gone, just like that. I can't believe it's not there any more." She watched her mother fiddling with her hair, pinning up blonde strands as the breeze fretted at it. "I can't believe you did that."

"I think we should eat inside," Matty said. "It's really not warm enough. There's a cold wind out here."

"How can things change so fast?" Luisa said, as they rearranged themselves at a table in the window. "One minute we have a home together, full of stuff, full of memories; full of Dad, apart from anything else." The waiter showed Matty the bottle of wine, and she nodded.

"That looks fine," she said.

"And the next minute I'm homeless, and you're installed at Arno's place."

"I don't like *installed,* baby. I'm not a washing machine."

As they laughed, Luisa saw something pass like clouds across her mother's eyes, her glance drifting aside, withdrawing for a moment into some private dismay. "I come and go," Matty said, brightening again. She took a sip of wine. "I'm not plumbed in, you know." They clicked glasses. "And don't worry about the flat; we'll get another. We'll get it all back. Lisbon belongs to us."

"*Paris nous appartient,*" Luisa said.

"What's that, sweetheart?"

"*Paris belongs to us.* It's a movie."

"Well, in real life it's Lisbon. *Lisboa é a nossa.*"

The waiter brought their order, setting out bowls of salad, bread-sticks, mineral water. Luisa watched her mother serve the food on to their plates, her movements nervily precise, the plastic implements clicking on the bowl.

"Tell me about you and Morgan," she said. "How did you first meet?" Matty leaned back in her chair, smiling.

"It was a long time ago," she said. "It was a very long time ago, in another world."

"Like all the best stories. Go on."

"We met at drama school," Matty said. "He was funny, he was a good talker. I'd never met anyone quite like him before; actually, I don't think I'd ever met anyone Welsh before. He was anarchic; he made me laugh." She trailed her fork across her plate, arranging spiky leaves of rocket and glistening

48

strips of beef into abstracted patterns. "We were rather a starry couple," she said. "When our year did *Romeo and Juliet,* guess who had the lead roles?"

"Were you in love with him?"

"Mind you, it was a very cut-down version; I think it only ran for an hour and a bit. Quite appropriate, really."

"Were you serious about each other?"

"I was nineteen, sweetheart. I wasn't serious about anything."

"You're not giving much away."

"I'm getting to it. We had a flat in Kings Cross." She shuddered. "A dismal part of town, really awful. And then one day I bought an evening paper, and there was this huge picture of a tank on the front page, and soldiers, and everybody waving and smiling and throwing flowers."

"*O vinte-cinco d'Abril,*" Luisa said. "*A madrugada que eu esperava.*"

"Of course. But I didn't know that at the time. It didn't mean a lot. I hardly knew where Portugal was." She took a sip of wine.

"Go on, mother."

"Then, over the next few weeks and months you saw more and more stories coming out: huge demonstrations in Lisbon; all the soldiers with long hair, like Che Guevara. It was on the TV all the time. It looked so much fun! It was a real Marxist revolution, you couldn't believe it was really happening. All the red flags waving, all the slogans: *O povo, unido, jamais será vencido!* Wonderful revolutionary songs - baby, it looked fabulous! It looked like the world's biggest party! Everyone wanted to be there. The summer after that, when we got to the end of June and the long vacation, Morgan and I took off." The waiter was clearing away their plates, sweeping up crumbs. Luisa poured the remains of the wine into their glasses.

"This is great," she said. "I love it."

"You cannot imagine the atmosphere in Lisbon," Matty said. "It was so exciting; people were so happy! They'd had forty years of miserable, suffocating dictatorship, and suddenly they were free; they were more than free, they were flying! Everyone was so friendly! We thought we'd have to find a youth hostel or something, but people just put us up for the night. I don't think we paid for a single night's sleep, not that we ever got much. They were so pleased to see us; we were the 'foreign comrades', the 'British comrades'. We were the first signs of the world revolution. People talked politics all the time, but it was so much fun. You could feel the world turning upside down under your feet. And Lisbon was full of Angolan weed, terrifying stuff; it made the hash we'd been used to in London seem like nothing at all. I shouldn't be telling you the naughty bits, should I?"

"It's funny," Luisa said. "I've never thought about how you might have been with somebody when you met Dad."

"And so much music," Matty said. "Rock and roll, and *fado*, and *Grandola*, and the *Internationale*, all mixed up together. *There was music in the bars at night, and revolution everywhere.*" She looked round for the waiter. "Let's get some coffee."

"What happened next?" Luisa said. "I sort of know, but I love hearing you tell it."

"Somebody told us about the collective farms," Matty said. "You know all this. Those huge estates in Alentejo; absentee landlords, real poverty, generation after generation. After *vinte-cinco d'Abril*, the people took them over. *A terra a quem a trabalha.* They collectivised the land, lived together communally. Someone told us about *Estrela Vermelha,* they said it was one of the biggest collectives. It was Morgan who really wanted to go; I was having too much fun in Lisbon." Outside the window, the crowds on the South Bank surged past in their holiday clothes beside the bright, cold river.

"But you went anyway?" Matty nodded.

"I can still feel that train-ride," she said. "All that heat; the varnish was boiling out of the wooden seats. We kept stopping in the middle of nowhere; nothing but brown hills, and cork groves, and white farm buildings on the sky-line; and the cicadas so loud it felt like they were inside your head."

"You're going slower than the train, mother. So then you got there?"

"So then we got there," Matty said. She shook herself, throwing off the lethargy of the journey. "And not long after that I met your Dad, and he was the handsomest man I'd ever seen."

"And then what?"

"You know what. You are a child of the Revolution."

"I mean, what happened to Morgan?"

Matty reached across the table and touched her daughter's hand.

"You are so like him sometimes," she said. "In the best way. You are so elegant."

"Thank you, mother. But what did Morgan do when you met Dad? Every time you've told this story you've left Morgan out."

"I don't really know," Matty said slowly. "That sounds terrible, doesn't it? We must have had rows, it must have been awful for him, but I blanked it out. Meeting José just blew everything else away. I dropped out of college; I went back to Britain to sort things out, say a few goodbyes, and that was it. All I could see was the future; everything else was like a door closing behind me."

"Haven't you talked about it with him now, in the last couple of days?"

"Perhaps we have, in a way," Matty said.

"He's probably been pining for you ever since."

"That's enough of your match-making, scheming daughter."

"I'm not. It's just that it's nice to see you with someone your own age, someone you share a past with." She looked at her mother over the rim of her coffee cup. "Maybe a future."

"*Chega!*" Matty said. "That's enough! It's nice, but I don't think I'm looking for commitment right now. Shall we go? Have we paid?" Outside, they linked arms and set off into the teeming streets.

"What would you like to do, mother?" Luisa said. She put her arm round Matty's shoulders and kissed her on the cheek. "I'm not meeting Sam until half-past five."

"I've had an idea baby," Matty said. "I've had a very good idea. I think you're really going to like it."

Chapter Six

. . .

Astring of ponies was ambling across the bridge over the Long Water, little riders slumped and swaying on their broad backs, anxious faces under oversized helmets. Matty glanced back at them as she and Morgan took the path down to the Serpentine.

"Sometimes I dream I'm riding my pony again," she said, watching them follow their instructor out into the traffic. "Did I say, I told Arno I was lining up another gig, so I'll be staying on in London for a while? And you never know, something might turn up; it's half true." She glanced at Morgan. "What's the matter?" she said.

"Are you really that accountable to him?"

"Of course not sweetheart. It's not like that at all."

"What is it like then?"

Matty took his arm, smiling up at him.

"I do believe you're worrying about me, Morgan. That's so sweet! But don't, really. I know what I'm doing."

On their left, rows of red and blue deckchairs lined the grassy bank, turned like beds of flowers to face into the sun.

"I need to keep everybody happy," she said. "He's paying for Luisa's film-school, did I tell you that? She doesn't know, she thinks I'm picking up the bills, but it's way too much for me. So it's complicated, do you see? I need to keep all the balls in the air."

They stepped aside as a girl and a boy on roller-blades swooped past them, leaning into their stride, arms swinging, shoulder to shoulder, intent. "That's what I do," Matty said. "I keep everybody happy." She took his arm again.

"And I'm good at it. Buy me an ice-cream, sweetheart." She tapped the back of his hand with a brisk, affectionate gesture. "I think I deserve one."

Stepping down into the dinghy, she held her dress out of the way with the fastidious poise of a ballet dancer. Morgan lowered the oars to the water as the boy pushed the little boat away from the jetty; he feathered them back, squared the blades and took a tentative pull, the movements instantly familiar.

"We've done this before," he said. "Do you remember?"

"Have we, darling? Are we allowed to smoke out here? That's one thing about this country I can't get the hang of any more: everyone's so law-abiding."

"You don't remember, do you?" Morgan said. "Why would you?"

"Remember what, darling? Don't be cross with me, I forget everything these days."

"It came back to me the moment I picked up the oars." A pair of Canada geese passed low overhead on noisy wings, honking, flaps down and feet extended, tearing a strip of spray across the glassy surface of the water as they touched down. "We were here just before we went to Lisbon," Morgan said. "I think Howard was with us."

"You're a good rower," Matty said. "You really know what you're doing."

"The weather was very hot," Morgan said. "This felt like the coolest place to be."

"Howard!" Matty said. "My goodness, I've just taken in what you said the other night. Howard Lockhart! Of course I remember him; he was so intense and weird, wasn't he? Are you two still friends?"

"We lost touch until a couple of years ago," Morgan said. "He got a job at my local uni. He was going to come to Lisbon with us, do you remember?" Matty shook her head.

"A lot of it's a blur," she said.

Morgan lengthened his stroke, the oars slipping in and out of the water as though they were liquid themselves, the long pull of the blades raising arabesques of swirling movement just below the surface, like muscles moving under the skin.

"Did you read the play?" he asked. Matty leaned forward, gripping the sides of the boat.

"Yes," she said. "Yes, I did."

"Tell me what you thought."

"I've had a wonderful idea," Matty said, her voice bright with excitement.

"Can you get copies made?"

"Copies?"

"Luisa has to make a film this summer," Matty said. "I told you, didn't I?" Morgan shook his head. "For the college; it's their final year project. She's talking about needing ten or fifteen thousand euros. Can you imagine? Sweetheart, I've been in despair. And then yesterday it came to me!" She clapped her hands. "She can film your play! It's perfect!"

Morgan had stopped rowing, the oars trailing in the water, the boat slowing in a half turn that left them drifting towards the bank.

"It's not my play," he said.

"Of course not, darling, you know what I mean. Don't you see? She can film at Arno's place: authentic locations, and no hotel bills! She wants to make a film about terrorism, or the credit crunch or something, but seriously, this is more subtle, don't you think?"

"More subtle?"

"To make a film about *vinte-cinco d'Abril*: all that hope, all that idealism, and look at us now. Look at the state we're in." The boat bumped against the paved edge of the lake. "It would really say something. And it would be so easy to hire extras. I think she quite likes the idea, but I need to get copies made. Could you get it digitised at your office, do you think? I'm so excited!"

Morgan reversed the boat and swung it round towards open water. "It would be such fun to do," Matty said. She lowered her voice. "And filming at Arno's place would get me out of a jam." She lit a cigarette, shrugging. "It doesn't say you can't," she said, waving the smoke away from her face. "I can't find the kind of money she says she needs; but I can't bear to tell her that. It's been bad enough the whole business with the flat."

She looked across the lake, watching the flotillas of pedalos and dinghies, a pair of swans chasing each other, mating or fighting, running on the water below splashing wings. "What is it?" she said. "What's that look, Morgan? You think I'm over-protective, don't you?" Morgan shook his head.

"No, I don't," he said. "I wasn't thinking that at all."

"You look at her and you see a young woman of twenty five," she said. "But I see a girl of fifteen who just lost her dad. I can't help it, I was made that way."

"I wasn't thinking that," Morgan said.

"What then? There's something." She leaned forward again, looking into his eyes. "I can tell," she said. "I'm getting to know you again."

Morgan concentrated on rowing for a few strokes, pushing the boat forward through the murmuring reluctance of the water. Matty dropped her cigarette over the side, watching him. "Talk to me," she said.

"Did you actually read it?" Morgan asked. "Did you read the whole play?"

"Of course I did, darling. That's why I thought of Luisa's project. Of course I read it."

"And what did you think of it?"

"Sweetheart, I just told you, it's perfect, it's just right."

"That's it? It's just right? That's your final answer?"

"What is this, Morgan? You're making me uncomfortable." Morgan took a breath, resting on the oars.

"Didn't it make you think about the past?" he said. "About us?" Matty looked at him.

"Oh sweetheart," she said. "Have I hurt your feelings? I'm so sorry."

"When Tessa meets Pedro, when she starts ignoring Chris, when she doesn't even try to hide it; when you were reading that, didn't it ring any bells at all?"

"I suppose I could see the parallels," Matty said. "But I was so excited about my idea for Luisa's film I wasn't thinking about the past; I really didn't make the connection. I'm so sorry, baby."

"You don't need to apologise," Morgan said. "It's a long time ago."

"I don't want you to think badly of me," Matty said. "You have to understand: when I met José, everything else faded away. It was like being on stage when the lighting comes up: you can't see the audience, and most of the time you don't think about them at all; they don't exist."

"I was in the front row," Morgan said.

"Everything seemed to happen at once," Matty said. "I was in such a rush. It was like running for a train that was already pulling out of the station. Do you remember, I came back to de-register, pack things up?"

"I do," Morgan said.

"I went home for a couple of days to tell Mum and Dad what I was doing, and all I could think about was getting back to Lisbon. I got obsessed with the idea that if I didn't get back, he'd go off, do something else, he wouldn't be there."

"But he was."

"My life began all over again when I got off the aeroplane in Lisbon,"

Matty said. Across the water, invisible beyond the trees, muffled traffic surged down Knightsbridge. "His parents were lovely; they were quite well off; we had a little flat. José was working in journalism, newspapers at first, then broadcasting; he got a job at *Rádio Clube Português.*"

"And you became a pop-star."

"Later on I realised they'd been dangerous times, those first couple of years, there could have been a civil war, but I never worried; I was too busy being happy." She drew her cardigan around her as a breeze stippled the surface of the water. Morgan turned the boat towards the jetty.

"Have you had enough?" he said. "Shall we move on?"

They picked their way between couples spread out on the grass, entwined or separate, slick with sun-block, turned towards the sun. As they left the Park a cuckoo was calling, its chime repeated like an unanswered doorbell.

"It took a long time," Matty said. "I got absolutely nowhere with acting, and it was years before I started getting decent gigs as a singer. I didn't sign with EMI-Valentin until 1983."

"We should have gone the other way," Morgan said. "I need to stop by the office. Do you mind?"

"The music scene was all beards and folk-singers," Matty said. "Not really my image." A cab U-turned across Bayswater Road; she put a hand on Morgan's arm as she stepped in and sat back into the deep, low seats. "How I love taxis," she said. "Where are we going?"

"Go on with your story," Morgan said. "How did you become rich and fabulous?"

"It was all a bit: *Matty James - The Wilderness Years,*" she said. "I thought I was doing well if I sang backing on a soap-commercial."

At the lights, the driver turned his head, speaking sideways through the gap in the plastic divide.

"I know you from somewhere, don't I?" he said to Matty. "Where have I seen you?"

"On a red carpet," Morgan said.

"Course I have, Oscars or Baftas or something, I'm right, aren't I?"

"You're so sweet," Matty told him. "You're adorable." She leaned back as the lights changed and the cab rattled forward into the traffic, showers of pink and white cherry-blossom dancing in the slipstream like a Hindu wedding. There was a bright red tour-bus parked outside the ASOS building, the motor bubbling softly. They took the lift up to Morgan's floor.

"This is my friend Matty," he said. "Matty James." Angie came round from behind her desk while Morgan went through the packs of brochures and itineraries from the store. He could hear the two women talking, their voices animated.

"If we ever do a Lisbon trip I'll keep you in mind," Angie was saying as Morgan came back into the room. "I love your dress."

"I love your hair," Matty said.

In Cromwell Place the Lycée was emptying out, the air bright and shrill with children's voices, a score of little kids monkeying up the cast-iron gates of the school-yard. "Did you see about getting copies made?" Matty asked. "So I can show the play to Luisa?" Morgan nodded.

"I'll ask one of the girls," he said. "See if they'll type it up for me."

"Thank you baby. I know it's a brilliant idea. I'm so excited about it." She took his arm as they crossed the road. "Where had I got to? And then one day I got five minutes on *Rock em Stock,*" she said. "One song and a two-minute interview. It was José pulling strings with radio-buddies of course, but something clicked. They liked me. They asked me back. I got myself an agent. Matty James was on her way!"

She stopped as they passed the windows of the Fiat showroom. "Look at those," she said, putting her arm through Morgan's and turning him towards the two little Cinquecentos. "Look at those! Aren't they beautiful? Like baby clothes."

"Would you like one?" Morgan said. Matty glanced up at him.

"The colour of birthdays," she said.

"You'd have to have both, though," Morgan said. "How would you ever choose between them?"

"Pink, darling. It has to be pink. Look at me, what other colour is there?"

In the sushi bar she sipped green tea, and picked at a saucer of nigiri, her chopsticks clicking with easy precision.

"You're very elegant with those," Morgan said.

"Thank you sweetheart. Where was I? I did a couple of gigs at *Rock Rendezvous,*" she said. "A big deal, take my word for it. And then my agent got me onto *TOP PLUS.*" She glanced at him. "That's a TV show; it had a huge audience in those days. Sweetheart, you cannot imagine how terrified I was. The act after me was *Heróis do Mar,* and they were massive! Can you imagine?

57

After that, people would come up to me on the street, ask for autographs. I suddenly realised I was famous."

She positioned a dot of wasabi on a flake of salmon, pushing the tiny construction through a tear-drop of soy. "I took less than a year off with Luisa," she said. "I feel guilty about that, sometimes." She laid the chopsticks down beside her bowl. "What now, sweetheart? Take me somewhere nice."

At the far end of the street the turrets and spires of the Museums rose up into the deepening afternoon light. "But she was always happy with José's parents, and my career was really taking off. What can you do? You have to follow your star. I went back to work and had two songs in the top ten in the next six months. And then I did *Flirting*."

"I remember hearing it on Mykonos," Morgan said. "With my first wife. They were playing it on the beach; and back in Athens it was on every jukebox in the Plaka."

"*I'm looking through your eyes at me. What do you see when you see me?*" Matty sang, her voice so low that it was no more than a breathy whisper. "*Am I still here when you shut your eyes?*" Morgan lowered his head towards hers, her voice just audible above the sounds of the street. "*Am I still in you, are you still in me?*"

They waited for a gap in the traffic, then hurried across the road. "I couldn't believe it when I didn't get Eurovision the following year," Matty said. "That was Dublin, in 1988. They gave it to Rosa, can you believe that? Rosa! *Sonho de Ti!*" She looked up at him, pulling a face. "*I dream of you!* Sweetheart, she was frightful! She shouted her way through that song like she hated it! *Sonho de ti, sofrei por ti! I dream of you, I suffer for you!* I think you'll find it was the audience that suffered, Rosa. Darling, it was painful! And she looked like a man; a man in a tight dress with a flower behind his ear. And we came eighteenth, out of twenty one. We got five points - *Cinq points!* I could have won it."

She stopped, pushing her sunglasses up into her hair, looking up at the towering facade of marble and red brick which stretched ahead of them. "Oh baby," she said. "I didn't realise where we were. That's the V&A, isn't it? I haven't been in there since I was a little girl. Can we go in, sweetheart? I want to go there now, can we please!"

"Of course," Morgan said. "I'll give you a guided tour."

"I shouldn't go on about poor Rosa," Matty said. "It was a long time ago."

Morgan led the way through the entrance hall and into the Sculpture Gallery, the immense length of the room lurid with naked bodies, bewildering orgies of breasts and thighs and writhing limbs, wrapped around each other in contortions of ecstasy and submission.

"When I look back, not getting Eurovision seems like a sort of turning-point," Matty said. "As though my career started to go backwards after that. But I didn't know that at the time, of course, and it didn't happen quickly. Years go by before you begin to see a pattern."

They were standing under the largest sculpture in the gallery, Eric Gill's *Mankind*: the kneeling figure of a naked girl, three or four times life-size, one and a half tons of glittering Derbyshire limestone, cut and polished to a luminous brilliance. The figure has no arms and no head, but it is not incomplete; it's as though Gill had carved her on the border-line between two worlds, where the specific disappears into the Absolute. She is kneeling, but she is not submissive; the curve of her body suggests that her arms are raised up, her head thrown back in some state of exaltation, sexual or religious, or both.

Matty looked up at the silky swells of flesh evoked in stone. "Isn't that beautiful?" she said. "It's so tender. It makes you want to touch it, to stroke it, to run your hands over it." She looked at Morgan. "Don't you want to do that?"

***

"You still move like a dancer; you're so beautiful," Morgan said. "*You have been mine before.*"

"Forget about the past," Matty said. "Let's just start from now."

"It's from Rosetti," he said. "Not a very good poem, but I've always loved that line."

"Look at me," she said, kneeling over him. "Look at me baby, and don't talk so much." She raised her arms above her head, the naked pose of the statue, and loosened her hair. She lowered herself over him so that they touched along every dip and swell of skin, tongue to tongue, pressing herself against him, whispering into his lips: "*I'm looking through your eyes at me. Am I still in you, are you still in me?*"

"No doubt about it," Morgan said.

Chapter Seven

. . .

"Listen to this," Luisa said, reading from the screen. "*What you call the government is simply the political wing of the banking system.*" She swivelled the laptop round on the table. "Come and look at this, Sam. *And the banking system is nothing more than the front-office of gangster-capitalism.* How great is that!" Sam turned away from the window.

"What have you got there?" he said.

"It's Dave Leaper's blog." She scrolled to the top of the page. "*The first thing we do is, let's kill all the lawyers.* That's Shakespeare, apparently, Dick the Butcher."

"There's a man who knows his own mind."

"Listen to this: *They're all criminals. The people that are actually labelled criminals are simply the ones who couldn't move on, who are stuck in the old, dying industries: drugs, prostitution, armed robbery.* How good is that!"

"I'm going to the supermarket," Sam said. "Do you want to come, or can I borrow your card?"

"Are you still thinking about that casting?" she asked. Sam shrugged.

"Can't win them all," he said. "And now that I didn't get it, it wasn't much of a part anyway."

At the news-stand on the corner of Lavender Hill, Luisa stopped to read the bill-board: *Markets turn on Portugal again.*

"Dave Leaper's right," she said. "Look at that."

"I thought you couldn't stand this Arno person," Sam said. "I don't understand why we're all going out to stay with him."

"It's partly for Mum," Luisa said. "I hate to think of her there on her own.

We'll be company. We'll dilute the atmosphere." Sam unhooked a trolley from the rank.

"I want meat," he said, raising his voice against the rumble and shriek of a train running into Clapham Junction. "Any more salads I'll go nuts."

"She really wants me to make the film there," Luisa said. "It's important to her, I don't quite know why."

"Or fish," Sam said. "Maybe that's a compromise."

"Anyway, apart from anything else, it's a way of keeping the connection with Morgan open," Luisa said. "*Red Hammer* is something they've got in common; I suppose it reminds them of the past. And I can tell, he makes her happy. I don't think she's quite admitting it to herself, but it's lovely to see it."

"Pork chops," Sam said. "Is that alright?" Luisa nodded.

"Morgan is bound to come and stay if we film at the clinic," she said. "It was his idea, really; he found the play."

"And fried potatoes," Sam said. "Now we're talking serious dinner. And a bottle of wine, don't you think?"

"I think she likes him a lot," Luisa said. "She's just scared of getting too involved. And I suppose Arno makes her feel safe; he's not threatening, she doesn't have to make any choices."

"Red or white?"

"I think we could turn it into a great film," Luisa said. "The last couple of days I've really started to see it. I want to narrow the focus right down; I want it to be dark, enclosed, claustrophobic, people whispering to each other, looking over their shoulders. And then you burst out of the darkness into the sunlight."

"Red then," Sam said.

"Into that fabulous light," Luisa said. "The beautiful south, I miss it so much! And crowds, and banners, and people marching! And anyway, I want to show you Portugal, it's my homeland, I can't believe you've never been there."

"Sounds expensive," Sam said. Luisa shook her head.

"Mum's right, I've been thinking about it. We can hire extras for pretty much nothing. Almost everything we need is either free or dead cheap. We keep the crew right down: maybe just me and Marley and Kate. We've got the locations, we've got the crowd scenes, most of all we've got the light!" Luisa was standing in the centre of the meat-aisle, her eyes shining as the frames spooled by inside her head, her hands slicing the air, a timid traffic-jam of shoppers behind her manoeuvring their trolleys, trying to get by. "We can really put the dollars on the screen," she said. "It's going to be epic!"

"I'm assuming I'm Chris," Sam said. "So I get dumped, of course."

"Of course," Luisa said. "It'll do you good." She moved her trolley out of the way. "You haven't met Kate, have you? Australian? She and Marley seem to be an item these days. She's good, you'll like her." She looked at him. "Seriously, you'll do a great job."

"Thank you."

"We need to find someone to play Tessa, someone with a bit of pulling power."

"Thanks again."

"Someone who's on the edge of getting noticed."

"Where do they keep the wine here?"

"Don't look like that. I mean someone like you, but a girl. Don't get your hair cut, by the way. This is 1975, I want it as long as possible."

In the flat, she went back to the website. She could hear Sam pulling open drawers in the little kitchen.

"I'm going to make *batatas bravas*," he was saying. "With loads of garlic. Where's that little sharp knife?"

"*The poison-toads of the Nazi press*," Luisa said. "I love the way he writes. Guess who the toads are: the *Daily Mail*, the *Express*, the *Sun.*"

"Look me up a recipe for these potatoes," Sam said. "Tonight we dine like kings. Where's the garlic?"

***

After the screen-writing workshop Luisa took the tube and met her mother in the foyer of the hotel. She led the way across Sloane Square and into King's Road.

"The place is a bit of a mess," she said. "You'll have to not mind."

"I know how artists live, sweetheart," Matty said. "Don't we want that cab?"

"So how are things, Mum? How's Morgan? We can get a bus from here."

"They're thinking about asking me back for a gig at Jimmy's Place," Matty said, finding a seat. "Jack's talking to them now, see if we can do a better deal. Wouldn't that be fun? *By popular demand!*"

"I ought to have a photo of this," Luisa said. "Mum on a bus."

"That's blackmail darling; *Paris-Match* would pay good money. The shame of it!"

"You're not answering me, mother. How are things with you and Morgan?"

"Look!" Matty said, pointing across the Thames as the bus surged over Battersea Bridge. "There's that power-station thing, where I did the first gig. I never really knew where I was: cab in, cab out, all a bit of a blur."

"This is our stop. And you're being very secretive."

In the flat, Matty went quickly from room to room.

"I'm not being secretive," she said. "Everything is fine, I just don't want you cooking up a big drama. I like things the way they are, I like being my own person." She scuffed the carpet with the toe of her shoe. "You could get a couple of bright rugs," she said. "Nothing you can do about the wall-paper." Luisa shrugged.

"I don't notice it any more. It's just a place, it's not like home or something."

"Don't make me feel guilty, sweetheart," Matty said. "How in the world do you cook in this kitchen? It's tiny!"

"What, mother? What was that look?"

"Morgan has an espresso machine in his kitchen," Matty said, smiling to herself. "And a cupboard full of Italian coffee. And there were six bottles of Cliquot in the fridge; and as far as I could see, nothing else at all, not so much as a packet of rice."

"So you've been in his flat! Is it nice?"

"He says he never eats at home. It's a funny place, rather anonymous; not very lived in."

"It needs a woman's touch."

"Stop that at once, baby!" She moved to the window, drawing aside a corner of grimy lace curtain, watching as a police car slid by in the street below. "It's in one of those huge mansion-blocks; when you step off the street and through his front door you feel as if you've disappeared, you've gone to ground. It's a nice feeling actually, very safe and secret. No one would ever find you there, behind so many doors."

"Are you alright, mother?"

"Of course, baby. What sort of question is that? I'm always alright."

"Sam and I are meeting Dave Leaper this evening," Luisa said. "After he finishes work."

"Dave Leaper?" Matty clapped her hands. "So you really are going ahead with the film? I'm so excited!" Luisa nodded.

"But you're not going to tell me anything juicy about Morgan, are you?" she said.

"Certainly not, sweetheart. He's taking me to the theatre tonight. I'm off to the gym for a work-out and a steam, and get my hair done; and that's all you need to know."

***

At half past five the office-blocks around Victoria were emptying out.

"Francis Street," Luisa said. "It should be down here - *The Grenadier*, is that it?" Ahead of them a crowd of young office-workers were spilling in and out of the pub, blocking the pavement in a convivial mass of bodies, clinking glasses, lighting cigarettes, shouting each other down above the uproar, packed closely together as though they were crammed into an invisible room. Luisa stood on the edge of the crowd, watching Sam work his way back out of the pub with their beers.

"How are we going to find him?" he said. "Didn't think of that, did you?"

"It was his idea. He said he was working in some office near here."

"We should have told him to wear a badge," Sam said.

"Wave a flag, more like."

"An anarchist banner: *Class War!* What sort of office? I'm guessing not a bank. "

"He said something about computers."

"Oh dear."

High above them a police helicopter hovered, its pale, reptilian underbelly rotating slowly, a blue light flicking irritably on the tip of its tail; it hung there for several minutes before moving away south towards the river. On the pavement, the crowd around them had expanded, drawing them in towards the centre as new drinkers circulated round the edge, as though creating a vortex.

"Yesterday, there were military helicopters over Trafalgar Square," a voice said, as the thudding of the rotors faded away. A man was standing a little to their right; he had been there, Luisa realised, since Sam had come back with the beers. "Helicopter gunships," he said. "Circling over Nelson's Column. Welcome to the Banana Monarchy."

Luisa took in a light-coloured suit, a lean, middle-aged figure, grey hair pulled back into a short stub of pig-tail. He had a heavy satchel slung over his shoulder. He held out his hand. "I'm Dave Leaper," he said. "This place will quieten down soon enough. They're mostly one-drink wonders around here."

"Do you work around here?" Sam asked.

"Short-term," the man said. "I work for myself. I've been re-synching a disc array for an insurance company round the corner here." Sam nodded.

"I see," he said. "Not really."

"I'm a systems engineer," the man said, shrugging. "That's the kind of thing I do."

Luisa reached into her bag and produced her copy of *Red Hammer,* passing it to him.

"We really like your play, Mr Leaper," she said.

"Dave," he said, abstracted, turning the spiral-bound script over in his hands. He ran a finger over the plastic covers, then riffled through the pages, stopping halfway through, frowning down at the lines of dialogue. "This isn't mine," he said. "I mean, you've had copies made up."

"That's what we wanted to talk to you about," Luisa said. "That's what I was trying to explain in my email."

"Everything's exactly as it was," Sam said. "Your copyright and everything."

"My mum's friend has got the original," Luisa said. "He had the copies made."

"Your mum's friend?"

"So we could work on the shooting script. I'll get the original back for you, if you like."

"It's too noisy out here," Dave Leaper said. "Let's find a table indoors. Start from the beginning. What are you kids drinking?"

Half an hour later they had the back bar to themselves. Sam came over to the table with a tray of beers. "After 1977 I went to the States," Dave was saying. "I needed to get out of Europe for a while; I ended up staying in the US for twenty-six years." He tapped the cover of *Red Hammer,* smiling. "So you're really going to film this thing."

"If that's alright with you," Luisa said.

"I've waited thirty five years for Hollywood to come knocking on my door; I'm hardly going to turn you down."

"It's not exactly big budget," Luisa said. "We won't fill all the production slots; we'll do a lot of doubling up. There'll only be three of us in the crew."

"So you're playing Chris?" Dave said. Sam nodded.

"The main thing is we've got the locations, and the extras." Luisa said. "We'll save a lot of money like that."

""So long as I get my fee," Dave said. "Only kidding. I'd like to come and watch you filming, though."

"Of course," Luisa said, aware of Sam glancing at her. "What?" she said. "There's loads of room, what's Arno going to say? Anyway, Dave should be there. It's his play we're working from." She turned back to him. "You and Mum and Morgan can be our historical advisors. I meant to ask, have you written anything else?"

"No more plays," he said. "Journalism, pamphlets, communiqués." He turned to the title page. "*Barricades Press,*" he said. "They lasted about eighteen months as I recall. And *Red Hammer* got two performances at the Ramparts; an audience of about forty people in both shows. My first night, I was so excited! I don't suppose the old Ramparts is there any more either. Listen," he said, turning to a page near the end, "This is Alvaro talking, the old communist: *You have the revolution, but maybe you don't keep it. You don't have the discipline. Only PCP have the discipline. The ultra-leftists call us social fascists. They think they are anarquista, but they are students, bourgeois, privilege.*"

He looked up from the page. "You've read it," he said. "You know it ends badly; that wasn't what people wanted to hear. They didn't want political truth, they wanted romance, and guns and flowers, and happy endings." He looked at Luisa. "You grew up there," he said. "You know what happened. The people made a revolution for a year or two, and then the bourgeoisie moved back in and repossessed everything. They took everything back."

"It's better than what went before," Luisa said. "It's better than Caetano, and Salazar, and colonial wars." Dave Leaper shrugged.

"Maybe," he said.

"No, really," Luisa said. "It really was an optimistic time. You should hear my Mum talking about it. Anyway, you were there, you saw what it was like. We got democracy, they didn't take that away. And decent education, and at least half-way decent health care. The revolution brought people happiness, it really did. That's what I grew up in: happiness. That's why I want to make the film, because now it really has got worse, like you say in your blog. I love the way you write, by the way!"

66

"Thank you."

"For me, that's what the film is all about: so much idealism back then, and now it feels like the world is being run by criminals, like you say."

"Maybe it's better like that."

"Or even if it's not being run by criminals, it's at the mercy of criminals. How can that be better?"

"No more smiling masks," Dave said. "The Beast is revealed."

"Magic!" Sam said. "That's so cool." Dave grinned at him.

"It is," he said. "Isn't it?" He got to his feet and shook hands briskly with each of them. "We'll keep in touch; I'll come and see you in Portugal."

They watched him make his way out of the bar, silhouetted for a moment in the bright frame of the open doors.

"Do you think he really means all that stuff?" Sam said. "He's quite a talker; hard to know what to make of him."

"You're quite free with invitations to Arno's place, aren't you?"

"Why not? It's all reinforcements for Mum; he's got a crowd of his own people there all the time: Bendt people. Anyway, I don't suppose he'll show up."

Chapter Eight

. . .

As Howard opened the side door of the Lecture Theatre and stepped up on to the stage, something moved through the shadows at the far end of the room, high up, above the top tier of seating. He switched on the lights and looked round the theatre with an obscure unease, seeing nothing out of place. His books and the lecture notes were still on the lectern where he'd left them, and he shuffled them into order and slipped them into his briefcase. He straightened up, still feeling the sense of movement in the room, a presence that was palpable, just beyond the periphery of vision.

As he turned towards the door, reaching for the light-switches, a barn-owl flew across the room above his head in a single curving swoop, on silent wings. It landed on the bracket of the video projector in the centre of the ceiling, flapping and clattering for a moment until it got a secure perch. Settling, it turned its white face, like a painted mask, towards Howard, watching him out of black, impenetrable eyes. Howard sighed.

"Now what?" he said. The bird shifted from foot to foot, long talons curled around the metal frame, its head perfectly still, staring back at him. There was one bar of signal on his mobile; he called the Estates Department.

He went for his weekly session the following day. Dr. Walters closed his notebook and looked up at him.

"Why do you think you felt so agitated?" he said. "It was just a practical problem, wasn't it? Apart from the mystery of how it got in there, of course."

"It gave me a shock," Howard said. "It was so out of place. It was so big. Maybe I was frightened of it; not frightened exactly, something else. I think I was a bit wound up already; I hate losing things. The lecture notes had some personal stuff in with them, and I really didn't want it all floating around the University. Do you know that feeling, when you lose something? You feel the whole structure of your life becoming unstable?" He looked out of the window. On the strip of lawn, a black cat was performing a series of ritual movements, sinuous and measured, like T'ai Chi. Dr. Walters leaned back in his chair.

"So you found your notes," he said. "But the feeling didn't go away?"

"The chap from Estates was new, or I didn't know him. I could tell he thought I was fairly odd."

"Why do you think that?" Howard shifted in his chair, trying to get comfortable.

"I was being rather hyperactive," he said. "There was a ludicrous side to it. We didn't have the slightest idea what to do. The windows in the Theatre are high up and very narrow; you can't get at them without a ladder, and anyway they were shut. I kept making silly jokes. I could hear myself, it was embarrassing." While he'd been talking, the cat on the lawn had caught a bird.

"How did you solve the problem?" Dr. Walters said. The cat flicked a paw at the bird, flipping it onto its back.

"We found a step-ladder," Howard said. "And the Estates chap came back with one of those nets on a long pole; they use them to clear leaves off the pond. The ladder was far too short." The cat had let the bird hop a few paces away before darting at it again, flashing its claws across it, knocking it to the ground.

"What did you do then?"

"We waved the net around, never got within a few feet of it. It was getting more and more agitated. It kept flying from the projector to the window-sills, but it couldn't get a proper grip there. It would start slipping off, and have to fly back again. I suppose it knew there was open sky on the other side of the glass."

"How was all this making you feel?"

"Very bad. It was so big, it was so out of place. And suddenly I started to get a terrible feeling: I suddenly knew that I had produced the owl myself. It was part of me; it had somehow broken loose, detached itself, as though a piece of myself had been torn out, as though my rib-cage had burst away from me. My ribs were wings, covered in blood and feathers, flying round the room." He looked across at Dr. Walters. "That's how it felt," he said. "Not a metaphor. I really thought that's what had happened."

The cat had gone. A couple of feathers lifted and fell in the breeze. Howard shrugged. "I don't feel like that any more," he said. "I haven't really gone nuts." Dr. Walters smiled.

"What happened to the owl?"

"Reinforcements from the Estates Department. They got a blanket over it, so they said. I was staying well away by then." They shook hands at the door.

"I'll see you next week," Dr. Walters said. "We'll come back to this."

Howard drove down to the bay and ran on the beach for exactly an hour; it was just under eight miles to the old coast-guard station and back, so he was well off the pace, but he'd only had the larger block in the backpack for a week, and hadn't adjusted to it yet. As it was he'd cut it a little too fine. He decided it would be better to turn up at the Exam Board meeting in his tracksuit, which was clean and smart enough, rather than make himself late by showering and changing.

The nurse had got Anne up and had left her in the wheelchair. Howard found her by the double doors leading out on to the terrace.

"I couldn't get them open," she said. "It's that bolt at the bottom, I couldn't get it. I should have asked Beverley to open them before she left." He parked her in the sunshine, and went to make a cup of tea. She took the beaker from him, holding it with both hands. "I think it's worse when the weather's nice," she said. "You know it's not going to last. It's a kind of cruelty." Howard nodded. "You start to relax," Anne said. "You can feel the sun lay its hands on you. And the next day it's raining and cold, and everything inside you shrinks."

"I saw Dr. Walters again this morning, talking of shrinks. I think its doing some good. I told him about the owl."

"I want one last time in the sun," Anne said. "I want to feel the heat pressing down on me. I don't want to die in the rain, Howard."

"It's like the fox the other day," Howard said. "Do you remember me telling you? It crossed the road in front of me just before the bridge, where you can't see round the corner. If I hadn't slowed down for it, I would have run smack into that lorry, right on the apex of the bend." He became aware of Anne staring at him. "I'm not going nuts," he said. "I'm not getting messages from the animals. I think what I keep seeing is the counterfactual world, the world of things that don't happen, the unrealised fraction of events, like a remainder in maths. It was the same thing with the dead cow. We're following a trail, but there's a network of paths spreading out on either side that we don't go down. Does that make sense to you?" Anne shook her head.

"Why won't you listen to me?" she said. "You have to do something. I don't want to die here in the rain."

"You won't," Howard said. "That's not going to happen."

Away to the west, an aeroplane was drawing perfect lines of silver across the sky. As he watched, the winds in the upper atmosphere began to break the trails into twisted fragments, like lines of code, a series of symbolic markings like a mutated alphabet, like notes on a stave, like the transcription of DNA, and for a moment he had a sense of what it might mean. Anne drank from the beaker.

"Pass me the tissues," she said. "I'm dribbling this everywhere." She smiled at him. "Don't look so panic-stricken," she said. "It's called emotional lability: wild mood swings. It's symptomatic."

"I'm not panic-stricken," Howard said. Anne turned the wheelchair to face the sun. She closed her eyes.

"I'm serious, Running Man, I want us to get away. I want you to do this for me. I want to wake up somewhere in the cool of the morning when the light is still sweet and fresh, and know that I need to make the most of it because in a couple of hours the air will be trembling with heat, and the light so bright it feels like a solid substance. I want to feel crushed by the heat all day, until at last the light turns golden, and the shadows lengthen, and a breeze comes down from the hills. And I want to know that it'll be like that every day, day after day, for as far ahead as I can see."

Chapter Nine

· · ·

Through the blurred lozenge of the window another aeroplane was cutting diagonally across the clouds, trailing smoke, a foreign body as black as grit in the oyster of the sky. Morgan's gin and tonic trembled on the plastic table as they bumped through its choppy wake. *The sky is a unity, as the sea is.* He read through the trip folder again, shaking his head. Angie had attached a note: *Sorry to spring this on you, Bob's mother's very ill. They might want to see Schindler's List locations - do your best, it's a small group and it's only a long weekend!* He put his earphones back in. Matty was singing *Broken Telephone,* just a piano and a slide guitar backing her: *The wind is singing in the wires...*

The tombstones in the Old Cemetery at Kazimierz were warm to the touch. His group followed him down the path between the graves, the grass and meadow flowers on either side of them knee high, stirring faintly as they passed, flickering with sulphur-yellow butterflies as bright as little stars. There were only ten of them, middle-aged to elderly, from Florida. Morgan could calculate the size of his tip just by looking at them.

"Before the war this was a place of pilgrimage," he said. "Thousands of people would visit every year. There are Rabbis buried here who were so powerful that just mentioning their name would heal the sick. The Germans used it as a rubbish dump." No one said anything.

They had lunch outside at a café across the square. "Spielberg filmed the ghetto scenes here because it was more picturesque," Morgan said. The subdued clatter of cutlery fell silent for a moment, then resumed. "The real ghetto, where the bodies were lying in the streets and the gutters were running with blood, was in Podgórze, on the other side of the river. So when he filmed the Jewish population being herded across the bridge, they were going the wrong way."

"Does it really make a difference?" Mrs Rickman said. Morgan gestured across the square.

"I think it's a metaphor about film-making," he said. "Imagine Spielberg coming here to film. He has all the glamour and wealth of Hollywood behind him; it's like the Second Coming. He has the power to re-order history. He's surrounded by assistants and secretaries, and runners and translators; the film-crew itself is like an armoured column. There are semi-trailers parked up full of rib-eye steaks and cold beer; there are coils of power-cables looping all over the square."

He paused, leaving space for a response; he was beginning to enjoy himself. There was a series of faint clinks as someone reached a carafe of water round the table, refilling glasses. "Through the magical power of Dreamworks, he can do anything he wants," Morgan went on. "He can re-imagine the past the way it should have been. He can raise the dead from their graves. He has absolute power over the SS; they sit around in groups, reduced to bit-part players, bored extras, smoking and playing cards, docile and submissive, waiting to be given the order for the next atrocity. And everybody comes back to life in the end. Film-making is an act of exorcism. By bringing them back over the bridge he is bringing them back to life. Death is on the other side of the river."

He smiled at his audience. It wasn't working; they really weren't getting it. He was beginning to feel that special euphoria that can sometimes happen on stage: you're off your mark, you've missed the cue; you don't know how to get back to where you're supposed to be. You can either freeze, or wade on in, hoping you find your feet again.

"I think he must have felt like the Messiah," Morgan said. "Bringing redemption. The trouble was there weren't many Jews left to appreciate the favour, and it's not clear that the Poles really wanted to be redeemed; but it's brought in a lot of tourist money ever since."

A column of Israeli high-school kids were queuing to go into the synagogue, waving flags and chattering. At the head of the line their minder was speaking into his throat-mike, amplified Hebrew booming out across the square, falling silent as the last of them filed through the doorway. "Did everyone enjoy their lunch?" Morgan said. "This afternoon we're going round the Wawel - the Royal Palace, the sanctuary of the nation: tapestries and state rooms and suits of armour, and the tombs of all the kings and queens of Poland. You're going to love it, I promise you!"

"I still don't see what difference the bridge makes," Mrs Rickman said.

Sometime in the night Morgan was woken out of half-sleep by the sound of footsteps in the room above his; a sound he had come to associate with his mother and with mental illness: that endless walking in the room above, footsteps knocking overhead, that restless, inconclusive pacing, end to end along the floorboards, hours at a time. The air conditioning was off, and the room was stuffy; he raised the window and looked down into *Westerplatte*. An empty tram was sliding past below him on its way to the depot, wheels grinding and shrieking as it took the curve, throwing out a crackling shower of sparks from its pantograph. Across the street, in the fringe of gardens that circled the Old Town, the survivors of a hen-party limped and staggered along the path between the trees, dragging broken heels, too drunk and tired to cry.

There was a message on his phone from Matty, her voice sleepy and low: *Hello from Lisbon, sweetheart. It's been 34° here today and it's still so hot I'm trying to get to sleep but I can't I'm just melting. Night night, baby. Dream about me.* He called her back, but her phone went straight to voicemail.

***

Long white curtains, almost transparent, were stirring in the breeze from the half-open doors. Matty brushed through them and out onto the balcony. Below her, a woman in a black bikini was lying on a sunbed by the swimming pool, a book open across her lap. At the far end of the pool, fifty metres away, someone was dipping a long net into the water to clear away fallen leaves. A peacock picked its way delicately along the ridge of the compound wall. Matty drew back into the bedroom and found a robe laid out on the chair. Pulling it round her, she unpacked her case, organised her make-up in the bathroom, setting out jars and bottles along the glass shelves, hung up her dresses, and left the room in a halo of Chanel. The hallway was cool and dim, vaulted ceilings and marble floors, a succession of tall mirrors briefly recording her as she passed.

She met Julietta coming down the stairs carrying a tray littered with breakfast debris. The girl beamed at her.

74

"Senhora Matty! Jà voltou! Vai tudo bem? A senhora quer o pequeno almoço?"
"Belissima, Julietta! Sim, faz favor!"

The sunlight on the top terrace was already dazzling. Below her the pool danced in glittering points of light as the woman in the bikini swam a length. A line of young palm trees threw deep shade over the cloisters of the guest quarters. Julietta arranged the little table, setting out yoghurt and honey, cherries, warm bread rolls, a pot of coffee. Beyond the walls of the compound the valley fell away between swathes of low hills, stepping down through orange groves and poly-tunnels towards the distant silver of the sea. On the edge of sight, white high-rise buildings crowded into a strip of horizon between the salt-flats and the airport.

Matty finished her coffee and lay back in the lounger. She closed her eyes as the sun pressed down on her, laying its weight and heat over her until she felt herself opening like a flower. In the vast dome of sound surrounding her she could hear the clanking bells of a flock of milking sheep a couple of fields away, the shrill buzz of a scooter further down the valley, the braying two-tone of the fish-man's horn. She didn't hear the hiss of Arno's wheelchair until he was right beside her. She sat up, putting on her sunglasses.

"When did you get back?" Arno said.

"I didn't want to disturb you," Matty said. "The plane from Lisbon was delayed." Arno nodded. He was wearing a bright blue silk robe, like a samurai war-lord, swarming with intricate dragons picked out in red and gold.

"Be careful not to burn," he said. "The sun is strong already, and your skin is so fair." He touched her forearm. "You will burn very easily." Matty looked at the dark fingers resting on her arm.

"I'm always careful," she said. He moved his hand.

"I am a salamander," he said. "I do not burn."

From far down the valley the rumble and crash of heavy equipment rolled back towards them, a plume of yellow dust rising from the unfinished apartment blocks that stood, unsold and boarded up, in oppressive circles around the church, the jacaranda-shaded central square, the market-place and the little cobbled streets of São Miguel do Monte. "Look at me," Arno said. "Let me see you properly; take off the glasses."

They looked into each other's eyes for a long moment, Matty smiling slightly, Arno nodding.

"Well?" Matty said. "What can you see?"

"You are happy," Arno said. "That's good."

"Thank you," Matty said. She put her sunglasses back on. "Thank you for the consultation, my dear Dr. Bendt."

"It is my pleasure, my dear Miss James."

"I'm happy to be here," Matty said. "And I had a wonderful time in London; so, yes, I'm very happy. Your diagnosis is perfect, as always. You know me so well, dear Arno."

"And how long were you in Lisbon?"

"I spent some time with my mother-in-law. She's so frail these days, she's such a darling. She shouldn't be on her own."

"Tell me, what was the best thing about being in London?" Matty looked at him.

"Being taken seriously," she said. "As a singer. And spending time with Luisa, of course. I must talk to you about that." A girl Matty didn't recognise cleared the breakfast things off the table, lifting the tray away with a quick, shy smile. Arno watched her as she crossed the terrace.

"There is something I need to ask you, Matty," he said, as the girl trotted lightly down the flagged steps and out of sight. "Will you drive me to the coast today, to Ilha Negra? I want to talk to the hotel people, and I must be near the sea for a little while."

Jorge brought the car to the front gates, stepping out and holding the driver's door open for Matty. It was a Mercedes, a red convertible; she hadn't seen it before. She watched as Arno levered himself out of the wheelchair and into the passenger seat with quick, easy movements, as agile as a gymnast on the parallel bars.

"I like this car," she said, swinging round the hairpin bends of the track, trailing a plume of red dust. On the motorway she pulled out into the fast lane and was doing 200kph by the time they reached the first viaduct, racing over a landscape of stunted cork-trees and abandoned farms. On the crest of a low hill the ruins of a Moorish fort were crumbling back into the red earth. In the deep leather seats there was hardly any wind-noise. Arno looked at her.

"You drive as you sing," he said. "You have panache."

"Thank you darling." They swung off the motorway and on to the coast road, passing kitchen-showrooms, and tractor-dealerships, and ranks of apartment blocks set in dusty vacant lots; past brick-stacks and piles of unused sand and towering, silent cranes.

"Tell me about your time in London." Arno said. "Tell me about being taken seriously, is that what you said?" They stopped on the edge of a traffic jam, some dispute between a bus and a lorry, a line of cars backed up and idling, radiating heat and rage.

"I was talking about the jazz-clubs I was playing," Matty said. "They were little places, but they had specialist audiences. Maybe only thirty or forty people, but they knew what they were listening to, and they liked me."

"Of course," Arno said. Matty shook her head.

"I mean they liked me as a singer, as a jazz-singer; not as a curvy little body in a tight dress."

"Maybe it's possible to like both."

"Thank you, darling, you're sweet. The thing is, I'm ten times a better singer now than I was when I was famous. Ironic, isn't it? Fat lot of good it does me." The cars in front of them were hooting their horns, a discordant, involuntary braying, as though the heat had reached some threshold beyond which it had to issue into sound. Matty sighed. "Such nice places, but they pay so little," she said.

"We will find you more work," Arno said.

At the hotel, staff in maroon uniforms fussed around the car, fetching the wheelchair out of the boot and setting it up for Arno to lift himself into, taking the keys from Matty, putting a plastic sheet over the front seats and driving it away to park underground. Matty sat in the shade by the hotel pool and drank mint tea while Arno had his meeting. It was still off-season, and the resort was nearly empty. A young Portuguese couple were splashing about in the shallow end of the pool with a little girl of eight or nine. They looked so happy, the little girl dark and skinny and shrieking with laughter; in a world of their own, in a little universe of three.

A breeze was coming off the sea; they took the old coast road for a few kilometres, running along beside the beach before turning inland. Arno was breathing deeply. "There is a year of life for every movement of the lungs," he said. "From the salt in the sea, to the breath in the chest, to the blood in the veins." Matty nodded, concentrating on overtaking a lorry.

"Jazz pays so little," she said. "But I'm an artist; the golf-hotels and resorts like this aren't good for me. I realise now those gigs last year nearly killed me, the few I actually managed to get. They don't pay enough for that."

"They like you here in Algarve," Arno said.

"They sit there glassy-drunk in their tuxedos, and the women in those unbelievable dresses, and it's just part of the meal: dessert, and fruit and cheese, followed by little me, trying to do jazz and give them something really good, when all they really want is cabaret numbers, all the standards."

"I think they like you very much."

"They don't get me, darling. They don't get what I'm trying to do. Most of them don't know who I am, and the few that do, they want me to stick to my eighties and nineties stuff. All they really want is *Bimbo-Boumbo* back again. Did you know that's what the fan-club used to call me? Can you imagine? It was the title of my first TV special."

"Take this turn here," Arno said, gesturing, the gold on his fingers catching the sun for a moment in a flash of light. "Let us go over the mountain; it is so beautiful."

"And those are the good audiences," Matty said. "As good as they get down here. The worst ones talk through the songs, or click their fingers for the waiter, or leave before the end of the set."

They drove through the little village at the top of the hill, narrow white streets stunned and silent in the heat. Beyond, range upon range of steeply-wooded mountains rolled away north towards Alentejo.

"There can be work for you here half the summer if you want it," Arno said. "I have talked to the hotel. I will talk to the Dona Margarita, also to the Flor do Mar. These hotels will like you, they will find work for you to do."

At eight o'clock, as the light deepened, Matty walked slowly down the stone steps to the terrace by the pool, concentrating on making an entrance. She was wearing the red silk dress, matching her lipstick, and she'd put her hair up in a thick and tangled mop of blonde. Charcoal smoke was blowing about in the evening breeze; she breathed in the sweet and pheremonal smell of lobster grilling on the barbecue, the scent of rosemary and wild thyme, of perfume and designer sun-block and, faintly, the odour of drains. There were a dozen people sitting at the long table under the arcade, all of them turning to watch her as she stepped down onto the terrace.

Arno presented her to the new guests, seated at the head of the table in another samurai robe, red this time, with purple dragons, bowing from the waist as he introduced the other guests. Julietta and Maria made their way round the table pouring champagne, bobbing and smiling. The woman who'd been swimming in the pool turned out to be Swedish, her name was Anita, she'd been here ten days.

"I begin to return to myself," she said. "Arno is bringing me back from far away, from a bad place."

"I'm glad to hear that," Matty said. "Where did you get the bikini you had on this morning? It's lovely, it must have come from a good place." Anita was methodically shredding a bread roll into a little pyramid of crumbs.

"Is Arno helping you also?" she said. Matty sipped at the icy wine.

"Arno helps everybody," she said. She raised her glass and smiled at him down the table. Anita touched her elbow.

"You see the man and woman on his each side?" she said, lowering her voice. "They have couple-therapy, two sessions a day, very intensive."

"I can imagine darling," Matty said.

"You have read *Sword and Silk?*" Anita asked her. "Arno describe the method, between the woman and the man." She added a fragment of bread to the top of the pyramid. "Or the woman and the woman. There is always who is sword and who is silk. I have read it in Swedish, of course: *Svärd och Siden.* It's very wonderful."

"I think I must have missed that one," Matty said.

The table had fallen silent; everyone was looking at Arno. He raised his right hand, two fingers extended in a gesture of blessing, the sleeve of his robe falling back to his elbow, his forearm as thin as a stick.

"We travel this road together," he said. "We find wisdom in each other. We take strength from each other. We find love through willing acceptance. Regret vanishes! Radiance pours down on us!" As he finished speaking he raised both hands, and at almost the same moment, Jorge began splitting the lobsters, driving in a knife behind the eyes, sawing back along the thorax and the tail, releasing sweet and salty juices that spurted out around the blade and onto the plates.

As the light faded to a greenish glow along the line of the hills, Julietta lit rows of lamps down the centre of the table, bowls of yellow glass burning lemon-scented oil. The therapy-couple were the first to leave the table. When Anita got up, murmuring and smiling to herself, walking quickly across the terrace and through the arch into the cloisters, Arno motioned to Matty. "Come and sit beside me," he said. "Come and talk with me." He nodded, smiling, as the last of the guests left the table. "Goodnight, Mrs. Donaldson.

We will make good progress tomorrow. *Schlaf gut!* Be full of strength!"

"Thank you, Dr. Bendt." She gestured vaguely at the dark pool, the globes of yellow light on the long table, the fading horizon of hills. "Thank you for all of this." Arno turned back to Matty.

"I will enjoy being a film-producer," he said. "I like your idea for Luisa. It will be good to have her here with us."

"She'll come with friends, of course," Matty said. "Her film crew, and actors; it's an important project for her."

"Of course. There is room for all here. We will find you a bigger space, I have been thinking. Your room is too small."

"I'm fine, dear. I like it where I am." She looked at Arno. "I like to be able to come and go," she said. "I want to try and find more gigs in Lisbon."

"I have told you Matty, there is work for you here in Algarve."

"I want to be taken seriously," Matty said. "And I also want to be paid decently. That's not too much to ask, surely?"

"We will talk to the hotels. I think they will pay more."

"And I want to go back to London. I need to expand my career - Paris, New York, why not? It's just a matter of self-belief."

"You have a good opportunity here."

"After all, darling, look at Marianne Faithfull! If she can do it, why shouldn't I? I was a bigger star than her once upon a time; she was just a pop-singer's girlfriend. How often did she get into the charts? But look at her now, she's huge, she's global, she's started all over again." She watched the lamp-flames dip and flicker in a breath of night wind. "I can do that too," she said. "I can start over again. And I sing better, too."

"Of course," Arno said. "But start here. Start with Dona Margarita and Flor do Mar."

"At Jimmy's Place I was doing what I do best," she said. "Here, half the audience isn't even listening. And it's not as though they pay that well. I used to get paid ten times what they pay me here."

"I told you I will talk to them," Arno said. "Also there is a lesson here, Matty: if we want to change our lives, we must start by accepting our circumstances as they really are, not as we would like them to be."

"I have to go to Lisbon," Matty said. "I want to talk to my agent. All I need to do is believe in myself."

Little moths and mites were circling the yellow flames of the oil-lamps, dancing in the updraught. As they watched, a moth passed too close to the heat, its wings shrivelling instantly, pinched out like a candle-flame between two fingers.

"It's a good opportunity for Luisa to make her film here," Arno said. "One must be prepared to seize the opportunity when it comes." He patted her hand as she flicked the tiny corpse off the table. "I have lived a long life," he said. "I know that chances come, and then they are gone."

"I think it's a fabulous opportunity for Luisa," Matty said brightly. "What would we all do without you, dear Arno! But you know, I've lived quite a long life too, darling, and I know that you have to believe in yourself; you have to follow your star. I always have done, and I always will."

Back in her bedroom, she opened the balcony doors and sat outside, watching the constellations wheel above her head. A shooting star sliced silently across the western horizon, and she made a wish. She smoked a cigarette, smiling as she pictured Arno's disapproval. A couple of miles away, headlights were sweeping along invisible roads in the dark hills, lorries bringing refuse from the resort hotels to landfill somewhere in the mountains. She fetched her phone from her bag, and sent Morgan a text: *Where are you now, sweetheart? I'm going to be back in Lisbon next week. Get on a plane, come and meet me there.*

Chapter Ten

. . .

"Stay at my place," Morgan said. There was a silence. "Howard?" he said. "Can you hear me? Stay at my place. When do you get in? I'll meet your train."

He saw him from a long way down the platform, toiling through the evening crowds, towing a suitcase that kept tipping over on its side.

"They put out a call for papers," Howard said. "I just bunged in an abstract because, you know, why not? I was a bit amazed when they accepted it."

"How's Anne? Is she at home?"

"It's at UCL," Howard said. "How far is that from you? I have to be there at 9.30 tomorrow: the Centre for Advanced Studies." His suitcase swerved off the pavement and he dragged it along in the gutter for several paces.

"Mind the traffic," Morgan told him. "They don't take prisoners here. You haven't got bricks in that, have you?"

"Books," Howard said. "I thought I better reference this thing a bit more; I did some on the train."

They stopped at the front entrance of Morgan's block. Howard looked up at the facade, five stories of red brick and tall bay-windows, elegantly shabby, nodding to himself as though some private estimate had been confirmed.

"I've got champagne in the fridge," Morgan said. "Let's have a drink, then we'll go and find somewhere to eat; there's nothing much in the flat." Howard bumped and dragged his suitcase up the front steps. "How is Anne?" Morgan said. "Is she at home?"

"I've been developing this thing about counterfactuals," Howard said. "The things that don't happen." He followed Morgan into the flat, the wheels of his suitcase jamming on the kilim rug and dragging it across the floor. "The aborted world," he said. "The children we never had." He went over to the window, looking out into a narrow well of brick wall. "She's having a week of respite care; she's in the cottage hospital." He looked around the room. "This is a nice place," he said. "Where's this drink of yours?"

By the time they left the building Morgan's side of the street was in deep shade; they crossed the road into vivid evening light. "She says she wants to go away," Howard said. "She says she doesn't want to die in the rain." He drew a breath, looking up into the bright stripe of blue above the shadowed blocks of flats and offices. Morgan nodded.

"You should go away together," he said. "It's what I was telling you in Llanbrychan. I'm going to organise something for you, something magical. I'll arrange everything; you two just get on a plane."

"Let me try and explain," Howard said. "Imagine an ice-breaker, forcing its way through the pack-ice. A channel opens up into the future, but it's jagged - a web of fractures radiates out on either side, like a broken mirror; fragments break away. These things are counterfactuals, the unrealised fraction of events, itineraries not taken."

"Sounds a bit like tour-guiding," Morgan said. They turned onto Edgware Road. "Where do you want to eat? We've got Indian, Chinese, Thai, Vietnamese, Iranian, Moroccan? Plenty of counterfactuals."

"Potentially," Howard said.

"Italian? Algerian? Iraqi? Egyptian?" He nodded to a group of men sitting at a pavement table in a cloud of fragrant smoke, the rise and fall of their conversation harmonising with the musical bubbling of a water-pipe. *"As-salaam alaikum,"* he said, and a couple of them murmured a response: *"Wa alaikum e-salaam."*

"It's good to be shot of that damn suitcase," Howard said. "The wheels are coming off." He gave a short laugh. "How appropriate is that?"

"What's the title of your paper?" Morgan asked. "How exactly do these counterfactuals of yours fit into English literature?"

"It's where all mythology comes from," Howard said. "As actuality drives on it releases hypotheticals, and those spaces are filled with heraldic beasts: chimeras, salamanders, owls."

"Owls?"

"You better believe it," Howard said.

"I know where we'll go," Morgan said. "You'll like this place."

They turned down a narrow sidestreet. In the window of a dimly-lit café a man was sitting at a table by himself, his head in his hands. Howard paused, looking in. "Not there," Morgan said. "We have to go a little further."

"Did you see his shoes?" Howard said. He shook his head. "Anyway, applied to literature, it means that everything is contingent. It's as though you were looking at a row of nearly identical books; you pick one out and start to read, and it's *Our Man in Havana*. Do you remember how it begins?"

"This way," Morgan said. They turned at an unmarked doorway, brushing through a curtain of metallic beads and up a steep flight of stairs. Howard was still talking as they climbed.

"Do you remember? Jim Wormold and Dr. Hasselbacher are having their morning drink at the Wonder Bar?"

The stairs brought them into a room crowded with long tables, set close together. At the far end a door opened into a kitchen. The place was nearly full: family groups, the men in dark suits, the women wearing the *hijab,* pale children with eyes as dark and round as owls. Morgan found a couple of empty chairs between two families, everyone smiling and nodding at them as they sat down. Howard was still talking. "They're drinking their daiquiris," he said, "and looking out the window at an old black man, who is walking slowly down the street."

The owner of the restaurant came over, beaming at Morgan, and set down two glasses of a thin and milky liquid, gesturing with elegant hospitality for them to drink.

"*Motshakeram,*" Morgan said. "*Merci.* It's called doogh, "he said to Howard. "It's made from yoghurt. Try it." Howard nodded.

"The old black man sells pornographic photos to tourists," he said. "Dr. Hasselbacher makes some comment about him to Jim Wormold, and they order more drinks." He shrugged. "Perhaps you go on reading for a while; then you put the book back on the shelf, slipping it in between all the others. You get on with your life, and Jim Wormold gets on with his."

"Try it," Morgan said, and Howard sipped, nodding.

"Good," he said. They were served their food: skewers of spiced lamb on flatbread. "As a matter of fact I'm starving." The family opposite him nodded and smiled, watching as he struggled with the skewers. "Where was I?" he said.

"The old black man?" Morgan said. "Jim Wormold?"

"That's right," Howard said. "Here's the thing: you picked out *Our Man in Havana*; you didn't look at the book immediately to the left of it. And in that book, the one you didn't open, a tourist buys a set of pornographic photos from an old black man in Havana." He paused, chewing. "The tourist is travelling on his own; he's recovering from a breakdown. The images in the photos penetrate his mind like poisoned darts. It's exactly as though he's been injected with a lethal pathogen. From the moment he opens the envelope and fans the photographs out on the table in his hotel bedroom and recognises the girl, he begins his descent into Hell." He looked around the room. "Where are we?" he said. Morgan looked at him.

"Off Edgware Road?" he said. "Near my flat?" Howard shook his head.

"I know that," he said. "Where's here?"

"This place? It's Iranian," Morgan said. "I've been coming here for years."

"Do you understand what I'm saying?" Howard asked him. "The book you didn't open is a counterfactual. It was never on the shelf. It exists only in the unrealised world, which is a world of infinite possibility, infinitely vast; but you can't get at it, however much you feel it all around you." He tore off a piece of unleavened bread, gesturing at Morgan with it. "There are an infinite number of books that are not *Our Man in Havana*. But Greene's book can only exist because of all those unrealised books. It's the same for every category of thing. Whatever exists in the realised world owes its reality to the unrealised. You can't have a path through the woods unless it's surrounded by woods where there are no paths." He waved the bread at Morgan. "But fiction cuts new tracks through the forest."

"I wish I could hear your paper tomorrow," Morgan said. "But I've got to be at the airport by midday."

"Never mind," Howard said. "I'll probably make a balls of it anyway." He leaned back in his chair. "Never mind all that," he said. "Tell me about Matty. What was it like meeting her again?"

***

In Avenida da Liberdade she took his arm, leaning into his shoulder.

"I want to show you the flat," she said. "Or walk past the building anyway." The immense width of the avenue was softened and shaded by palm trees and jacaranda, the cobbled pavements laid out in geometric patterns of black and white marble, mosaics of squares and diamonds and arabesques like musical notation, the choreography of her footsteps beside his.

"I thought I'd remember it better," Morgan said, watching the ceaseless flow of traffic as it flickered between the trees, flashes of sunlight spangling on windscreens. "I don't recognise anything." They were walking past jewellery stores and designer boutiques, little palaces of mirrors and replications, a dream-world of lacquer, gloss and shadow. From the foyer of a hotel a doorman, sweating under a top-hat and braided frock-coat, saluted Matty as they passed, and she turned and blew him a kiss. "Maybe the trees are bigger," Morgan said. "They must have grown in thirty years. Maybe that's why it looks so different. It's hard to imagine thousands of people marching down here. It's hard to imagine there ever was a revolution." Matty nodded. *"So much music in the bars at night,"* she said. *"And revolution in the air.* So long ago."

Ahead of them, the avenue opened up into the vast space of Marquès de Pombal, a distant ring of high-rise buildings under a bright blue dome of sky, the Marquess stepping forward into emptiness from his marble pedestal in the centre of the square, a bronze lion crouching at his feet, the plinth surrounded by plough-oxen and fecund women and the fruits of the earth and the sea. They turned off the Avenida onto a side-street. A gypsy woman was squatting in a doorway, hunched over a tin cup. She looked up and murmured something, offering a little spray of dried flowers.

"Don't, sweetheart," Matty said. "There's no point encouraging them."

"Two euros," Morgan said. "How much encouragement is that?" He dropped the coin into the cup. They had stopped in front of a medium-rise block of flats, steel and marble, a short flight of steps leading up to glass doors and a row of bell-pushes. Matty looked up.

"We were so happy here," she said. "It's a very good address. We moved here in 1986; Luisa was a year old, my career was really taking off. That's our balcony there, do you see, on the sixth floor? We were complete; we were a little universe of three. It's so strange to think of someone else living here; that I can't just trot up those steps and let myself in." She sighed, gripping his arm. "Oh baby," she said.

Over her shoulder, Morgan looked at the gypsy, crouched over her cup; the woman stared back at him. A bus blew past them in a gust of warm air. Matty shook herself, still holding on to him, a little shiver running up his arm. "That's enough of that," she said. "There's a taxi-rank on the next block.

Let's grab a cab and I'll show you the sights, see how much you remember. My turn to be the tour-guide. Have you got cash on you?"

In the back of the cab she put her arms around him, burying her face in his neck. "Let's be in the same hotel, baby," she said. "Arno booked me into the Avenida Palace, but it's only a single, it's better if I come to you. Let's be together tonight."

Morgan paid the taxi off below the walls of Castelo São Jorge, the steep and narrow alleys of Alfama behind them.

"I remember this," he said. "I remember these little streets." They climbed to the top of the ramparts, through gardens dense with oleander, peacocks picking in the dusty shade. Below them, Lisbon lay folded into its seven hills in glimmering variations of pink and ochre and gold.

"Look, you can just see our building," Matty said. "See it catching the sun there. We had such fabulous views! I'll probably have to look for somewhere further north next time." She clutched his arm as a peacock shrieked at them from somewhere in the shrubbery.

"Next time?" Morgan said.

"The next flat we get," Matty said. "I hate not having a base here." A male bird wobbled unsteadily across the path in front of them, the great fan of its tail swaying.

"I'd forgotten the peacocks," Morgan said. "They're coming back. I remember smoking dope with you up here, that Angolan weed, do you remember? It felt like there were peacocks everywhere."

"Do you, baby? That's so sweet." She patted his arm. "I need a good relationship with two or three jazz promoters in Lisbon," she said. "Not just clubs; bigger venues, full-scale concerts - imagine me at the Gulbenkian! That's mainly why I'm up here; and to see you of course, sweetheart. Then a couple of gigs in Algarve from time to time, just to keep Arno happy."

Away to their left, an aeroplane was crossing the Tagus above the statue of Christ in Majesty, hanging low over the rooftops of Lapa and Rato, heading north to the airport, the roar of sound modulating as the landing-gear came down. "They used to come right past our building," Matty said. "Luisa and I would wave at them from the balcony. She was sure the pilots were waving back." The peacock had turned his back to them and was treading from one foot to the other in a ponderous little dance, his tail waving from side to side in iridescent sweeps.

"I think he likes you," Morgan said.

"Then I need some proper backing from a record company," Matty said, watching the aeroplane as it crossed the city, slipping away to the size of a toy on the northern horizon. "I'm seeing Isabella tomorrow. I want her to get in touch with Valentim de Carvalho, and CBS. There must be people there who still remember me. Or maybe one of the indie labels. I need a web presence. I need to get a real publicity machine behind me. I need to work on my fan-base; I need to get it all back again. I know I can do it."

In the narrow streets and court-yards and steep flights of steps below the Castle they passed the dark entrances of tiny shops and bars, hobos and derelicts sleeping or unconscious on the cobble-stones, gypsies begging, groups of Angolans gathered on street-corners, illegals from Eastern Europe, *clandestinos,* drunkards selling lottery tickets, washing strung in ragged lines from balcony to balcony. Morgan stopped to read a communist party poster: *Basta de injustiças! Dà mais força ao PCP!* "An end to injustice," Matty translated for him. "More power to the PCP! That's the Communist Party, do you remember?" She took his arm. "Let's keep going," she said. "This isn't a good neighbourhood."

They emerged into an immensity of blue and white space in Praça Dom Pedro, flags snapping in front of the marble colonnades of the Dona Maria Theatre, the pavements crowded with café tables. "I'll buy you a coffee at my favourite place," Matty said. The waiter beamed at her as he led them to a table.

"Senhora Matty," he said, flicking out a clean table-cloth and adjusting the umbrella so that the shade fell on her. *"Senhora Matty, graças a Deus!"*

"You really do belong here," Morgan said.

"Of course I do darling. This is my town!" She watched the rushing traffic and the teeming crowds. "How I love it," she said. "I'll never leave it. This is where my heart is." She reached across the table and took his hand. "And it's so special to be here with you," she said. The waiter brought them tiny cups of coffee and saucers of little cakes, as sticky and yellow as egg-yolks. "Come to Algarve with me Morgan; come and spend some time with me. Get to know Luisa better; she'll be there next week."

"What about Arno?" Morgan said.

"Arno will be fine," Matty said. "You and I are old friends, that's all there is to know. Anyway, it's true. We go way back sweetheart, don't we?"

A group of musicians set up on the pavement next to their table: violin, squeezebox, guitar. "Romanians," Matty said. "You see them everywhere in Lisbon. Bucharest must be empty." A little girl was with them, selling carnations. She offered one to Matty, bobbing a curtsey as the band struck up a wobbly, unrecognisable serenade.

They walked up to Restauradores so Matty could collect an overnight bag from her hotel, then took a cab back up the Avenida to the Tivoli. In the lift going up to his room she reached up and drew his head down towards hers, touching his lips with the tip of her tongue. "I haven't given you my full attention yet," she said. "Did you know that, baby? There's a lot more of me still to come."

***

The city resisted his memories of it. Wheeling sea-gulls, their gullets full of fish, swung in from the estuary to feed their squalling chicks on warehouse roofs around the docks. Morgan stood near the water's edge in Praça do Comércio looking out across the Tagus, watching the commuter ferries pushing back and forth across the river from the suburbs and dormitory towns on the other side - Cacilhas and Barreiro and Montijo, the bright water chopping in the breeze. Down river a white cruise-ship, improbably vast, disrupting the laws of perspective, was moored at Alcántara, at docks where the troop-transports had carried away a generation of young men to futile wars in Angola and Moçambique.

Walking down through Baixa from the hotel, Morgan crossed Rua do Arsenal, the street where Capitão Salgueiro Maia had confronted units of a tank-brigade loyal to the Caetano regime - main-battle tanks, as big as dinosaurs in a museum, gunning their engines in plumes of blue exhaust - climbing down from his armoured car, his arms raised high above his head, walking under the muzzles of the guns and calling on the tank-crews to join the revolution: the exact intersection of history and the individual.

Morgan waited for a gap in the traffic, hurrying across the street between tour buses. In the vivid sunlight, through tunnels of deep shade, swifts and house-martins flashed through the arcades on the north side of the square. Everywhere, in the surging traffic, in the shops and cafés, in the ceaseless intensity of the murmuring crowds, the glittering, elaborate surfaces of the morning lay like an impenetrable lacquer over the past. Deep below, unreachable at the bottom of a well of time, Morgan and Matty's ghosts ran through the city like drowned children.

Back in Dom Pedro he ordered a beer from the same waiter, the old man bowing and smiling. He saw her as she waited at the traffic lights across the square, recognising the clothes he'd watched her put on in the hotel room that morning, a white dress splashed with blossoms of bright red, white stockings. The night came back to him, salt and sweet. A moment later she saw him and waved extravagantly, standing on tip-toes. She arranged a collection of bags around her as she sat down, waxy, lacquered, chocolate, lime-green and pink, rustling with tissue paper.

"A little bit of therapy," she said. "It's been a long morning." The waiter brought her a glass of white wine and she smiled up at him, shading her eyes. "I had coffee with my little mother," she said. "José's mother, that is. I did a bit of shopping for her. Then the rest of the morning with Isabella. That woman can be so negative sometimes." She reached into one of the carrier bags, drawing out a shivering length of multi-coloured silk. "Look at this," she said. "Isn't it gorgeous? And I could wear it at a gig, so it's a business expense, really." She looked up at him. "Are you alright sweetheart?"

"You're very extravagant," he said. "I worry about you."

"Baby, you're adorable," she said. She looked down, rotating the long stem of her wine glass, smiling to herself. "You were particularly adorable last night," she said.

"No, really. You should be more careful." He took her hand, slipping her fingers between his. "And anyway I'd like to buy you stuff myself."

"I am careful darling, really I am." She sipped her wine. "Anyway, I went on insisting with Isabella, and finally she got through to someone at CBS, nobody I knew. Everyone from the old days seems to have gone. We set up a meeting for tomorrow. What else to tell you? I made her talk to three or four jazz venues. I thought this afternoon I could look in on a couple, let them see what they're missing. And then on the way here I bumped into Elisabetta. I said we'd have lunch with her tomorrow; I'd love you to meet her, sweetheart, she's such a darling, you'll love her. And she'll love you." She looked out into the traffic. "I ought to think about another agent," she said finally. "I ought to think about firing Isabella."

A sports car drew up at the kerb, lipstick-red, and a young woman got out, waving as the driver gunned it away. Matty watched as the girl sashayed up the street. "She was happy enough to take her cut when the money was rolling in," she said. "But these days she really doesn't give it a hundred percent.

You can make anything happen if you want it badly enough."

"Why don't I get you one of those," Morgan said. "Why don't I buy you the reddest Alfa-Romeo in Lisbon?" Matty laughed.

"Why, Morgan," she said. "I never realised you were so competitive!"

"Competitive?" Morgan said. "What does that mean? Who am I competing with?"

"Don't be silly, sweetheart. You know what I mean." She drank some wine, a faint click of glass against her teeth. "Don't look at me like that, sweetheart. Come with me this afternoon, come round the clubs with me. Please baby, I really need your support right now."

Chapter Eleven

. . .

"Holy crap, it's hot," Sam said. "I don't think I slept at all. There doesn't seem to be any air-conditioning."

"Arno doesn't believe in it," Luisa said. "He has a thing about it." She turned as the door opened. "Get the fuck out of here, Marley!" she said

"Sorry, Luisa."

"And shut the door!" She turned back to Sam. "How does he do that?" she said. "Every time I take my clothes off, there he is, popping up like some little skinny gnome, like a meerkat." Luisa went to the door, calling out into the corridor. "What time does Kate's flight get in today?" She waited, listening. "Marley, where are you?"

"He's terrified of you," Sam said.

"It's alright, Marley," Luisa said "I'm dressed now." They heard him clearing his throat.

"Fifteen twenty," he said. "Local time."

"Of course it's local time, pinhead. What else time would it be?"

"I'm starving," Sam said.

Matty and Arno were sitting in the shade of an umbrella by the side of the pool. Piano music was playing somewhere in the house, faint, hesitant, melancholy, like something from a French movie.

Arno leaned forward, releasing something that he'd been holding on his lap: a little dog, stick-thin and completely bald, its skin hanging in wrinkled folds. The creature trotted to the edge of the pool and stooped to drink.

"Go to the top terrace," Arno said. "I will send Maria up to you with breakfast."

"Don't, Sam," Luisa said, murmuring to him as they turned away. "Just don't, alright?"

Matty joined them as they finished breakfast, hidden behind sunglasses and a floppy hat. "Where's your friend, darling? What was his name again?"

"Marley?" Sam said. "Hiding, I expect. He'll be alright once Kate gets here."

"How was Lisbon, mother?"

"Beautiful, sweetheart." She got to her feet. "I have some work to do with Arno," she said. "Shall we meet at lunchtime?"

They lay on sun-loungers by the side of the pool, muffled by the heat, drowsily aware of the life of the clinic running through its functions around them like an intricate machine: the bubbling of the pool's filtration system, the rasp of a stiff broom as someone swept a terrace on the other side of the cloisters, the sound of the postman's van in the front yard. Julietta passed by, pushing a trolley of tinkling bottles.

Sitting up, squinting in the fierce light, Luisa watched as a little green snake, slim and elegant, slipped into the pool, swam an unhurried length and slid out onto the warm paving at the far end. Arno's horrible little dog appeared out of the shadows of the cloisters, stood watching her for a few moments, then turned and disappeared back into the shade.

There were twenty of them at lunch, Arno sitting at the head of the long table dressed in a turquoise robe, his wheelchair framing him like a throne.

"We find love through willing acceptance," he said, and Luisa caught Sam's eye, shaking her head. "Regret vanishes! Radiance pours down on us!"

Marley sat between Sam and Luisa, hardly looking up from his plate. Across the table, Matty introduced them to the woman sitting beside her.

"My friend Anita," she said. "From Sweden. The other guests are new, I haven't met them yet." She smiled brightly round the table. "Then there's Manólo, of course, in the black T-shirt, and the girls."

"In the very tight black T-shirt," Luisa said.

"And the girls?" Sam asked.

"In the white uniforms," Matty said, nodding in their direction. "Arno's assistants."

"Are they nurses?"

"Manólo is very skillful," Anita said. "He has wonderful hands."

"And very big arms," Luisa said.

"They're sort of nurses," Matty said.

"And Manólo?"

"He is chiropractor," Anita said.

"He gives massage," Matty said. "Isn't that right, Anita?"

"He is chiropractor," Anita said.

"Can we borrow a car, mother?" Luisa asked. "We want to pick Kate up from the airport. She'll have a lot of stuff with her, film gear."

Maria and Julietta served coffee in the walled orchard, at little tables set out under the trees, the sunlight dancing through the leaves.

"The Mercedes is available," Arno told them. "Shall I have Jorge drive you?" He raised his voice over the murmur of conversation around them. "*Manólo!*" he called out. "*Ich möchte bitte mit Jorge sprechen.*"

"There's no need," Luisa said. "I'm happy to drive."

"Luisa's an excellent driver," Matty said. "Aren't you, sweetheart? She gets that from me." Arno shrugged.

"As you wish," he said.

Jorge brought the car round from the stables; as he got out he touched a button on the dashboard and the roof folded itself away like the wings of a bird.

"Fasten your seatbelt, Marley," Luisa said. "Hang onto your hat." From the back seats Marley said something they didn't catch, swept away in the rush of warm air as the car surged down the steep track, gravel cracking and spitting under the tyres. "Now we're making movies!" Luisa said. "Next stop Cannes. Maybe Arno's got his good points after all." They swung onto the main road.

"Is that dog meant to be like that?" Marley said. "That dog we saw?"

"Manólo," Luisa said. "What sort of name is that? He's German, isn't he?"

"Austrian," Sam said. "I asked him."

"Do you think his hair really is that colour?"

"I didn't ask him that."

"What would you call that style? Elvis in blonde?"

"Was it born like that?" Marley said. "Is it a breed?"

"What, Manólo? I think he's a one-off."

"You're sort of driving in the middle of the road, by the way," Sam said. Luisa corrected the car with a brief shriek of tyres as a lorry rushed at them round a curve in the road, air-horn blaring.

"I'm an excellent driver," she said. "I'm where I want to be."

"Me too, babes. How about you, Marley?"

"Welcome to the Hotel California," Marley said.

Kate's plane was late, and she was hot and bad-tempered, struggling with an airport trolley piled with cases. When she saw Marley her eyes filled with tears, and she hugged him so hard that his heels lifted off the ground.

"How have you been, you little creature?" she said. "Did you miss me?"

"There's this dog," Marley said. "Wait till you see it."

"Wait till you see the whole thing," Sam said. "Wait till you see Arno, and Manólo."

"Fuck this damn thing," Kate said as the trolley dug its heels in, wheels turning sideways. "Thanks for leaving me to bring all the heavy stuff. Do you know how much excess I had to pay? We'll have to sort that out, Luisa."

"Did everything get here safely? Where's the camera?"

"Here," Kate said. "I never let it out of my sight."

"Did you speak to Enid before you left?" Kate nodded.

"Our star awaits your call," she said. "Sitting by a white telephone, having a manicure."

Matty met them at the front gates of the compound.

"I've put Kate in with Marley," she said. "Is that right, dear? You'll want to freshen up. Baby, take everybody over to the annexe. Jorge will bring the bags." She seemed about to say something else, and they stood in the gateway for a moment, the afternoon light dusty and golden, scented with honeysuckle. "Arno wants to introduce you to the group," she said. "At dinner; he wants say a few words, so you need to be there at eight." She caught Luisa's eye. "Be nice, sweetheart."

Julietta finished lighting the lamps and stood back from the table, waiting with her hands folded in front of her, her head slightly lowered.

"We travel this road together," Arno said. "When the heart is healed, all things are possible. All that is willed shall be fulfilled. Radiance pours down on us!" As he finished speaking he drew his hands over his face and through his hair, the gesture of a swimmer emerging from the water. He raised his glass towards the far end of the table. "We have new travellers with us on the journey," he said. "I hope we will be good companions. They are artists and creators. The act of creation and the act of healing are both acts of love." Sam put his lips to Luisa's ear.

"Jesus creeping shit," he whispered.

"We will nourish each other," Arno was saying. "We will draw love and strength from each other. We will drink from the same well." He took a sip of wine, and a murmuring echo ran round the table as the guests drank, as though responding to a toast, raising their glasses, nodding and smiling down the table.

"*The same well*," someone said. "*Love and strength*."

"There, that wasn't so bad, was it?" Matty said softly, as the silence bubbled up into sound and movement, like a jug being filled until it overflowed. Anita leaned forward across the table.

"And your film," she said to Luisa. "It's a love story, of course?"

"Last time I had champagne was when my mum got married," Marley said.

"And you've got your star now, haven't you baby?" Matty said. "Your co-star, that is, your leading lady. What was her name?"

"Enid Farmer," Luisa said.

"That's right, such a funny little name!"

"She's been on British tv," Luisa said.

"In *Eastenders*," Sam said. "She bought a top off Stacey down the market, or was it a skirt? She didn't have any lines."

"And *Grazia* said she was 'one to watch'," Luisa said.

"So did *Heat Magazine*, in their own special way."

"That wasn't her fault," Luisa said. She turned back to Anita. "My film is about the past. It's about what brought us to where we are."

"It's about love as well though, don't you think?" Matty said. "Like all the best stories?"

"This is what I think," Anita said. "All stories are about love."

"And jealousy, of course."

"Jealousy is deeper than love," Marley said. "Because jealousy goes further in the apprehension and interpretation of signs." He drank, emptying the glass. Kate kissed his ear.

"Marley!" she said. "You clever little bugger! How did you come up with that?" Marley shrugged.

"It's a quote," he said. "It's Gilles Deleuze, not me. Where's that girl with the champagne?"

"Film brings the past to life," Luisa said. "Peter Brook said: *Representation*

96

denies time. Something that once was, now is." Marley was examining the food on his plate, prodding at it with a fork.

"What is this?" he said. "Is it some sort of a crab? What was it when it was alive?"

"I don't think that's right," Sam said. "Representation presents what isn't there. That's the whole point."

"It's a lobster, pinhead."

"This is too deep," Anita said. "I must understand with my heart, not my head."

Later, the four of them sat in Luisa and Sam's room, the doors onto the balcony wide open, the night breathing softly, stirring the long curtains. From somewhere far away in the compound a bell rang, and a dog began to bark. Marley sat at the little desk, rolling joints.

"I don't think that's my weird little friend," he said. "I don't think he can bark, I think he's mute. Bald, and mute, and weird."

"We need to start working tomorrow," Luisa said. "We need a proper schedule."

"I think Arno's got something," Kate said. "There's something about him?"

"We've got to be completely organised before Enid gets here. We need to start visualising the script in real locations."

"It's his eyes though. They're so blue, they're so empty; it makes you think: what's behind them? What's in there?"

"And we need to think about extras. Maybe we'll have to talk to Arno about that."

"I watched him talking to that German woman, and something was happening, you could feel it, he really has got some sort of power."

"I don't want to drink from the same well as him," Sam said. "Thanks all the same."

"Your mum's beautiful," Kate said. "She's really nice."

"Thank you," Luisa said. "Yes, she is."

"That dog-thing drinks from the swimming-pool," Marley said. "Puts you off a bit." He lit a spliff and passed it around.
"Probably pisses in it too," he said. "Welcome to the Hotel California."

***

They borrowed the Mercedes again the next day and drove down to São Miguel.

"This place ought to suit us," Luisa said. "Mum says it's just an ordinary little town."

They drove through an outer ring of construction sites and vacant lots, past half-finished apartment blocks, boarded up and shrouded with debris-netting, the road unsurfaced, a cloud of yellow dust following them. In the main square a stray dog lay in the middle of the traffic, bony chest heaving, a halo of flies around its head, kids on mopeds making wobbly detours around it. A woman came out of a shop and chased it away with a broom. Sunlight flashed blindingly off windscreens and shop-fronts. A bus was idling in the road, the driver winding up a new destination in the window.

Luisa drove slowly round the square, looking for somewhere to park. Under the awning at Café Central half a dozen customers sat motionless in their chairs, old men in black homburgs, their eyes following the car as it murmured past them. Luisa stopped in front of the church. When she turned the cold air off, the heat fell on them like a solid weight.

"Chris keeps trying to find ways of being alone with Tessa," she said. "In the middle of all this revolution, all this marching and waving banners, he's in a personal nightmare of his own. I want to find dark corners where they whisper to each other."

"Another challenge for the lighting cameraman," Kate said. "Are you listening to this, Marley?"

"I don't think they see a lot of Mercedes in town," Sam said. "Not open-top red ones, anyway. Are we having a beer?" They looked across the square at the café.

"I'd like a warm one, please," Kate said. "With a fly in it."

There was a communist party poster on the side wall of the chemist. *"An end to injustice!"* Luisa translated. *"More power to the PCP!"*

"So we're going to walk in there and hire extras," Kate said. "Is that the plan? Marley, are you up for that?"

"I don't think we're quite at that stage yet," Luisa said. "There must be more to this place than we've seen. Let's drive around a bit more."

They watched themselves reflected in shop-windows, the immense length of the car, fire-engine red, slipping noiselessly through the streets like a barracuda in a fish-tank, their four heads turning as they passed, staring back in amazement at themselves.

"Look at us!" Marley said. "We're beautiful!" They parked in a smaller square, shaded with trees, one side taken up by the train station, a café facing it. Luisa sat at the bar, chatting to the woman running the place.

"Doesn't she look Portuguese?" Kate said, as they settled themselves around a table outside, watching her through the open doorway of the café, perched on a high stool, vivid, animated. "It's seeing her here; I never thought about it in London."

Two old men walked slowly across the square and sat on a bench in front of the railway-station. One of them opened a paper bag, and a pigeon hurried over, then several more, flapping and clattering around their feet. From an upstairs window across the street, a small child in a string vest stared down at them. Luisa slipped off the bar-stool and came out to join them.

"This is typical," she said. "*A vila esta profundamente dorminda* - the whole town's fast asleep." She stirred her coffee, looking round the square. "There's only a couple of trains a day: one to the coast, and the other joins the main line to Lisbon. Not many people use it."

"Look at that car," Marley said. "I've got to have a photo of it."

"She said a lot of little shops are closing. People use the supermarket out of town, in the *centro comercial*."

"Maybe we can use it in the film," Marley said.

"Brilliant," Sam said. "A Mercedes that time-travels back to 1975, you pinhead!"

"Don't call him a pinhead," Kate said.

"How do you go back in time?" Luisa said. "How do you get all that optimism, all that excitement, how do you make it visible? How do you get the revolution up on the screen?"

"I only meant it's a photogenic car," Marley said. "It ought to be in a movie."

"She said nearly all the construction projects have stopped," Luisa said. "Did you see all those building sites, on the way in? All speculative, she said; they've all gone bust. How could you film a revolution here? How can you make the past come alive?"

"Just not this movie," Marley said. Luisa looked round the little square, torpid in the afternoon heat.

"She said there's a lot of unemployment," she said. "A lot of small firms going bankrupt. In Portuguese it's *quebrado* - broken." She stirred the dregs of coffee in her cup. "It sounds a lot more final put like that, doesn't it?"

"That ought to make it easier to hire extras," Sam said. "I don't mean to be brutal."

"She told me the foreigners still seem to have plenty of money," Luisa said. She glanced over her shoulder at the Mercedes. "She was looking at the car when she said that. She said there are lots of Germans and English around here, but they live up in the hills. They don't live in town, and they don't shop in town."

"Have we paid?" Sam asked.

"She said they don't even shop in the *centro comercial*, they spend all their money in the hypermarkets on the coast."

"Have we paid?" Sam said again. "I have a serious suggestion: let's go to the beach."

They parked the car in the shade of umbrella pines, and followed the scoured and salty boardwalk through the dunes until the sea opened in front of them, beyond a blinding crescent of white sand splashed with beach umbrellas, the blue of the ocean dotted with wind-surfers and jet-skis.

"Laurel and Hardy," Luisa said, watching Marley and Kate as they danced about at the water's edge in their shorts, skinny legs and big legs, skipping in and out of the foam as it surged and withdrew. She pushed her feet into the sugary sand, feeling the rasp of tiny shells as pink as fingernails between her toes, letting the cry of gulls and the bright voices of children wash over her above the placid breathing of the waves. Far to their right, the glittering towers and ramparts of resort hotels rose up on the horizon.

"Let's eat down here tonight," Sam said. "There's a beach café back there, and a dance-floor. We'll survive one evening without Dr. Bendt's radiance pouring down on us, don't you think?"

***

Whispering noisily, wheezing with suppressed laughter, they crossed the entrance hall, padding across the marble in bare feet towards the corridor leading to the annexe, carrying their shoes. The lights were dimmed very low, a faint radiance repeated in the dark mirrors lining the walls, and they didn't see Matty until she spoke, a figure in a white robe, emerging from the shadows.

"I need a quick word, sweetheart," she said to Luisa.

"Why are you up so late, mother? You weren't waiting up for us?"

"Of course not, baby, I was restless anyway. I couldn't sleep; I heard the car."

"I'll catch you up," Luisa said to Sam. "Goodnight, you guys." She turned to her mother. "Is there a problem?"

"No darling, not at all. It's just that Arno was a little bit sad you weren't there at dinner."

"Sad? A little bit sad?"

"Not quite so loud, baby."

"I rang you! I rang you from the beach!"

"I know, sweetness, but it was quite short notice. Please keep your voice down." She drew a breath. "The evening meal is very important to him. It binds the group together."

"For Christ's sake mother, I'm not part of his group."

"Please try and understand, baby. I need you to help me with this. He wanted me to speak to you." Across the hallway, a tiny dot of red light was blinking irritably as the security system re-armed itself.

"I don't see how this is going to work, mother."

"Don't say that, baby, please. We just need a bit of a compromise. It means so much to me, having you here."

"I know that. I wanted to be here."

"You're as free as the wind, baby. You can come and go as you please. This isn't a prison! We just need to know what you're doing, that's all, a little ahead of time. You can do that for me, darling, can't you?" Luisa sighed, putting her arms around her mother.

"I suppose so," she said. "I suppose I can." She kissed her, drawing her closer. "Have you been losing weight, mother? You need to look after yourself."

"I do, baby. I look after myself very well."

"It'll be alright," Luisa said. "We can work it out. We need to be more disciplined about this whole thing anyway. We didn't have a very productive day today."

***

"With your permission," Manólo said. The seat beside Kate was empty, and he sat down, moving plates and cutlery to one side, resting his elbows on the table cloth, his hands clasped in front of him. "We have a club in São Miguel," he said. "It's very nice." Luisa caught Kate's eye, watching the muscles moving in Manólo's forearms as he pressed his hands against each other, squeezing and rotating as though softening a ball of clay. "Dr. Bendt has asked me to tell you about it," he said.

"That's nice," Kate said. She glanced at Luisa, looking quickly away. "That's nice, isn't it Marley?"

"We start it five years ago," Manólo said. "We Germans, and some English." He smiled at Sam. "I am Austrian, as it were."

"As it is," Sam said.

"Every year we make a small production, it's very nice."

"And Dr. Bendt asked you to tell us this?" Sam said. "That was very nice of him."

"This is like him," Manólo said. "He think always of the other." Luisa looked up at the far end of the table; her mother and Arno were talking, heads close together. Matty tapped the old man's wrist, laughing at something.

"This Christmas it was *Der Fröliche Geist* - 'Blide Spirit,' but we don't have this word 'blide.' In German we say: 'The Cheerful Ghost.' You know this play? By Noel Coward?"

"Of course," Sam said. "Amateur dramatics! You put on plays!"

"Of course!" They looked at each other, nodding and smiling. "And it's a club, also. We have German beer, and discussion."

"So you're an actor!" Sam said. "Just like me!"

Manólo shook his head.

"I am not so much," he said. "I help production, build sets. But in our club we have many fine actors. This is what Dr. Bendt is thinking: maybe we can help you with your film." Arno was signalling from the head of the table, arm raised, a pecking gesture between forefinger and thumb. "He calls me," Manólo said, getting to his feet. "I must be with him. One night we go to the club and I show you to my friends. *Ciao-ciao!*"

Matty brought her coffee over and sat with them.

"I think we may have found a good location," Luisa said. "Julietta was telling me about this village she knows, Cova da Viúva, up in the hills towards Alentejo, her aunt lives there. She says it's totally stuck in the past, nothing has changed there for years, it could be thirty years ago."

"Cova da Viúva?" Matty said. "The Grave of the Widow? What a cheerful name! Can you imagine the night-life?"

"I know. She says you still see donkey-carts there. It sounds just right. We're planning to check it out this afternoon."

"That's lovely, sweetheart. And listen, Arno said to tell you: take the Mercedes whenever you want, treat it like your own car. You see, he really wants you

102

to be happy here." Matty leaned back in her chair, closing her eyes, smiling.

"You look happy, mum," Luisa said. "You're looking beautiful."

"Thank you darling, so are you. And yes, I am."

"Anything in particular?" Matty nodded.

"Everything in particular," she said. "You being here, that's so special. And I just heard from Morgan; he's coming to visit."

"That's great, mother, I'm happy for you." Luisa turned to Sam and Kate. "Time we got moving," she said. "You too, Marley, wake up!"

"Yes, boss."

"We'll probably be out late tonight, mother," Luisa said. "We won't be at dinner, anyway. Just so you know."

Chapter Twelve

. . .

None of the rental firms had an Alfa-Romeo, and for a single beat of the heart Morgan thought about going into the city centre and buying one. There weren't many convertibles available at the airport, mostly Mini-Cabriolets, and he was too old for a Mini. Portocar had a BMW z4, an open two-seater, steel-grey, and he filled out the paperwork while someone went to fetch it.

Driving out of the airport into the dazzling southern light he worked his way round the ring-road system until he joined the A2. The motorway rose up on elevated sections, the city dropping away to his left as he crossed the river on Ponte 25 d'Abril. Far below him the commuter-ferries pushed back and forth across the Tagus; there was another cruise-liner moored at Alcántara. Glancing to his left, Morgan picked out the tumble of red roofs and steep streets in Alfama, and above them the Moorish ramparts of Castelo São Jorge, where the peacocks were picking in the shade. Across the river the motorway swung south under Christ's outstretched arms, and Lisbon disappeared from his mirrors.

He settled into the driving, getting used to the car and the surging traffic all around him, staying in the middle lane at a hundred and thirty, pushing past columns of heavy goods trucks in the right-hand lane. From time to time bigger, flashier cars swept past him on his left, or peeled away on slip-roads. Distance was measured in the steady register of the car's tyres over joints in the concrete road-surface, and the sudden modulation of the buffeting wind as he passed under road-signs and traffic information, high on elevated gantries. The satnav warbled incomprehensibly at him in Portuguese; he passed signs for

Palmela and, far away to the west, the teeming agglomeration of dormitory towns around Setúbal. After Aguas de Moura and Castro Verde the motorway swept south across empty plains of dried up pasture and wheatfields and the rolling, low brown hills of Alentejo. He passed stony riverbeds and groves of cork-trees, and the sudden familiarity of white farm-buildings on the skyline, a landscape remembered but unreachable, seen through glass at a hundred and thirty kilometres an hour.

The hills became steeper and the fields stonier; the sign-posts scaled down, pointing to smaller and obscurer destinations, places with evocative, musical names - Purgatório, Laranjéira - finally the name that Matty had emailed him: São Miguel do Monte. He left the motorway and swung through a couple of roundabouts, finding himself suddenly on a country road, in a dusty landscape of shrubs and stunted oak and untended fields. The wind-noise dropped away, letting in the high-pitched rasp of the cicadas, the sound that the heated earth makes as it breathes, the sound of heat itself, scented with wild thyme. He stopped the car.

From a distance, the clinic looked like a fortress, built on the summit of a hill, slabs and blocks and towers of dazzling white rising above the parched scrub. A woman and a little girl, waiting at a bus stop on a long stretch of empty road, pointed ahead to where a roadway led up through the trees. Morgan scrambled the BMW round the steep bends of the track, trailing a plume of red dust. When he stopped at the entrance to the clinic the dust hung in the air around him for a few moments in a halo of dancing light. Through the steel bars of the gates, he could see a woman in a black house-coat, deadheading a wall of climbing roses.

Matty had shown him to his room, hanging on his arm, her high-heels clacking as he trailed his suitcase down a long corridor, dimly lit, lined with dark mirrors. She drew the curtains and opened the doors onto the balcony. Stepping out into the immense brightness, Morgan took in the glittering length of a swimming pool, the water restless as though someone had just got out; terraces and courtyards, shuttered windows, cloisters shaded by trellised vines, sprays of bougainvillea purple and scarlet against whitewashed walls, an avenue of cypress trees. She drew him back into the bedroom.

"I'm three doors down the corridor," she said, reaching up on tiptoes to kiss him. "Just so you know."

***

From the top terrace, Morgan looked out across the compound. Beyond the dusty landscape that surrounded it, waves of hills rolled away north towards Alentejo, hazy with distance. He could feel the motorway vibrating inside him, still travelling. He turned as a set of lift doors hissed open in the wall behind him. Dr. Bendt rolled silently out across the terrace, Matty following him.

"Arno, darling," Matty said. "This is my old friend Morgan. We've known each other since we were eighteen, we went to drama school together, we're like brother and sister, can you imagine!"

At dinner he sat across the table from Matty and next to Manólo, a heavy-set young man with a pompadour of blonde hair. Dr. Bendt sat at the head of the table, two girls, buttoned up in white uniforms, on either side of him. Morgan counted eighteen people around the table, more than half of them middle-aged or elderly women. He had caught Matty's eye while Dr. Bendt was making his little speech before the meal, but she hadn't responded.

"I think you are a film-maker?" Manólo said. Morgan shook his head.

"Luisa and the kids are away most days," Matty said. "But you'll see them tomorrow morning. It's such fun having them around."

"I think they are very passionate," Manólo said. "This is why I ask if you are a film-maker also, or perhaps you are a writer?" Morgan shook his head again.

"I'm very passionate," he said. "But that's as far as it goes." A young Portuguese girl moved down the table lighting little oil-lamps, globes of yellow glass burning with a scent of lemons. Morgan and Matty looked at each other through the soft golden light.

"I also am very interested in theatre," Manólo said. "We have a little club in São Miguel, I hope to present Sam and Luisa there. I think it's very fine she is political, although for me it's more important comedy."

"I'd like to see how they're getting on with the film," Morgan said. "The revolution seems a long time ago; it's time people thought about it again." He looked across at Matty. "How strange to think of Howard finding that play in a second-hand bookshop in Llanfrychan," he said. "It's like the Arabian Nights. Old Howard rubs the magic lamp, and look what jumps out." He gestured around him. "All this," he said. "The enchanted palace, and the beautiful princess." He raised his glass. "Here's to the beautiful princess," he said.

"And the brave prince!" Matty said, clicking glasses with him. "Was it the prince? Who was it that rubbed the lamp? Maybe it was a thief. My memory, sweetheart, too awful!"

"For me, it's Noel Coward," Manólo said. "For me he is the prince."

"Manólo is very popular here," Matty said. "Everybody says he's a wonderful masseur."

"I am chiropractor," Manólo said. "For me, the revolution it's in here." He patted his chest with the flat of his hand.

"I'm an actor," Morgan said. "Some of the time, anyway."

"I knew!" Manólo said. "I knew this! I see the passion, like Sam!"

"Arno was talking about this yesterday," a woman said from across the table, sitting next to Matty. "He was talking about the crisis, the economic crisis? He said there is always a cyclic, a rise and then a fall. People want too much luxury, too much material things. They turn away from things of the spirit."

She looked up, nodding, as the young Portuguese girl offered her more champagne. "This Julietta, for example," she said, lowering her voice as the girl moved on down the table. "Once, her family is farming, and she would be content also: keep a pig, grow a little vegetables. But now it's as Arno says, everybody wants too much." She shook her head, sipping her wine. "They don't want the simple life, they want a car, and an apartment. But it's too much. They can't have everyone car and apartment. And so we have credit crunch, it's simple!"

"I don't think I've ever heard it put more clearly," Morgan said.

"*Ich auch*," Manólo said. "I also."

She came to his room an hour after he'd gone up.

"I wasn't sure if you knew which was my door," she whispered. "Can't have you creeping into someone else's bed."

She put her arms round his neck. "This makes me feel about sixteen," she said. "Padding about in the dark like this. Isn't it exciting!"

"I want some time alone with you," Morgan said. "Let's go off for the day tomorrow. Let's go and have lunch somewhere, go to the beach."

"We're always alone together," Matty said. "Whoever else is around, it's just the two of us. Don't you know that, sweetheart?"

"I hope so," Morgan said. "Don't you feel this place might be bugged? We might be on camera right now."

"Let's give them something worth watching, then," Matty said. "Rub my lamp, baby."

He woke up alone, the curtains stirring in a faint breeze. From somewhere in the compound he heard the shriek of a peacock and closer, the gasp and splash of someone diving into the swimming pool, the water slapping musically against the sides. When he went down to the pool the surface was still restless; a track of wet, bare footprints led away towards the arcade of the cloisters. As Morgan watched, they evaporated off the hot flagstones of the terrace, lifting away like the footprints of a ghost. At the far end of the pool, Dr. Bendt appeared through an archway in his wheelchair, crossing the terrace with unnerving speed, the two girls in their white uniforms hurrying along behind him, trotting to keep up. Morgan raised his arm in an uncommitted gesture, but the old man didn't see him.

Matty was in the walled orchard with Luisa and Sam and a couple of kids he hadn't seen before, sitting around a table in a companionable litter of coffee cups and plates of croissants, in the dappled shade of a walnut tree. He watched them for a moment before they looked up and saw him, the white of Matty's dress lit up by globes of dancing light refracted through the leaves, the exact look of an impressionist painting, a Monet or a Pissarro.

They drove to the coast and walked along the beach. The wind was up, red flags flying, the waves dark and solid, spray combing off the crests. The life-guards sat hunched and bundled into wet-suits at the top of their towers, staring out to sea. No one was swimming. Along the horizon a rampart of cloud, the colour of steel, hung between water and sky.

"I hate it when it's like this," Matty said. "Let's go back into the hills."

"Where did you get to last night?" Morgan said. "I didn't hear you leave."

"Julietta brings me coffee first thing," she said. "A girl has to keep her secrets, darling. Anyway, it's a Cinderella thing." As they drove back inland the wind softened, the air warm and benign. "Take me to lunch," she said. "I know exactly the place."

They had coffee on the hotel terrace, looking out over the gardens, a fountain playing, the sea glinting on the horizon. "A person could get very relaxed here," Morgan said. He put his hand over hers. "Don't be despondent about those Lisbon clubs," he said. "It's funny how often when people say *we'll get back to you*, they really mean it."

"I know, sweetheart, although Jimmy's Place never got back either. But me, despondent? Not in my vocabulary, darling." She lit a cigarette. "I told Arno we'd be in for dinner," she said. "I hope that's alright." Morgan sighed. "He'd like to talk to you baby, get to know you a little."

"Can we be fashionably late, at least?" Morgan said. "So we miss the sermon. I'm not sure I can handle that again. Does he do it every night?"

"It's his way of making everybody feel included," Matty said.

"I'd rather be included out." Matty took his hand.

"Please baby," she said. "Don't be like that. Do it for me."

***

Arno had them sitting with him at the head of the table. Watching Matty, Morgan took in how carefully she'd prepared for the evening, dramatic in red silk, her nails lacquered, her lips scarlet and glistening, her make-up perfect, her hair elaborately piled up. The kids were further down the table, beyond the guests, sitting with Manólo and the Swedish woman. The two girls in the white uniforms had also been moved down; the skinny kid, Marley, was sitting between them.

The old man touched a napkin to his lips.

"I first came here forty years ago," he said. "It was a different world." He took a sip of champagne. "Let me tell you a story," he said. "Perhaps it will help you understand." He paused, waiting for their full attention, an actor's trick. "When I was first here, in 1970, I was invited to a family farm, here in the hills." Another pause. Morgan nodded. "They were serious, hard-working people. They offered me refreshment, and brought a water-melon to the table; a big one, it must have been ten kilos or more." He looked at Matty. "You have heard this story."

"That's alright," she said. "Go on."

"When they cut the melon open, it was not ripe," he said. "Do you understand what this means?" Morgan shook his head.

"No," he said.

"A melon so big," Arno said. "Wasted, a catastrophe! These people are not rich, they cannot afford to waste food. Do you know what happened next?"

"Probably not," Morgan said, careful not to catch Matty's eye.

"They said to me: *It doesn't matter, we will give it to the pig. The pig will grow, and in the autumn, when we kill him, he will give us back our melon.* Do you understand?"

"Yes, I do," Morgan said. "A bit gruesome, perhaps. Not for vegetarians."

"There is a profound lesson here," Arno said. "You are not allowing yourself to hear it."

"Explain it to me," Morgan said. "Please do."

"I learned something then that has stayed with me all these years," Arno said. "When it is lived correctly, life is a cycle, a state of perfect balance in which nothing need be added or taken away. This is the truth in all my books. This is the whole of my teaching and my practice here at the clinic."

"*Com a sua licença,*" Julietta said, bobbing at them as she collected their plates. Matty smiled at her, stroking her arm.

"*Certamente, menina,*" she said.

"We have lost this way of living within the circle," Arno said. "I have watched it happen here in Algarve. First the communists, and then the socialists: the people lost their way."

"So you were here during the revolution?" Morgan said.

"And finally the bureaucrats, or as we say, the Eurocrats."

"Did the revolution have a big effect on your life here?" Morgan asked him. Arno shook his head.

"The revolution is here, only here," he said, touching a finger to his forehead. "In those years I had business elsewhere. I set up my first clinic in Germany, then in Brazil."

"They were exciting times," Morgan said. "It'll be fun to see what Luisa and her friends make of it all." Arno nodded.

"A worthwhile subject," he said. "It is good that young people think about it. So much chaos, so much desire."

"Desire?" Morgan said.

"The circle is broken," Arno said. "The balance is lost. People want what they cannot have."

"Your Swedish friend was saying something similar last night," Morgan said, looking across the table at Matty.

"Anita," Matty said.

"Modern life is driven by an engine of desire," Arno said. "A terrible motor that draws everything in, like a whirlpool. Everything is wanted, everything is needed, more and more and more!" He dabbed at his mouth again, closing his eyes and leaning back in his chair. "Look at those apartment buildings in São Miguel," he said after a few moments. "Monuments of unobtainable desire!" He shook his head. "And yet people are shocked that the motor over-heated, that the machine stopped. First they are shocked, and then they look about for who to blame."

He shook his finger, the sleeve of his robe falling back over a forearm as brittle as a stick, burned nearly black by the sun. Morgan stared at him. "They blame the bankers, but they should blame themselves," Arno said. "They should blame nobody but themselves."

In Morgan's room the long curtains stirred, translucent in the moonlight. Matty raised her arms as he lifted her nightdress over her head.

"I don't think I can go through that again," Morgan said. "The old bastard can talk up a storm though, can't he? An engine of desire!" Matty put her arms around his neck. "Everything is wanted!" Morgan said, his voice muffled, breathing in the scent of her skin. "Everything is desired!"

"You're desired," Matty said, reaching up on tip-toes, her lips nipping at his. She stepped back, watching him, her smile deepening. "I want every bit of you."

"Sweetheart," Morgan said through searching tongues; tight and sweet and rolling in the heat, and sleek release and coming in her, twisted sheets and pearls of sweat and coming in the scarlet of her mouth and sweetheart, she said, sweetheart. The heart is joyful, and the limbs are swift and clinging; every bud of every bush is bursting into song: sweet pea, wet petal, salt and honey on the tongue.

Chapter Thirteen

. . .

The road to Cova da Viúva was steep and narrow, a strip of tarmac barely two cars wide, working its way in a series of hairpin bends across ridge after ridge of cork forest, slowly climbing towards Alentejo. In places the edge of the road had crumbled, dropping away into steep ravines of tumbled rock, choked with oak and eucalyptus.

"Hope we don't meet a bus," Sam said.

"I want to see the cork factory," Luisa said.

"I thought cork grew on trees," Marley said. "I thought that's what all these trees were for. Why would you need a factory?"

"It does grow on trees," Sam told him. "That's why they're called cork trees."

"So why do you need a factory? What do you actually do in a cork factory?"

"Make corks, you pinhead."

"Don't worry about it, Marley," Kate said. "And don't call him a pinhead."

"Julietta said to ask in the shop," Luisa said. "Where we had those beers yesterday."

"Maybe it's time for a couple more?"

"Work first," Luisa said. "Let's get something done today."

"There's not a lot for me to do until Enid gets here," Sam said.

"You need to immerse yourself in the part," Luisa said.

"That's what I mean, a couple of beers."

They waited in the car, watching her brush through a curtain of plastic strips in the doorway of the store. A boy came by on a moped; when he saw the Mercedes he twisted the throttle open and did a wheelie past them, the tone of the engine rising to a shriek.

The main street of the village was not much wider than the road through the mountains, rows of low, white-washed buildings facing each other across it. Opposite the shop there was a filling station and further on a little dusty church, set back from the road on a square of parched earth lined with dispirited trees, drooping in the heat, casting no shade. In the foothills beyond the village, a new road led up to a development of white villas, built around a swimming pool.

"I really like the sound of this," Luisa said, thumping the car door shut. "Listen to what she told me. The cork factory closed two years ago, but there's an old man in the village who has the keys. She thinks he'll let us in if we talk to him nicely."

"I still don't see what's so great about a cork factory," Marley said. "And it doesn't even make cork any more."

There were three locks on the rusting double doors, and it took the old man five minutes to get them open, trying one key after another before he got it right, pushing them inward with a look of triumph, the hinges shrieking.

"He used to work here," Luisa said. "He's called Manuel Oliveira. He's sweet." The man gestured at her, and the two of them set off into the building, the others following, picking their feet up cautiously through a rubble of broken bricks and fallen timber. The place had been gutted, although several huge, incomprehensible machines still stood against the walls. Columns of sunlight, falling from holes in the damaged roof, danced in clouds of dust as they moved about, disturbing the debris. On the far side of the building a door opened into a yard, one side of it stacked with piles of old, greying cork.

"He says this factory was always the main employer here," Luisa said. "There was a German consortium wanted to turn it into riding stables last year, but that fell through; the same people who built the development up on the hill. But this is the best bit: during the revolution the workers took it over. They kicked out the bosses and ran it as a co-operative. How authentic is that!"

"I don't see how we can film inside the building," Marley said. "How would we ever light it?"

"Just think," Luisa said. "The revolution really happened here! This was a workers' co-operative! This is holy ground!" She punched the air with her fist. "Down with the bosses! Smash capitalism!"

"What would I know," Marley said. "I'm only the lighting cameraman."

113

"Power to the people!" Luisa said, laughing. "*A luta continua!*" Manuel Oliveira took his hat off and rubbed his forehead, smiling and shaking his head.

"*A luta continua,*" he said softly.

"What does that mean?" Kate said. "What did you both say?"

"It means the struggle continues," Luisa said. "The fight goes on. I've told him we'll see him again tomorrow. I wonder if I ought to give him some money?"

"Why don't we have a look round the rest of the village?" Sam said.

"The struggle continues in the pitch dark," Marley said.

"A look round the rest of the village could include a beer or two?"

"We'll mainly film outside," Luisa said. "We'll use natural light. And indoors we'll have pools of light in the darkness; that's the look I want anyway. You'll see, this place will really work for us."

On the track back up to the clinic another car passed them coming down, an open BMW, both vehicles raising clouds of dust. They heard it toot its horn as it disappeared round the bend.

"That was Morgan's car," Luisa said. "I wonder where he and Mum are off to." Kate glanced at her.

"Are your mum and Morgan, you know, having a thing?" Luisa nodded, smiling. "Isn't that sweet!" Kate said. "I thought so, but I couldn't quite tell."

***

"You aren't the skinniest person on the set any more," Kate said. "But I love you just the same."

"Don't distract him," Luisa said. She looked up at the back wall of the cork factory, flipping through the script on her clipboard. "This is where they had the first demonstration," she said. "The day before this scene." She turned over a page, reading aloud. "*The same location in front of the big house, no one around. Tessa and Chris enter stage right, walking slowly. Chris sits down on the front steps of the house.* We'll do that in six shots."

She rattled an aerosol can, stepped forward and fired off a sequence of bursts of spray, writing in quick, sweeping movements, her arm outstretched: *A LUTA CONTINUA!* in bright red letters a metre high.

"Aren't they going to mind that?" Kate said. Luisa wrote again: *VIVA O PCP!* Marley adjusted the camera on the tripod, stooping to look through the eyepiece.

114

"Shows up fine," he said.

"That's what I mean."

"We'll wash it off," Luisa said. "Paint over it or something." She stepped back to look at the slogans, nodding.

"That red is unreal," Marley said.

"What's wrong with it?"

"I mean Enid's hair." The three of them looked back across the yard.

"It's real," Kate said. "Trust me."

Sam and Enid were sitting on folding chairs, the girl shaded under a striped parasol, her face reduced to a triangle of white under the black lenses of her sunglasses.

"We'll do the whole thing in long shot first," Luisa said. "Then we'll break it down. Let's get set up."

"How can anyone have skin that white?"

"They're going to walk from right to left in front of the building," Luisa said. "Then when Chris sits down, you see the slogans above his head."

"She's a bit too clean for someone working on a commune," Kate said. "We'll have to dirty her up a bit."

"Me, please," Marley said.

"You stay behind the camera, you pervert. You belong to me."

Sam and Enid walked across the yard; Enid's T-shirt was grimy with dust and sweat, sticking to her; Kate had rubbed it into the scrub at the side of the road and dribbled lemonade on it.

"I'm here now, aren't I?" she said. "You wanted to talk, so here we are. We're talking."

"Cut!" Luisa called out and they stopped, turning to look at her. Marley straightened up from behind the camera. "You're walking too fast," Luisa said. "You're depressed and irritable, remember? You're not going anywhere, you're just walking. Drag your feet." She held the clapperboard in front of the camera. "Let's go again. Action." Kate raised the boom of the mic; Sam and Enid walked slowly across the yard. Enid kicked at a pebble, scuffing the ground with the toe of her desert boot.

"I'm here now, aren't I?" she said. "You wanted to talk, so here we are. We're talking."

"We're not talking," Sam said. "I thought we were together."

"We are together," Enid said.

"I want a close-up on Chris now," Luisa said. Marley set the camera up again, Kate standing at his shoulder with the boom raised. "Let's do it again," Luisa said. "Action."

"You wanted to talk, so here we are," Enid said. "We're talking."

"We're not talking," Sam said. "I thought we were together."

"We are together," Enid said.

"Are you sleeping with him?" Sam said. "While we're on the subject?"

"Go again," Luisa said.

"Are you sleeping with him?" Sam said. "While we're on the subject?"

"Come on Chris, you know what I mean," Enid said.

"Good. Now it's hand-held, Marley. Keep it fluid, longer shot; we need a better sense of where we are."

"Come on, Chris," Enid said. "This place, here and now, this moment in time - music in the bars at night and revolution everywhere!"

"That's good," Luisa said. "What's the matter?"

"I need to get out of the sun for a minute," Enid said. "I need to cool down." She ducked under the shade of the parasol, reaching into her bag for a towel.

"It's a collective farm," Luisa said. "In Alentejo. You're doing physical work. Of course you're hot."

"I can act hot," Enid said. She dabbed at her face with the towel. "I need to rehydrate; I need a cold drink."

On the far side of the yard, a couple of kids on bikes had stopped in the road and were watching them through the main gates. Marley swung the camera round on them and they shrieked and pedalled away, their voices high and bright with excitement. "And I burn," Enid said. "I go bright red. So if you want to properly fuck up your continuity, go right ahead."

"We'll take five minutes," Luisa said.

"You have no idea how bad this feels," Sam said. He put his head in his hands.

"I want to go right in on Chris there," Luisa said. "Big close-up."

"Please don't," Enid said.

"What, feel bad? Don't feel bad?"

"Yes," Enid said. "Don't feel bad."

"We'll do that again," Luisa said. "On Tessa this time."

The kids had come back, bringing some older children and teenagers with

116

them, restless, whispering, pushing and crowding into the gateway, peering on tiptoes over each other's shoulders.

"Yes," Enid said. "Don't feel bad."

"What am I supposed to feel?" Sam said. "You dump me, in public. You don't talk to me about it, you just go off with someone else."

Luisa walked over to the kids in the gateway; they could hear her voice, low and urgent; she put a finger to her lips. The kids nodded, shuffling their feet.

"I thought the revolution was about being free," Enid said.

"Very convenient," Sam said. "Free to hurt other people."

"Free to be yourself," Enid said. "I'm not setting out to hurt you."

"Why am I hurting then?" Sam said. "Why aren't you free when you're with me? Do I stop you being yourself?"

"I want a two-shot now, Marley," Luisa said. "Two-shot mid-shot."

Gunning the engine in rasping bursts, a young man on a moped pushed his way through to the front of the little crowd in the gateway. He planked his feet on either side of the machine, the motor grumbling between his legs.

"Crap," Luisa said. "Cut. Anyway, we're beginning to lose the light. We'll go through the rushes tonight on the laptop."

***

"Why am I hurting then?" Sam said, his voice distant and tinny through the laptop speakers. "Why aren't you free when you're with me?" Luisa adjusted the angle of the screen, leaning closer.

"Some of this is really good," she said.

"I think I love lobsters," Marley said. "And those things we had tonight, crayfish. I even like the claw things and those little dangly bits, those little legs they have, like aliens." Luisa dragged the slider fast-forward through the thumbnails, her face lit by the soft glow of the display.

"Tessa has the power," she said. "She's detached. She's backing away into mid-shot and long shot, keeping her distance, where Chris is all needy and pushing forward in close-up. The rhythm is just right, this'll edit beautifully; and the shooting ratio is looking great."

"So salty," Marley said.

"I like the cicadas," Kate said. "The way the sound rises and falls, the way it punctuates their conversation."

"Look at Enid," Luisa said, swivelling the laptop round on the desk. "Look how she comes alive in that shot. Look at the way the light falls on her; she has the most beautiful skin. That reflector was perfect, she looks fabulous. Good boy, Marley."

"Did someone tell her where we'd be tonight?"

"It's so good to have something in the can at last," Luisa said. "It finally feels like we're getting somewhere."

"Move over," Kate said, climbing on to the bed. "Make some room, I need a cuddle."

"I had an email from Dave Leaper," Luisa said. "Did I tell you? He wants to drop by, see how we're getting on. At least we've got something to show him now."

"I had a dream about Arno's dog," Marley said. "Manólo was in it too. We were in his club; the dog was doing cabaret, Lisa Minelli-style." He shuddered.

"Does Enid know where we are?" Sam asked. "Shall I go and find her?"

"What do you expect?" Kate said. "You fill your skinny little body with lobster and champagne every night, and smoke dope on top of that, you're going to get bad dreams."

"She said she wanted an early night," Luisa said.

"She's not very, you know, friendly," Marley said.

"This is a strange place to find yourself in."

"Welcome to the Hotel California."

"It's impossible to tell what she's thinking."

"She's professional," Luisa said. "She's at work, it's a job. It pays, thanks to Mum. She's not here to socialise: she'll do the job and leave."

"But you can never leave," Marley said. "You can check out any time, but you can never leave."

***

The next morning there were thunderclouds massing over the mountains to the north.

"That's your idea of revolution, is it?" Sam said. "Dancing?"

"What's the problem?" Enid said. "Why can't you do both?"

"We had some aeroplane noise in that one," Kate said. "Do you want to do it again?"

"Go again, Marley," Luisa said. "On Tessa this time. Longer shot, hand-held. And maybe you should be bopping about a little, Enid, nothing too much."

"What's the problem?" Enid said. "Why can't you do both?"

"What, dance your way to socialism?" Sam said. "Boogie on the barricades? What a great achievement. World capital must be shaking in its boots. Keep on dancing!" He shook his head. "Until the bankers and the lawyers turn the lights off. Kill them all."

"Good," Luisa said.

"I don't really know why I say that," Sam said. "It's a bit abrupt, isn't it - *kill them all*?"

"He's confusing the personal with the political," Luisa said. "I like it. You got it just right."

Enid plucked at her T-shirt, pulling the damp cotton away from her skin. "Can we take a break, please?"

"Ten minutes," Luisa said. "I'm worried about those clouds." The three of them walked across the yard to where her mother and Morgan were sitting together at a table in the shade. The old man, Manuel Oliveira, had joined them. Luisa watched her mother turning from one to the other, translating for Morgan.

"It's so exciting to watch you work," Matty said. "Thank you for letting us on the set, baby." She smiled at Enid, making room for her on the bench. "Sit with me," she said. "You're so stunning, darling, you're just so gorgeous. Isn't she perfect?" She turned to Manuel Oliveira. "*Que beleza! Que perfeição!*" The old man nodded and smiled.

"*Com' uma princesa num conto de fadas.*"

"He says you're like a princess in a fairy-tale."

"Tell him thank you," Enid said. She looked across the table at Morgan. "I hear you're an actor," she said.

"Where are the rest of your crew?" Matty said. "Where are Kate and Marley?" Sam looked over his shoulder.

"They must be in the factory building," he said. "Don't ask."

"That reminds me," Luisa said to Morgan. "Would you take a small part for us? Just a couple of afternoons shooting?"

"I'd be honoured," Morgan said. "I've got a tour coming up, I'll be gone for about ten days; will that fit in with your schedule?"

"No problem."

"Senhor Manuel has just been telling me a wonderful story about this place," Matty said. "Listen to this, you three, you'll love it." Morgan reached across the table, pouring out tumblers of iced water.

"Thank you," Enid said.

"There used to be a Carmelite Convent here, about ten kilometres north of the village," Matty said. "It was a very secluded order, very cut off from the world. In 1975 the people of the village occupied the big estate and started running it as a collective farm. Then the workers took over this factory and chased the bosses out. Word eventually got through to the nuns, and they panicked. They thought the red hordes were on the rampage, godless communists, raping and killing. They barricaded themselves in."

"*Foram apavoradas,*" Manuel Oliveira said.

"They were terrified," Matty said. "Senhor Manuel here was the chairman of the Action Committee, and he and the mayor went to the convent and managed to persuade the Mother Superior to let them in. They asked her if the nuns would run a crèche, so the local women could drop their children off while they went to work in the fields. The Mother Superior agreed and, imagine, it was a huge success, it was like a fairy-tale! Everything was transformed! The nuns were so happy, it was as if they'd been let out of prison! They adored the children, they became part of the life of the village. He says they were like god-mothers to the whole community - *as madrinhas da aldeia!* Isn't that sweet!"

"*Dias de alegria,*" Manuel Oliveira said. He shook his head. "*Há tanto tempo.*"

"Happy times," Matty said to Enid. "So long ago."

"Back to work," Luisa said. "We need to use the light while we have it."

Chapter Fourteen

· · ·

Rhodri snipped the end off a matchstick, dipped it in glue and tweezered it into position.

"There!" he said, looking up at Morgan. "The west front is now complete."

Seventy miles away down the coast the sprawling cruciform of the real cathedral was slipping, very slowly, towards the sea. At the end of a two mile slope the lifeboat station, in a notch of bay like a missing tooth in the cliff, looks out across the sound to where the guillemots and razor-bills wheel and shriek below the cliffs in bursts of spray. Further out to sea, the glassy water wrinkles and slides across hidden rocks.

For seven hundred and fifty years the tower has been leaning slowly to the west, pushing the arcades of the nave out of the vertical, cramming the lower arches into narrower, gothic forms. "The ground is so wet," Rhodri said. "It's just not stable."

He stepped back from the kitchen table, nodding, chin in hand. "I told you about the slope from east to west," he said. "Do you remember? The last time you were here; so they could sluice away the mud the pilgrims brought in on their feet? But the way the foundations have shifted, that's another matter." He went over to the sink and washed his hands. "That's proper subsidence," he said over his shoulder. "The same thing that's caused those cracks in your back wall out there."

"Where did you get that idea?" Morgan said. "Who told you that?"

"It's well documented," Rhodri said. "You can look it up. Shall I put the kettle on?"

"Look it up where?" Rhodri reached up into the cupboard beside the sink.

"You can google it," he said. "Tea or coffee? And there are plenty of books." He raised his voice against the sibilance of the kettle. "The tower has always been unstable. It collapsed in 1220, and they didn't do a good job of rebuilding it."

"I'm not talking about the cathedral," Morgan said.

"Although I think the real problem is they built too close to the river. There just wasn't enough room, it nibbles away at the footings. The west front has fallen down twice, did you know that?"

Morgan looked around the room, at the paint flaking on the metal window frame over the sink, the tiles behind the cooker sticky with fragments of food, the lampshade in the centre of the ceiling black with half a lifetime of soot and grease: a map of the dispirited years. "Tea or coffee?" Rhodri was asking.

"Neither," Morgan said.

"Have you never noticed the way the paving slabs have buckled at the front of the house?" Rhodri said. "They thought it might be tree roots, but it's the same fault; it runs right under the building." He poured boiling water into the tea-pot, his glasses misting. "An underground water-course, they think, or even old mine-workings. Are you sure you won't have a cup?"

"Who thought it might be tree roots?" Morgan said. "What are you talking about?"

"The survey your buyers asked for," Rhodri said. "Your former buyers. Rees and Lowry did it for them. Adrian Rees is my cousin, did I ever tell you that?" Rain rattled against the back window. "Or there's coffee if you'd rather."

In his mother's bedroom a section of wallpaper by the window had detached itself, hanging limply away from the wall. Morgan sat on the arm of the chair. He shut his eyes, going back to the smell of wild thyme, and heat, and cicadas singing. He went downstairs.

"I'm sorry to hear the sale fell through," Rhodri said. "It was the survey, I suppose, put them off." The front door rattled on its hinges as Morgan flipped it shut behind him. Someone had taken the estate agents' board down and propped it against the side wall. At the bus stop, in the scudding rain, he noticed that the house three doors down from his was boarded up.

"Why take the bus?" Howard asked him. "I would have come and got you. Why didn't you ring me?" They had moved Anne's bed downstairs, into the living room; the table was folded up and pushed against the wall.

Howard settled the pillows behind her as she struggled to sit up, gripping the bed-covers. She was thinner, her eyes deep and dark. There was a faint, medicinal smell in the room, camphor, or disinfectant; institutional, like a waiting-room.

"I suppose I wanted the full masochistic experience," Morgan said. "Waiting for the bus, in the rain, without an umbrella. Hello sweetheart, hello baby." He sat on the edge of the bed.

"Don't you start," Anne said, taking his hand. "I have enough masochists in my life. I want to hear about Arno Bendt. I've been looking at his website, and I'm reading one of his books."

"I bombed at UCL," Howard said. "I'm glad you weren't there, it was embarrassing. They really didn't get it."

"A year ago I would have made fun of it," Anne said. "It's something to do with you being there; it made it seem real."

"They didn't understand about the owl," Howard said. "I probably should have left that out. I was under-prepared, I suppose."

"I suddenly got a sense of what it might be like," Anne said. "When I watch the video I can feel the heat, and the light, and the stillness, and all of a sudden his book started to make sense. I began to understand what he was saying to me."

"But they didn't respond to the Graham Greene stuff either," Howard said. "In the end I got one question, after like a minute's silence." He left the room and they could hear him clattering plates and cutlery in the kitchen. "There's food," he called out. "Give me a minute. You'll be glad to know it isn't beef." The oven door banged shut, pushing a warm breath of roasting meat into the room. "Or owl," he said.

"Tell me I'm not being silly, Morgan," Anne said, gripping his hand. She sighed, speaking very softly. "I feel so positive about him, about the clinic. Tell me what you really think. Am I being ridiculous?"

"It's chicken," Howard said. He and Morgan sat facing each other across a little table at the foot of the bed. "You'll have to take my word for that. Damn, forgot the wine, wait there."

"It looks so beautiful," Anne said. "So peaceful. Is it really like that? Or am I just getting desperate? Tell me it's really as beautiful as it looks."

"So there was this long silence," Howard said, pouring the wine, fetching a beaker for Anne. "And finally Professor Duvall said: *So tell me Dr. Lockhart, this notion of yours, the counterfactual world? It's everything that doesn't exist, have I got that right? Isn't that rather a wide field of enquiry?"*

"It is," Morgan said. "It really is beautiful. You're not being ridiculous." Howard cleared away the plates. They could hear him murmuring to himself in the kitchen.

"People say he really helps them," Anne said. "Do you think that's possible? I feel like it's my last chance. I want to get there before it's too late. Am I being stupid?"

"I didn't have a quick answer to that," Howard said. "I've been working on it since, and in the end it comes back to the trails in the forest, do you remember?"

"I know that people in my situation clutch at anything," Anne said. "I can see myself from the outside, doing just that, and I'm not impressed." She cleared her throat, pressing a handkerchief to her lips. "But I'm drowning, Morgan. How can I not clutch?"

"Howard found the magic lamp," Morgan said. "It's my turn to bring on the magic carpet." He took her hand, smiling at her. "I'll get you there. I'll make it happen."

***

London was gritty with stale heat and swept with the whoop and shriek of police sirens, patrol cars racing down the Edgware Road. There was a message on the answer-phone in his flat, a wrong number; an old man's voice, speaking in a papery vibrato: *I often wonder where you are, Terry, and what you're doing these days. Perhaps you'll call me.* Morgan deleted it.

He walked to the office. In Hyde Park he picked his way between cricket games and picnics and people throwing sticks for dogs; a football thumped across the parched grass in front of him and he booted it back in a long, satisfying loop. Cutting through a side street behind the Lycée, he found himself passing a line of half a dozen police vans, riot screens lowered, black-helmeted heads turning to watch him through the meshed glass as he hurried past. In the Fiat showroom the little pink Cinquecento was gone from the window, replaced by a grey one.

"Don't you get the papers down there in Wales?" Angie asked him. "Read that." She pushed a folded copy of the Guardian across her desk.

"GBH Global Asset Management is the largest mutual fund manager in the world," Morgan read out loud. He looked up at Angie. "Why am I reading this?"

"Go on," she said. "You have a nice voice."

"*It has major offices in London, Chicago, New York and blah-blah,*" Morgan continued. He looked up again. "They have assets of three and a quarter trillion dollars," he said. "What is a trillion, anyway? How many noughts is that?"

"Turn back to the front page," Angie said. "Read the headline."

"*Bomb at London investment bank,*" Morgan read. "*One dead.*" He scanned quickly through the story. "That still doesn't explain why there are riot police round the corner here in South Ken," he said. "This GBH outfit is in Holborn."

"There are coppers everywhere," Angie said. "They're in a panic. It'll blow over in a few days; just don't get yourself shot in the meantime."

"*One dead,*" Morgan said. "Not much of a billing, poor sod. Talk about a bit-part."

"How was Wales, anyway?" Angie said. "Are you selling your house?"

"I don't know if I can," Morgan said. "They're talking about condemning it." He shrugged. "I suppose that's one way of getting shot of Rhodri."

He walked over to the window. Below him, across the street, a girl was striding along the pavement, dodging round the tables set out in front of the pub, long robes flowing around her, waving her arms in florid gestures, her mobile tucked into her hijab, talking hands-free. "Has it always been called that?" he said. "The pub opposite?"

"Called what?"

"The Shallow Grave," Morgan said. "When did that happen?" He turned back into the room. "What have we got in the pipeline for the autumn?" Angie shrugged.

"Not a lot, as it happens; next season looks even worse." She tapped the newspaper with a bright green fingernail. "And this sort of thing doesn't help bookings."

"Good nails," Morgan said.

"Still, you've got Rome now," Angie said. "And then Paris. Make the most of it. Have you had the final itinerary yet? I never knew all that stuff about the Pope, what a bastard."

"I know," Morgan said. "A horrible man, a glove puppet with a hand-washing mania: the Pontius Pilate of his day. His reason for not protecting the Italian Jews was that he didn't want, and I quote: *to make things worse.* You have to laugh."

"Do you ever do a tour without finding a Holocaust dimension?" Angie said.

"*L'épouvantable, c'est partout,*" Morgan said. She looked at him. "The unspeakable is everywhere," he said.

"You're not wrong."

She shuffled papers around on her desk, quick, precise movements punctuated by the thump and clack of the stapler, slipping documents into plastic files, sealing an envelope with a pink flick of tongue. "How's the new girlfriend by the way, your jazz-singer?"

"I'm seeing her after the trip next week; I'm going back to Portugal."

At the end of the afternoon, in the descending lift, their reflections caught each others' eyes, smiled, glanced away.

"Let's give the Shallow Grave a miss," Morgan said. "Where shall we go?" Angie glanced at him as they passed the Fiat showroom.

"Any news of Gabriella? She didn't send the car back I presume?" Morgan shook his head. "You should have stuck to chocolates and a long-stemmed rose," she said. "Does Matty have a car?"

The Antelope was filling up, a noisy, Friday evening rush of office-workers spilling out on to the pavement. A police car nosed slowly down the street; through the open window they could hear the nasal fizz and crackle of the radio. "*One dead,*" Angie said. "Apparently it really was a walk-on part." Morgan looked at her. "Your bit-part player at the bank?" She pointed at the Metro billboard across the street.

"*Bank Bomb - The Wrong Man?*" Morgan read. "What does that mean?"

"The chap who got blown up," Angie said. "He was just somebody's assistant."

"Now there's an epitaph," Morgan said.

"He worked for some big-shot fund manager, one of those billion-dollar-bonus types we all admire so much. They're saying he may have been mistaken for his boss, that they were trying to kill his boss."

"Tell me what happened to James," Morgan said. They took their drinks outside. Angie turned and said something to him, her voice baffled for a few moments by the harsh clatter of a helicopter passing overhead.

"I'd forgotten you missed all that," she was saying. "She pushed the Red Button, very exciting. They wanted to parachute you in to terminate him, but I told them you were on down-time, couldn't be disturbed. How's that

126

all going, you and Matty? Do I sense a bit of commitment?"

"Tell me about James."

"One bit of advice: when you find yourself passing car-showrooms, look the other way."

"Tell me what happened to James. Start at the beginning."

"It's important to recognise your areas of weakness, that's all I'm saying. With me it's shoes; bad enough, but the gap between impulse and regret is smaller and cheaper. Shoes and hair."

"Bob started to tell me, but we got interrupted. All I know is someone pushed the Red Button."

"That would be head-teacher Val Driscoll, of Hamilton High. They were in Paris, thirty kids and two teachers from upstate New York. James made a pass at Ms Driscoll, on a *bateau parisien*. They were on the Seine, it was twilight, heading towards Notre Dame, they were going under Pont Neuf. You know the way you get all that booming and echoing when you go under a bridge in a boat, and the light is bouncing and reflecting off the water, and the vaulted stone is so close above your head? It's very sexy."

"I think I do," Morgan said.

"That must have been what set him off," Angie said. "They were at the back of the boat, just the two of them, away from the others. I say he made a pass at her, but if it was rugby you'd call it a high tackle. He just dived at her." She looked at him over the rim of her glass. "At first she thought he was trying to push her overboard."

"How do you know all this?" Morgan asked. "I like your hair, by the way; I thought you were going to go green, but that red suits you."

"I'm working from effects to causes." She brushed her hair off her forehead. "You don't think it's too bright?" Morgan shook his head. "Also I saw a bit of the report afterwards," Angie said. "And the rest I'm making up. Anyway, he got his hand inside her blouse, which made his intentions clear at least, but once they were out from under the bridge she fought him off. The minute they got back to the hotel she pushed the Red Button, and all the alarm bells started ringing in the Paris office, and then here in London and then in Seattle, and within a couple of hours Luke Skywalker was flying in to Charles de Gaulle and poor old James was on his way home."

"Poor old James," Morgan said. "Whatever got into him? Maybe he really was trying to push her overboard, maybe it was one of those trips; we've all had one. You made up the bit about the blouse though, didn't you?"

"You're looking good, Morgan. I think not being with Gabriella suits you."

"Thank you, I think it does too. How about you? Did you go out with Paulo again?" Angie pulled a face.

"We haven't had enough drinks to get on to Paulo," she said. "What is it with these Italians?"

"What?" Morgan said. "What's that look?"

"More drinks." They pushed their way to the bar, pressed close together by the crush of bodies around them, buffeted by the roar of talk and laughter. "I always wondered about that job in Milan," Angie shouted into his ear. "Gabriella must have known about it for weeks before she left. She must have known about it before you gave her the car. Did that ever cross your mind?"

"Cross my mind?" Morgan shouted back. "It laid an egg in it."

Outside, the pavement was still in bright sunshine, the pub windows spangling with golden light. The far side of the street lay in shadow, elegant Georgian facades reduced to dark silhouettes against the deepening blue of the sky.

"Did you hear about the Madrid office?" Angie said. "Did you know they're talking about closing it?"

Chapter Fifteen

· · ·

Julietta brought a jug of fresh lemonade and little bowls of wild strawberries to the terrace.

"I don't understand," Matty said.

"I don't like to see you have these debts," Arno said. "You were paying too much interest on that account, it's not good finance. Better to pay it off."

"How could you access my account?" Matty said. "Of course I'm grateful, darling, but how did you even know about it? How did you know what I owed on it?" Arno shrugged.

"You're account is with my bank," he said. "It's simple."

"How is it simple? It's supposed to be confidential, isn't it?"

"Do you like these strawberries? In German it's *walderbeere,* they remind me of my home." Arno refilled her glass, the jug musical with ice. Matty watched an aeroplane coming in to land at the sea's edge, between the salt-flats and the high-rise buildings ringing the city, burning like a star as the sun caught it.

"It's sweet of you to worry about me," she said. "But a girl needs her privacy, darling. That account was between me and my bank manager, can't you see that?" Arno patted her arm.

"My dear Matty," he said. "You are beautiful and talented, and I like to be able to help you."

"And I appreciate what you do," Matty said. "You're a darling. But I've always made my own way; I've always followed my star." Another aeroplane was taking off, the roar of acceleration softened by distance as it rose steeply into the sky. "I've always looked after myself," she said.

"Of course," Arno said. "However, the payments were very high. You were not keeping up."

"That was just temporary, sweetheart. I have a lot in the pipeline."

"Temporary is good," Arno said. "But my solution is final, and so it's better, isn't it? Now the account is no more to worry about; closed, forget it. Try the *walderbeere*, please."

One of Arno's assistants crossed the terrace towards them, her uniform blindingly white, creaking with starch. She had a sheaf of papers in her hand. Arno riffled swiftly through them. "*Danke, Steffi,*" he said. "*Wo is die Eva?*"

"*Noch mit Frau Gordon, Herr Doktor,*" the girl said. Arno nodded, dismissing her. He turned to Matty.

"So we say no more about this, are we agreed?" Matty watched the girl as she walked away, holding herself very straight, her heels clacking on the brick floor. "And the young people?" Arno said. "I didn't see them today. The filming is going well?" He swung the wheelchair through half a turn with a powerful movement of his arms. "I have a group session now," he said. "I will see you this evening." The little dog jumped off his lap and minced stiffly across the terrace into the shade.

Matty turned off the clinic track onto the São Miguel road and stopped the Range Rover, lowering the window. To her left, a flock of milking sheep were grazing the dried underbrush in a grove of olive trees, bells clanking as they moved. A shepherd was sitting on a rock, his back against a tree, arms folded across his knees. He pushed his hat back on his forehead and greeted Matty, pointing up the hill on the other side of the road. She looked, seeing nothing but cork trees, and low stone walls crumbling back into the red earth, and the blue dome of the sky where a bird of prey was circling.

From somewhere out of sight, amplified by a fold in the hills, she could hear the clink and thud of a mattock as someone turned over the stony soil, and the murmuring of slow country voices discussing crops, and drought, and livestock. The heat was drawing out intense odours of tar and sweat, sheep-dung and wild herbs. Behind her, framed in the wing mirrors, the towers of the compound rose like battlements above the summit of the hill. She waved goodbye to the shepherd and drove on.

She picked up the motorway below Loulé and turned into the sun, heading for Sagres and the end of the world in a soft, enclosing roar of air-conditioning and jazz and black leather and tinted glass, a capsule heading west at a hundred and sixty kilometres an hour. At Cabo de São Vicente the dark Atlantic boiled in surges of spray at the foot of the cliffs. Matty parked the car between tour-buses and walked to the lighthouse on the headland. Further out, the ocean was sliding and shifting in vast silver sheets under the westering sun, dropping away over the curvature of the world towards America.

To the north, the rollers were booming and breaking along fifteen hundred kilometres of coastline to the Spanish border at Caminha, barrelling in along the surf-beaches, or shattering in rainbow cascades over rocky headlands. And at secret, unforeseeable intervals, a freak wave: a sinister and anomalous monster building up from half way across the Atlantic, a thousand miles of power tightening like a muscle until it burst roaring up onto the rocks in blinding sheets of spray, dragging back into the ocean, leaving nothing behind it on the empty shore.

Back at the clinic she opened an email from Isabella. There'd been nothing from Hot Clube de Lisboa or Jazz-Box. Suzy Q had filled their slots through to the New Year; perhaps something could be arranged for the following summer, they would make contact nearer the time.

Arno sent for her to sit with him over coffee at the end of the evening meal.

"I have exciting news," he said. "You remember I had a meeting at Ilha Negra, with the hotel people at the golf-course, you drove me there?" Matty nodded, smiling up at Julietta as the girl set a coffee pot between them. "This afternoon they telephoned me," he said. "They want you to sing there, next Saturday, at the Flor do Mar."

Out of the evening sky, an owl crossed the terrace in a swooping curve, turning its white, astonished mask of a face towards them for a moment, skimming above the surface of the pool before banking away into the shadows. Matty heard herself repeating Arno's words.

"Next Saturday?" she said. He poured coffee and slid the tiny cup across the table to her.

"It's short notice," he said. "They had a cancellation. There isn't time to get it in the magazine, but maybe in the news-sheet. And I've talked to them, they'll put posters up all over the hotel, all over the resort. It will be good." Matty looked at him.

"Sweetheart, this isn't how it's done. I have an agent darling, everything goes through her. Arno, dearest, I'm not an amateur, I've been doing this half my life."

She was aware of Mrs Wanner and her daughter glancing up the table at them, and lowered her voice. "Dear Arno, I know you're trying to help, but this isn't the right way forward for me. I've told you how I feel about those places. That isn't where I want my career to go. I need to sing jazz, not cabaret. I need to get into clubs where I'm appreciated." She drew a deep breath. "Like in London," she said. "Or Lisbon."

"It's not a problem," Arno said. "You can tell your agent, she can be involved, she can take her percentage." He sipped at his coffee, watching her. "And you can sing jazz," he said. "That's a condition. They don't tell you what to sing; you sing whatever you want, I stipulated this. I have come to an agreement with them, do you understand?"

Looking up, Matty saw Luisa and Sam crossing the far end of the terrace, keeping to the arcade, appearing and disappearing in the archways, Kate and Marley following them; then Enid a few paces behind the others. Marley stumbled and nearly fell over, sneezing with suppressed laughter, the others hissing at him in sibilant whispers.

Arno watched them for a moment. "I have good news for Luisa too," he said. "I can find her twenty, maybe thirty people for her crowd scene, her demonstration. She can have them for as many days as she wishes. They will not want too much money; I will see to it all."

***

Half way through the rehearsal the hotel combo at the Flor do Mar suddenly came alive. They had trudged through the first forty minutes: three middle aged guys on keyboard, drums and electric bass. Matty took them through the first few songs of the set, and they nodded and chatted and cracked jokes, and paid her little compliments. They gave her plenty of space; they were quick to follow changes of mood, or pick up the pace. Sometimes they anticipated where she was going, and led into the phrasing with quick satisfied glances at each other. They were competent, professional, doing the job.

They took a break and drank coffee, and chatted about her career. Gil remembered *Flirting at the Funeral,* and picked it out on the keyboard in a Euro-poppy, double-time riff. They went back to work. They did *Cry me a river;* in the middle eight she duetted with the electric bass, feeling the dark thud of the rhythm in the pit of her stomach, her voice silvery above it, shimmering with vibrato, aware of something sparking across the gap

132

between her and the musicians.

They did *The Dark End of the Street;* as she sang the lines: *They'll never find us, they'll never find us,* she caught Gil's eye and they segued into the key shift in an exhilarating surge of pace and tone, like dancing together. As they finished the number the four of them looked at each other in a silence that was full of laughter and recognition.

On Saturday Matty sat between Arno and Luisa in the back of the Range Rover. Jorge was wearing a chauffeur's cap, experimenting with the fit as he drove, pulling it forward so that the peak half hid his eyes, then setting it further back on his head, tilted to one side, checking his reflection in the mirror. Eventually he pushed it right to the back of his head, the peak vertical. Sam nodded from the front seat.

"That's the look," he said. "You've got it now."

"I have heard from your friend Morgan," Arno said. "He has made a booking at the clinic for a friend of his. Were you aware of this?"

"Are you nervous, Mum?" Luisa said. "I'm picking up butterflies." Matty shook her head.

"Not nervous, baby, I think it's going to be good. The band is lovely. But you need an edge; you have to stay sharp." She half turned in the seat. "My dress is in the back, isn't it?" she said. "I put it in, didn't I?"

"Of course," Arno said, patting her hand. "Everything is taken care of."

"We used to have a Range Rover," Luisa said to Sam. "Didn't we Mum? You never saw them in Lisbon in those days, we may have been the only one. It felt really special."

"We were special, baby," Matty said. "We were royalty."

They took the exit for the resort, the slip-road peeling away from the motorway, running through groves of umbrella pines towards the sea. On either side, service roads branched off into suburban loops, clusters of little white villas built among the pine trees, a chemical flash of swimming pool, lawn-sprinklers lethargically dribbling onto balding patches of grass. At every intersection billboards advertised new developments: more villas, luxury apartments, club-houses, restaurants, riding schools, health-spas.

In a gap in the trees, seen for a moment as the car swept past, a dark-haired woman in a long skirt was nursing a baby, squatting in front of a shack made of sheets of tin and lengths of discarded carpet.

"*Clandestinos,*" Jorge said, his glance flicking across them. "*Miseráveis.*"

The hotel itself appeared at the end of an avenue of cypress trees, a terraced cliff of white marble and brushed steel blocking the horizon, like a cruise ship beached on the sand. They drew up in front of a colonnade of horse-shoe Moorish arches framing the foyer, flood-lit in the evening sunlight, the vaulted ceilings supported by brass columns cast in the form of palm trees, the air cooled by the splash of alabaster fountains.

"You see how Arabic we are becoming once more, here in al-Andalus," Arno said. Hotel staff in white jackets hustled round the car, setting up the wheel-chair, holding the doors open for Matty and Luisa, one of them fetching a rustling length of silk and cellophane and tissue-paper from the boot of the car. Arno set off towards reception, the others following. "Unfortunately it's Saudi money," he said, gesturing around him. "They did not study the Alhambra. There are lessons of elegance and balance that have not been learned here."

Matty's dressing-room was filled with white lilies, enormous fleshy blooms lolling in jars and vases, filling nearly every shelf and surface. She hung up her dress, switched on the lights around the mirror and started setting out her make-up. Luisa put her head round the door.

"Can I do anything for you, mother?" Matty gestured at the flowers.

"Look at all this," she said, smiling. "Isn't it ridiculous! Dear Arno!"

"Are you sure you don't want something to eat?"

"Don't fuss baby. I have everything. I just need to centre for a while." She sat down at the make-up table. "I must have told him lilies are my favourite flowers. I don't think I've ever seen so many at once."

"Be careful what you wish for."

"Perhaps you could find me some herb tea," Matty said, speaking into the mirror, puckering up her lips. "Camomile, if they have it." She turned as Luisa started to leave the room. "While you're here, sweetheart, help me put some of these flowers out into the corridor. They're making me sniffle."

She heard the combo starting up, slick and relaxed, Gil running trickling arpeggios up the keyboard. The three of them had helped Luisa carry the lilies out into the corridor, telling her how happy they were to be working with Matty. *"A tua mae é um' artista formidável,"* they told her.

She checked herself out in the mirror, misted more Chanel around her and went out into the corridor, walking down an avenue of lilies to where the MC was waiting in the wings, bulky in a white tuxedo. He smiled briefly at her, and they exchanged air-kisses with quick bobbing movements of the head.

"They gonna love you," he said. Beyond the music she could hear a faint drone of conversation and movement, the chink and click of cutlery and glass. The band started into *Flirting*. After a few bars Ernesto produced a crashing flourish, sticks clattering on the snare drum, the bass rumbling. "This is me," the MC said, pushing through the curtain.

Matty took her three deep breaths. "*Flor do Mar proud to present,*" she heard. "*International singing star!*" Ernesto was speeding up the drum-roll, flicking rim-shots, pumping shimmering clashes out of the hi-hat. "*The very lovely!*" The MC paused, the drummer dropping the volume to an urgent whisper of brushes on the snare. "*Matty James, ladies and gentlemen! Matty James!*" Matty counted slowly to five, drew the curtain to one side and stepped out on to the stage as the band surged into the chorus. They cut it short with another drum-roll; in the hush, Matty could hear a rustle of applause. She glanced at Gil, and he led her off into the opening chords of *To Love Somebody*.

Above her head a disco-ball revolved slowly among the spotlights, sparking off shards and flashes that flamed and shimmered in the sequins of her dress, wrapping her in glittering fire. Ernesto was hitting eight beats to the bar, nervy, fretful, syncopating over the heart-beat of Bobby's bass. She sang the line: *I see your face again,* lost in the music.

There were perhaps thirty tables, not all of them taken; couples and parties of three and four lit by dim globes of amber light, the room receding into shadowed distances. She held the last note, sliding off it as Gil ran a spiral of ornamentation down the keyboard. He caught her eye and smiled, murmuring to himself.

As the chord died, waiters appeared out of the shadows, clearing plates, topping up glasses of wine. Someone whistled piercingly above the subdued applause, and she picked out Luisa and Sam sitting on either side of Arno in the centre of the room. Sam put his fingers to his mouth and whistled again and the applause intensified for a moment, then died away. Matty cupped her hands around the microphone and breathed into it.

"Thank you, ladies and gentlemen," she said, her voice barely rising above the clatter and buzz of the room. "I'm so happy to be here tonight."

They did *The Second Time Around*, taking it in a slow, lilting waltz-time, Ernesto's brushes dragging softly across the snare like the last couple on the dance-floor. Waiters moved furtively between the tables, pouring drinks, taking orders. Balloons of cognac were appearing, glowing like night-lights. Matty slid over to the keyboard, putting her head down close to Gil's. He nodded, running off a quick phrase in the high notes; she took the mic off its stand and they did *Flirting*, low and melancholy, the four of them reading each other as though they'd been playing together for years.

She sang the last verse unaccompanied, standing alone at the front of the stage: "*Am I still in you, are you still in me?*" From somewhere near the bar a glass broke in sharp and dissonant fragments of sound, and a ripple of distraction ran round the room, someone hissing for silence. The old waiter who'd been pushing the dessert-trolley from table to table stopped in front of the stage and beamed at her, clasping his hands above his head.

"*Maravilhosa, Senhora Matty!*" he said. "*Perfeição!*"

"*Muinto obrigada!*" Matty said, bobbing at him. She caught Luisa's eye and blew kisses at the three of them, stepping back to re-join the band. They did *Loving Arms,* and *I Can't Stand the Rain.* As the song ended, she became aware of a slight commotion from somewhere near the centre of the dining area, someone calling out. She saw Arno turn in his chair, glaring.

"*My Way!*" the voice called out again. "Sing *My Way!*" She took in a party of eight or ten women crowded round a table, big, gaudy girls in bright clothes and short hair, vivid with lipstick and eye-shadow, heavy with ropes and chains of jewellery. She leaned over the keyboard again.

"*Vergonha,*" Gil said, pulling a face. "*São bébedas. Em Inglés é 'hen-party', não é?*" Matty tapped out a short sequence of notes, and he nodded, elaborating it, getting Ernesto and Bobby's attention. They doodled a couple of bars, and Matty took hold of the mic stand and drew it towards her.

"I'm going to sing this one in Portuguese," she said. "*O tempo volta para trás.* Time turns backwards. This is for an old friend. If I shut my eyes I can still hear his voice." Gil had the keyboard on soft electric piano, and she sang it the way she remembered it, as though someone was singing in another room: locked out, lost.

They did *Where or When,* the four of them playing for each other, getting almost nothing back from the audience. "We're going to take a short break now," Matty said. The MC hurried onstage out of the wings, buttoning his tuxedo.

"Matty *James*, ladies and gentlemen! Matty *James!* We'll be right back!"

They waited to go back on, listening to the MC bigging it up; Gil held his arms out wide and the four of them hugged, putting their heads together like footballers in a huddle. As they came out on stage she heard Sam whistling again, loud enough to hail a taxi, and waved back at him. She adjusted the mic on its stand, blowing a kiss at Arno, looking round from table to table as she waited for the band to get settled, wondering for a moment what was different about the atmosphere in the room: in the ten minutes they'd been backstage about half the audience had left.

The last of the twilight was fading to a greenish glow along the western horizon as they drove away from the resort. Looking out the back of the Range Rover Matty watched the hotel recede down its dark avenue of cypress trees. They had finished the set with *My Guy*, taking it fast and raucous, Matty clapping her hands above her head. She got nothing back: faces full of rich food, cross-eyed with brandy, staring dumbly up at her or wobbling unsteadily between tables on their way out. Even the acoustics of the room seemed to have gone dead.

"At Jimmy's Place people got up and danced when I did that song," Matty said. Ahead of them, the outline of the hills was softening against the dome of the night-sky, the stars beginning to dance, shivering as though reflected in water. "I think the universe is trying to send me a message," she said, leaning back into the dark leather. "But I've decided to ignore it." Arno took her hand, stroking it.

"It is important to learn," he said. "You must listen to the message in order to understand it."

"The band loved you, Mum," Luisa said. "You worked so well together."

"I know, baby."

"You must look at the audience," Arno said. "You must ask yourself: what do these people want?"

"They want butter and cream, and cognac," Luisa said. "And foie gras and smoked salmon, and more cognac."

"And *My Way*," Sam said from the front seat. "Don't forget *My Way*."

"You are an entertainer," Arno said. "You must work with your audience, not against them."

"They want to get plastered all night," Luisa said. "And then lie by the pool all morning, greasy with sun-oil."

"I was trying, darling," Matty said. "Believe me. They weren't an easy audience. Trust me, I've known a few; I'm not new to this."

"Like pigs on a barbecue," Luisa said.

"You must find music that will work for them," Arno said. "Also I will talk to the hotel myself. There are changes we can make. This can be made to work better."

"Crap will work for them," Luisa said. "Mum's an artist." She looked across at Arno. "But you don't really care for music, do you?"

Chapter Sixteen

. . .

"I am very happy to see you again," Manólo said. "I didn't expect you back so soon. And they say you have a part in the film?"

"A bit part," Morgan said.

"A big part?"

"*Olá querida,*" Matty said as Julietta brushed past them, lighting the oil-lamps. Maria was working her way down from the other end of the table.

"It's an important rôle?"

"I play an embittered old communist."

"He's brilliant," Matty said. "You should see him."

"And Sam plays me." Manólo looked at him.

"You are in the story?" he said. "I don't understand."

"Only kidding," Morgan said.

"The young people come to my club this week," Manólo said. "Don't you Sam? To find more actors perhaps."

"We need soldiers," Luisa said. "We'll need to hire some army uniforms."

"It's not a problem," Manólo said.

"And guns, I suppose. They'd have guns, obviously." She turned to Kate. "Why didn't we think of that? Can you do guns, Manólo?"

"There's a lot of new people here," Morgan said. "I don't remember any of them from last time. Where's Anita?"

"Poor Anita," Matty said.

"What happened to Anita?"

Matty shrugged, exchanging a glance with Manólo.

"Arno tells me your friend Anne is coming here," she said.

"And Howard," Morgan said. "He's coming too, I told you. The original cast gets together again. I wonder who'll play Howard in the revival?"

"What is this original cast?" Manólo asked him.

"It's the remake," Morgan said. "Very fashionable these days."

"We've had a brilliant idea," Kate said, raising her voice above the murmur and drone of conversation around them. "Or Marley has, didn't you, babe. Tell them."

"Mixed-doubles," Marley said. "A mixed-doubles tennis tournament. We'll play it over the next few evenings, after work."

"And Leni Riefenstahl agrees," Sam said, patting Luisa's hand. "She says it'll be good for team-building."

"Have they got a court here?" Enid said.

"Have they got a court?" Kate said. "They've got four clay courts; they've got changing-rooms, and a gym, and a bar. The whole place is immaculate, it looks like the French Open. Marley and I had a knock-about first thing this morning."

"Those clay courts are funny," Marley said. "Very slippy, I kept falling over. The bar wasn't open, by the way."

"You'll have to join in, Mum," Luisa said. "You and Morgan are a team."

"Purely for comic effect, baby."

"You used to be good, mother!"

"Now I know what I'm having on my tombstone," Matty said. "*I used to be good.*"

"Me and Marley," Kate said. "You can hide behind the net, babe, I'll look after you. Sam and Luisa, obviously." She looked across the table at Enid. "Who are we going to pair you with?" she said. "How do you fancy Manólo?"

"And this is the best bit," Marley said. "This is where the whole idea comes from." He raised his wine-glass in a toast. "We all knock each other out," he said. "And the last pair left standing play the Barbies!" He finished the wine in his glass.

"Who are the Barbies?" Enid said. Marley gestured towards Arno's end of the table.

"Steffi and Eva," he said. "Arno's assistants, down there in the white uniforms. I've talked to them, they're very happy to take us on." He lowered his voice. "Have you watched them in action?" he said. "They are so toned, it's unbelievable." He looked down the table at them, shaking his head. "Nothing wobbles," he said.

140

Matty and Morgan sat on the balcony, the night air soft and warm, musical with the warbling of crickets and the bubbling of the pool's filtration system, the constellations wheeling and unfolding above their heads.

"How was Rome, sweetheart?" Matty said. "Do you know, I've never been there?"

"Maybe we'll go there together one day. We'll sit at a café table in Piazza Navona and watch the water gushing out of that crazy Bernini fountain, all those buttocks."

"That Enid's a funny little thing," Matty said. "Like a china doll. I was never like her, like Tessa, that is."

"I hope I wasn't too much like Chris," Morgan said. "I don't think I was. All the same, it's a bit strange, playing opposite your younger self."

"You weren't, sweetheart. And I was never a flirt. Things happen when you least expect them, that's all. You look up and you find that everything has changed. That's the story of my life, you could say." She watched the navigation lights of an aeroplane pass overhead, towing a distant rumble of sound across the sky. "You know Arno's trying to set up a concert for me?" she said.

"That's good, isn't it?"

"No, baby, it's not good at all. He's been talking to the damn resort people again. He wants to hire the theatre, put on a show, starring me!"

"How is that not good? Morgan said.

"It's awful, sweetheart, it's truly frightful. It's amateur, it's all the wrong way round. You don't buy your way in - you don't hire the theatre - they hire you. How is he going to handle publicity? He doesn't know anyone in the business, he doesn't know any promoters or journalists. He thinks that money can buy you anything. Is he going to buy an audience?" She sighed. "It makes me feel cheap; it makes me feel like my career is over."

"But it isn't."

"I know that, darling. I've been a star in my time, and I will be again. I just need to take control of my life. I've been thinking about getting a new agent, someone who really understands me." She lit a cigarette and blew a plume of smoke at the stars. "I wish we still had the boat," she said. "I wish we could just sail away."

A light came on in the block beyond the pool, dimming as someone drew the drapes across the window. "That's one of the treatment rooms," she said.

"Arno's working late tonight." She stubbed out the cigarette. "He can probably smell it," she said. From beyond the walls of the compound a dog started to bark, a sequence of harsh yelps, then a silence as though it was waiting for an answer, even the cicadas pausing their incessant backing track. "I'm being hard on him," she said. "He's doing it for me; he's only trying to help." The dog started barking again.

"I haven't quite worked out how you and I are supposed to be with each other," Morgan said. "Around other people, I mean. Why aren't we just together? Is there a problem with that?"

"Just be yourself, sweetheart," Matty said. "Like I do."

"Maybe that's easier said than done," Morgan said. "Or easier for you than for me."

"The kids are alright," she said. "There's no problem with them. Luisa likes you a lot." She gestured towards the arcaded terraces below them. "It's only down there we have to be a little more careful." She stroked his cheek.

"Careful?" Morgan said.

"Discreet, then. You know what I mean. But we have all night, baby; we have every night. All of this belongs to us." A shooting star flared silently overhead, leaving a line of light on the retina behind it, and then a line of darkness. "Make a wish," she said.

Chapter Seventeen

. . .

The city grows incessantly, in secret increments, a mushroom pushing up through stony soil. Day by day the periphery expands into wastelands of access roads and brick-stacks and equipment dumps, where diggers and cement-mixers wheel and turn in clouds of white dust under enigmatic cranes. High-rise blocks of offices and apartments follow each other, stepping ponderously on towards the sea.

The airport is built on the last available stretch of solid ground, reaching into the edges of the salt-flats and lagoons that form a dissolving margin between land and sea. The Airbuses and 737s approach from the north, but the city blocks their descent; the pilots have to overshoot the runway and turn back over the sea, banking so steeply that the left-hand windows are full of cresting waves and wind-surfers.

Flaps down, the planes drop over the lagoons, mud and rushes flattening under the slip-stream until at the very last moment the reaching wheels find concrete and the bump and shriek of touching down; control towers and terminal buildings, mis-shapen airport vehicles, bored police with sub-machine guns, heat, and light, and the scented air of the south.

From the airport the motorway races out through tracts of industrial development: warehousing, dealerships, construction sites, shimmering in mirages of heat; then on through citrus-groves and vineyards, and irrigation systems throwing out rainbows of spray over green crops. Slip-roads peel away, heading towards the resorts along the coast, or north into the mountains. Dave Leaper followed the signs for São Miguel do Monte.

Just off the main square, the side wall of the bus station was covered with the remains of a vast, faded mural, painted in 1975 to celebrate the revolution, almost completely obliterated by time and weather and forgetfulness: tattered figures of soldiers and farm-workers, and the word *Unidade,* in faint red script. Everything else leached, bleached, the paint decayed or flaking away, little plants pushing through the surface, and from the top of the wall cascades of bougainvillea and morning glory hanging down, smothering the revolutionary slogans. *A terra a quem a trabalha:* the land belongs to those who work it. He parked the hire-car under the mural and went to look for a hotel and a cold beer, and directions to the clinic.

At the end of the afternoon a young girl led him along cobbled alley-ways between white-washed buildings, through courtyards shaded with trellised vines, past arches opening onto terraces and gardens; a blue flash of swimming-pool, the water restless, throwing off dazzling bursts of light.

"*Está muito calor,*" he said, fragments of language coming back to him, and she turned and beamed.

"*Está calor, sim,*" she said. "*É verdade! Dizem que faz trinta graus.*" From somewhere ahead of them, beyond a line of cypress trees, he could hear the elastic smack of a tennis racket, the scuffling thud of footsteps and a rattle of laughter and applause. He followed the girl through an opening in the trees. "*Olá menina!*" she called out. "*Está aqui um senhor perguntando para você!*"

Luisa missed the return, but the ball was going out anyway. Someone was standing by the veranda with Julietta, and she crossed the court to see who it was, not recognising him until she found herself shaking his hand. Dave Leaper had grown a beard, cut short and close, and was wearing mirror sunglasses. She peered at her reflection, distracted for a moment, her face flushed and spoon-shaped in the convex lenses. She wiped a wrist-band across her forehead, getting her breath back; she turned and called Sam over. On the other side of the net, Marley and Kate stood watching them, swinging their rackets.

"Get Julietta to open the bar," Marley said. "We're going to need a drink after this."

"You can't stop now," Kate called out. "We've got two set points."

There was a girl sitting in a deck-chair under the palm-thatched roof of the veranda, the shade so deep after the blinding glare of the tennis courts that he didn't see her at first: skinny, pale, very red hair.

"What is this?" Dave Leaper said. "The rich at play, while the storm-clouds of the revolution gather?" She gave him a thin, bored smile.

"I'm Enid," she said, holding out her hand for him to shake. He set up another deck-chair and sat down beside her.

On the baseline, Sam tossed the ball up and hit it at the top of his reach, serving out wide to Kate; she ran a few strides at full stretch, picking it up in the tramline and looping it back. From close in under the net, Luisa volleyed it back-hand across the court.

"Are you involved with the film?" he said. "I'm Dave Leaper." Enid nodded.

"I'm an actor," she said. The ball hit Marley square in the chest and he dropped his racket, hugging himself.

"Come here, you poor little bugger!" Kate said. "Are you alright?"

"Thirty forty," Sam called out.

"Oh my goodness," Enid said. "You're Dave Leaper? I'm Tessa!" she said. "I play Tessa!"

The players changed sides; heat-mirages bloomed and pooled on the baking surfaces. Cypresses lined the perimeter of the courts, elegant and melancholy; above them, at a vast height, a pair of eagles were circling. Dave Leaper looked at Enid, nodding.

"Interesting," he said. "I think I can see it."

All four players were up at the net, the ball flicking over and back in a crescendo of shots, gasps of laughter floating up to the veranda.

"I hope so," Enid said. "It's going to be a bit unnerving, playing in front of the author."

Marley flailed across the court, skidding up to the net; he played a drop-shot, picking the ball up like an egg in a spoon. He dropped to his knees, holding the racket above his head in triumph.

"I'm not unnerving," Dave Leaper said. He turned to look back at the tennis courts, his sunglasses panning across Enid, across the little bar at the other end of the veranda, out of the shadows and into the intense light of late afternoon, the dark silhouettes of the cypress trees swaying in the lenses as he moved his head.

"An audience takes you as you are," Enid said. "But you're the writer, you must have a picture of Tessa in your mind." He looked at her, sunglasses tracking back from light to shade. She could see herself, a dim outline, replicated. "I hope I match up," she said.

"There's beer, obviously," Kate said from the hatchway of the little bar.

"White wine, gin, tonic, whiskey, brandy." She held up a bottle, rotating it to look at the label. "Lots of whatever this stuff is. There's enough booze here to start a revolution, guys."

"Did you see my drop-shot?" Marley said to Enid. "Did you see how perfect it was? It ought to be on YouTube."

"This place is huge," Dave Leaper said. "Who exactly is this Dr. Bendt?"

"It's Hotel California," Marley said.

"We're filming in a village up in the mountains," Luisa said. "Come with us tomorrow."

"And you're all living here?" Dave said. "How did you manage that?"

"Do you play tennis, Mr Leaper?"

"Dave," he said.

"I've had a moment of genius," Sam said. "You could be Enid's partner. What do you think, Enid? Instead of Manólo."

"It belongs to a friend of my mother's," Luisa said. "Dr. Bendt's an old friend of hers."

"I've just realised who you look like in that head-band, Marley," Kate said.

"Jimi Hendrix?" Sam said. "Bjorn Borg?" He looked at Marley. "Somehow I always see Marley in long underpants."

"Lucky you."

"We're working on the scenes between Alvaro and Chris," Luisa said. "You can see the rushes if you like, come up to the clinic. Morgan is doing Alvaro for us, and Sam is Chris, of course."

"Alvaro," Dave said. "The old Stalinist; I think he's my favourite character, I'm pleased with him. And who is Morgan? I need more gin in this."

"It's a really good part," Enid said. "I love the way you've written him."

"He's a friend of my Mum's," Luisa said. "He's an actor. He's good, isn't he Sam?"

"What do you think, Dave?" Marley said. "A couple of games? The Barbies will thrash us in the end, anyway. Resistance is useless." He swirled the ice-cubes in his glass, leaning back in the deckchair. "What a good idea this is," he said. "Gin and tonic, who thought of that? This is what my mum drinks."

"I met a lot of people like him," Dave said. "The Communists were the best organised, but they were living in the past."

"That really comes across, the way you've written him," Enid said.

"Cuñhal and the others were real Moscow types," Dave said. "What they wanted was centralised power. That whole socialism-with-a-human-face thing left them cold; all that euro-communism." He drank, crunching a piece of ice between his teeth. "They were right of course; what a load of crap it all turned out to be."

"It'll be great to have you on the set," Luisa said.

"They may have been right about the socialists, but they were dinosaurs themselves," Dave said. "They thought they could take political control." He laughed, gesturing around him at the tennis courts, at the laid-out grounds beyond them, at the clinic buildings glimpsed between the cypress trees. "As this place clearly demonstrates, they didn't," he said. "Nobody did."

"He's not a monster though," Enid said. "The way you've written him he's a really interesting character. Don't you think so, Sam?"

"Nuanced," Sam said.

"And you get food here?" Dave asked. "Is it like bed and breakfast?"

"Food?" Marley said. "We get lobster! We get lobster nearly every day! I dream about them at night, all those claws, and wavy bits."

"We'll be moving on to the bigger mise-en-scènes soon," Luisa said. "Meetings, demonstrations, the stuff in Act Three. It'll be great to have your input, sort of eye-witness expert stuff, help us keep it real."

"I can see that'll be a challenge," Dave said.

"And be Enid's partner," Marley said. "We need you for that."

"Did I see a swimming pool back there," Dave said. "When the girl was showing me the way? Was that part of this set-up?"

"Come on the set with us tomorrow," Luisa said. "We'll collect you from your hotel."

"Everything is part of this set-up," Marley said.

***

Matty stayed behind at the compound the following day, working with Arno; Morgan collected Dave Leaper in the rented BMW. They kept up with the Mercedes for the first few kilometres out of town until Luisa accelerated away up the mountain road, the big car sweeping into the bends, spitting gravel and raising a trail of red dust.

"How do you fit into all this, Morgan?" Dave Leaper asked him, glancing sideways at him, his expression unreadable behind mirror shades.

"It's a long story," Morgan said. "It begins in Portugal, of course. You and I must have been here at about the same time."

"Perhaps. Were you in Lisbon?" Morgan nodded. "Were you on the May Day march?"

"We didn't get here until the summer vacation."

"You should have been there. It was chaos, it was beautiful, a week after the régime collapsed; the fat cats were still packing gold bars into suitcases and booking flights to Ipanema. Six hundred thousand people marching through Lisbon."

"No, we saw some big demonstrations, but we didn't get here until the following year," Morgan said. "The summer of '75."

"That makes you a tourist, I'm afraid," Dave said. "How long were you here for?"

"I suppose it does," Morgan said. "I stayed for less than a month; that's pretty much a package-holiday, isn't it? It didn't feel like that at the time."

They were passing through a swathe of mountain-side that had been burned off in a forest fire; steep slopes of blackened earth and splintered, incinerated stumps of trees on either side of the road, the car's slipstream raising spinning dust-devils of cinders and ash behind them. "You take yourself more seriously at that age," he said. "I thought I was serious about politics; I thought we were going to change the world."

"And then you became an actor?"

"That's exactly right," Morgan said.

***

They had cleared out a corner of the main factory building and set up a couple of tables and chairs. Enid and Dave brought in folding chairs and sat watching from the far side of the room.

"I'm not in this scene," she said. "This is a back room of the café, but I'm next door, drinking wine and flirting with the boys. They'll overdub the sound-effects later. Chris and Alvaro are sitting here in the gloom and there's a party going on in the big room through there, lots of music and dancing." A little group of village kids were peering in through the doorway, whispering and shuffling; she put a finger to her lips and made a fierce face, getting back gappy smiles. Dave had a copy of the play open on his lap.

An old man appeared in the doorway, murmuring to them, tipping his hat. He had a reel of power cable with him, unrolling it as he walked the length of the building to where Marley and Luisa were setting up a pair of tungsten lights on tripod stands. "He's sort of the caretaker here," Enid said. "This is a critical moment: do we have electricity?" The old man was crouching on the floor; as he straightened up, light blossomed, golden, filling half the room, casting deep diagonals of shadow. "The blondes are alive," Enid said. "We have power!" The old man beamed, taking a bow and stepping back into the darkness.

"I want more light on Chris, and less on Alvaro," Luisa said. "Bring the shutters this way. Are we ready? Quiet please, let's go."

Sam poured himself a drink; he offered the bottle across the table but Morgan shook his head, putting a hand over his glass.

"The people here need the discipline," he said. "They don't have the class conscious, there are years of propaganda from the fascists. PCP have vanguard role, we need to lead the people, we need to make the revolution." Dave nodded, his finger following the lines on the open page.

"The acoustic is very hollow," Kate said. "There's a bit of reverb. But I guess anything we can't fix here we can do in the edit."

"You need to look over at the door to the big room, Sam," Luisa said. "You too, Morgan. They can hear everyone fooling about in there, and music playing; Chris recognises Tessa's voice, her laugh. It makes him very tense. We'll need a cut-away on the door, Marley, we need light spilling out under it."

"They like to play at revolution," Morgan said. "They call themselves anarquista, but they are bourgeois, privilege."

"More emphasis," Luisa said. "More disdain, more contempt!"

"They are bourgeois, privilege!" Morgan said.

"Can't you get rid of people like that?" Sam said. "Can't you take direct action?"

"Direct action?" Morgan said.

"Can't you just execute them?" Sam said. "In the name of the people? Like the Baader-Meinhof?"

"We'll break there," Luisa said. The little world of the set disintegrated, resolving into individuals, the lights shutting down.

"I'm starving," Sam said.

"Senhor Manuel says he'll stay here and keep an eye on things," Luisa said. "So we don't have to take everything down." She shook the old man's hand. "*O senhor é um gênio!*" she said. "Bring the camera though, Marley. Don't leave that behind."

They went for lunch at the only café in Cova da Víuva, pushing through the curtain of plastic strips into the dark interior, a narrow room with a zinc-topped bar down one side and six little tables taking up the rest of the space, football flickering on a television high up in a corner of the back wall. Two old men were playing dominoes, and there was a group of four at another table, construction workers in paint-spattered overalls, their hair white with cement dust, sitting round plates of sardines and bread and bottles of wine. Luisa led the way, watching as everyone in the room silently counted them in, one of the domino players whispering the total: *Sete!* She spoke to the woman behind the bar, and, closely observed, they dragged tables together, the legs screeching on the concrete floor, and set chairs around them.

"Chris is really losing it," Sam said. "Am I getting that right? He's sounding fairly deranged."

"He's tormented," Luisa said. "He's in a private nightmare." She went up to the counter.

"And he's drunk," Kate said.

A little girl floated a paper cloth over the table and set out a basket of bread and bowls of olives. Across the room, one of the builders raised a glass of wine in a toast, directing it at Enid.

"But he's right," Dave said.

"There are no more sardines," Luisa said. "There's goat stew, or they can do omelettes."

"But Alvaro says that the Baader-Meinhof were just hooligans," Sam said. "He calls them the children of the bourgeoisie."

"That's the party line," Dave said. "Alvaro can't step outside of the Communist perspective, but Chris isn't tied down to that."

"Omelette," Kate said. "And salad."

"All the Communists could think about was political power," Dave said. "And there's no such thing. All that talk about party discipline: it's just a farce."

"Who's having stew?" Luisa said.

"But you said that the Communists were the best organised," Enid said. "Just salad, please."

"Am I going to find an eye-ball in this?" Marley asked.

"This isn't Saudi Arabia, you pinhead."

"Don't call my boy a pinhead."

The construction workers were leaving, picking up their hard-hats, tipping back shot-glasses of aguardente as they paid the bill at the bar, coins counted out and clinking on the zinc top.

"*Isto e que faz bom!*" one of them said as they passed, gesturing at the bowls of stew. "*Bom apetite! Bye-bye!*"

"They're working at that development up the hill," Luisa said, watching them as they brushed through the plastic curtain. "More holiday villas for foreigners."

"Politics is just a puppet-show," Dave said. "The Communists were the best-organised puppets, that's all."

"But in political terms Alvaro is more serious than Chris, isn't he?" Luisa said. "That's how I read it, anyway."

"Chris is a tourist," Morgan said. "I think that's the correct term." Dave grinned at him.

"Alvaro can't see that the revolution has no chance of surviving," he said. "If the Communists had seized power in 1975 it would have made no difference in the long run. Portugal is a tiny country on the very edge of Europe; it has no hinterland, no defence in depth."

"Defence against what?" Morgan said.

"Global capitalism," Dave said. "Do you think Wall Street was going to allow a Communist state in Western Europe? The revolution was doomed to be overwhelmed; it was only a question of method and timing."

"Have we got time for coffee? What about those little cakes on the counter?"

"It's our friends the gangster-capitalists again," Sam said to Luisa.

"Did you know that Franco wanted to invade Portugal in 1975?" Dave said. "He was going to send his armies of the night across the border and crush the revolution. Can you imagine, that blood-thirsty, rotting corpse, kissing St Teresa's mummified fingers, dragging his pustulating carcase round the corridors of the Escorial?"

"Fantastic," Sam said. "This is better than the website."

"He sent his Prime Minister to talk to Kissinger's deputy, asking for US support," Dave said. "He needed more dead children." He got up and went to the bar. "I like the look of those little brandies," he said. "Anyone interested? Morgan?"

"Long afternoon ahead, Dave," Morgan said.

"What's that about Mother Theresa?" Kate asked.

"Saint Teresa," Dave said. "Saint Teresa of Avila. Franco stole her mummified hand from the Carmelite convent in Ronda during the Civil War. He kept it with him wherever he went, for the rest of his life." He knocked back the little shot of brandy. "The Americans weren't impressed with Franco's plan," he said. "They'd propped that fascist zombie up for long enough; he didn't make them look good. And anyway, they had a better solution."

They finished shooting the scene in the café two hours inside schedule. Luisa looked at her watch.

"I don't want to go on to the next page today. Let's take an early finish; we can look at the rushes and start thinking about colour-correction."

"We can get a couple of games in," Kate said. "Me and Marley are on a roll. Let's play Enid and Dave, how about it?"

"You can get a cab back to your hotel later, Dave," Luisa said. "Save you bringing your car. Or Jorge could drive you."

Morgan waited in the rental z4 outside Dave's hotel while he picked up shorts and running shoes.

"Nice little car," he said, glancing at Morgan as he eased himself into the leather seat. "Not as big as Dr. Bendt's, of course."

"I didn't know that story about Franco," Morgan said. Dave nodded.

"It gets better," he said. "The guy Franco sent to talk to the Americans was in the job because his predecessor had been assassinated by ETA eighteen months before: Admiral Carrero Blanco, ring a bell?" Morgan shook his head.

"I'm a tourist, remember?"

"They dug a tunnel under Calle Claudio Coello, in downtown Madrid," Dave said. "Filled it full of explosives, rigged for remote detonation. They set off fifty kilos of Gelamex as the Admiral drove over it in his armoured limousine, it blew the car clear over the top of a five story building; it landed on a second floor balcony of the Jesuit monastery in the next street. *Olé!* I wish I could have seen that."

They waited at the main entrance to the compound as the heavy steel gates slid open.

"Enjoy the tennis," Morgan said.

***

Matty slipped her arm through his.

"Come with me, baby," she said. "Julietta's going to bring me something cold and delicious. *Traga mais um copo para Senhor Morgan, querida.*" She led him down the steps into the walled orchard, leaning against him in a dress

152

splashed with red flowers. "Come and sit with me, sweetheart. I'm exhausted, we've been at it all day." He sat opposite her at one of the little tables under the fruit trees.

"What do you do exactly, when you work with Arno?" Morgan said.

"That's a little abrupt, sweetheart!" Julietta set out a jug and tall glasses full of fruit and crushed ice, misted with cold. Morgan shrugged.

"It's something you say," he said. "*I've been working with Arno.* I never really thought about it before."

""It's nothing sinister, baby," she said. She sipped at her drink. "Try it," she said. "So refreshing! Wasn't it hot in Cova da Víuva?" She shuddered. "That name!" she said. "*The Widow's Grave!* Imagine having that as your address. Did you make good progress? Is Luisa happy? I'm so sorry I missed your scene today. Are you happy with it? Perhaps Lulu will let me see the rushes. You look so handsome!" She drank again, watching him over the rim of the glass. He smiled at her, raising his own.

"Here's looking at you, kid," he said. "I'm interested, that's all."

"We discuss his work," she said. "Nothing confidential, of course. He says I have good instincts about people. We talk about ways of improving the guest-experience. And he advises me about my career." She pulled a face. "I don't always agree with his advice," she said. "But he wants the best for me, and it's good to hear another point of view. Isn't this delicious? My own secret recipe!"

She turned, watching a peacock pick its way between the trees as though following a trail of clues. "And he helps me," she said. "He gets me to talk about what's on my mind, what's worrying me. I'm not one of his patients, it's not like that. He listens, that's all."

"And that helps?"

"Don't be like that, sweetheart. Yes, it does."

"So you talk, and he listens," Morgan said. "Is there a couch involved?" She leaned across the table and took his hand.

"Baby!" she said. "Baby, look at me! Don't be silly!"

"So what was on your mind today? Or shouldn't I ask?"

"I was thinking about the boat," she said. "I don't know why. I've told you about the boat, haven't I? And all of a sudden a day came back to me, I hadn't thought about it for years."

"It's alright," Morgan said. "You don't have to go through it all again for me."

"It was the summer of 1992," Matty said. "Luisa was seven. I'd done a TV special in May; it went really well, fabulous reviews, the album was in the top ten." She shut her eyes, leaning back in the chair, the afternoon light dancing through the leaves. "We were on the coast for the summer holidays. We used to take the boat out all day, far out into the ocean, you couldn't see the shore at all. We'd shut the motor off and drift. We trailed fishing lines over the side, and every so often you'd get that wonderful moment when the line tightens and beads of water drop off it like diamonds. We had a little charcoal-burner on the deck, and an ice-box full of beer and lemonade; we'd grill whiting and red mullet, straight out of the sea. I can taste them now. I can see the smoke on the water."

Through the fruit trees a peacock shrieked, and she opened her eyes. "I was really back there for a moment," she said.

"Go on," Morgan said.

"So there we were, alone in the middle of the ocean, and suddenly everything changed," she said. "If Lulu hadn't been there I would have started screaming."

"What happened?"

"It was a panic attack," she said. "I could feel all that water underneath us, down and down and down. It was like vertigo, I couldn't understand what was keeping us up there. It felt like we were about to slip off the edge of the world." She glanced around the orchard. "I need a cigarette," she said. "That's the one thing I can't do when I'm with him."

"What did you do?"

"I couldn't do anything," she said. "I was completely frozen; all I could do was try not to let it show, I didn't want to frighten Luisa." She waved smoke away from her face. "José was up at the front of the boat, pulling up one of the lines, but he must have sensed something was wrong, because suddenly he came back and sat beside me in the cockpit and put his arms round me."

She stubbed the cigarette out on the ground, scuffing it into the sandy soil. "Then he started the motor and turned the boat towards the shore. He told Luisa he wanted her to steer, she'd never done that before. He showed her how the compass worked, and explained how to keep the boat on the right heading. You have never seen anyone look as proud and happy as she did; I can see her now, squinting into the sun, checking the binnacle every five seconds. José sat beside me and held me tight. After an hour you could see

154

a faint line along the horizon, and then the blur of the mountains behind it, and then the white hotels on the beach."

"You're right," Morgan said into the silence. "I can see how it must have helped to talk it through."

Matty refilled the tall glasses. "And now I've told the story twice," she said brightly. "Double-therapy!" Behind her, the peacock stepped delicately along the top of the orchard wall. "I knew you'd understand, baby. So you see, that's what I mean by working with Arno." She stroked his hand. "I do nearly all the talking; he doesn't say much, but he's a wise old bird. He told me that sometimes I try to be too strong, too independent. He said my subconscious was reminding me that we all need someone to lean on; we all need someone strong to look after us and make things right for us."

"Did it ever happen again?" Morgan asked. "Getting a panic attack like that?" Matty shook her head.

"Never like that," she said slowly. "But it didn't go away either. It's still out there somewhere; it took my husband from me, after all."

"*A senhora deséja qualquer coisa?*" Julietta called down to them, standing at the top of the steps. Matty turned to Morgan.

"Do you need anything?" she said. "Julietta's asking if she can get us anything."

"I'm fine," Morgan said. Leaning across the table, Matty clicked her glass against his.

"These days, the real bottomless abyss is my bank balance," she said. "*A nossa*, sweetheart, let's not worry about it. Happy thoughts!"

***

"Bugger!" Kate said. "He's way better than I was expecting. And Enid's quick on her feet too. We're going to have to raise our game, Marley." They touched knuckles and walked back to the baseline. Dave bounced the ball half a dozen times before throwing it up and serving down the line to Marley. On the veranda, Luisa leaned forward in the deckchair.

"I've just seen what's different about him," she said. "He's cut off that pigtail, that little matador thing."

"Major improvement," Sam said. "Do you think he ever takes those aviators off?" Enid was up at the net, crouched over, shifting her weight from foot to foot. Marley caught the ball at the top of its bounce and sent it back down the line, following it into the net, calling out a running commentary to himself.

"And that's a masterly return," he said. "This young player's on fire."

"I'm so pleased with what we did today," Luisa said. When she shut her eyes she could see the darkness around the pool of light the men were sitting in, Alvaro's austere features half in shadow, the curling cigarette smoke as viscous and heavy as oil in water, Chris hunched and miserable, nervy and full of bluster.

"Forty fifteen!" Dave called out.

"I wasn't sure what it would be like having him on the set," she said. "But he makes the political stuff come alive, in a bizarre way."

"Young Enid plays a skilful shot," Marley was saying. "She slices it across the court, where it's intercepted by Marley at full stretch. He whistles it back-hand down the tramlines for the point."

"You and Morgan worked well together," she said. "There was a real dynamic going on."

"Thank you," Sam said. "He's good, isn't he?"

"Yes he is," Luisa said. "And he's good for Mum too. They're sweet together, don't you think?"

"What do you think Arno makes of it?" Sam said. Luisa shrugged, turning to watch the tennis.

"They're old friends," she said. "Why would he make anything of it?"

"And Marley serves, fighting to stay in the game."

"Net!"

"We need to start planning the demonstration," Luisa said. "If Manólo can supply a few soldiers, we can make up the crowd numbers with Arno's people."

"A beautiful cross-court volley," Marley said. "Look at the power in that shot! Let's see the replay!"

"Except it was out," Dave said. "Sorry about that. Game Dave and Enid."

They watched the light grow pale between the cypress trees, a single star hanging above the swaying tops.

"I was thinking about Chris banging on about Baader-Meinhof," Sam said. "I looked them up; I hadn't realised it was all happening at more or less the same time."

"Of course," Dave said. "That's why his argument with Alvaro is interesting. It's a historical tipping point. He's right, and Alvaro's wrong."

"Why do you say that?"

"It's a debate between the past and the future."

"And Baader-Meinhof were the future?"

"Exactly."

"It may have looked like the future back then," Sam said. "But it didn't go the way they wanted."

"Baader-Meinhof's analysis was correct," Dave said. "They understood that you can't get at the real sources of power through politics, even revolutionary politics. Terrorism is the only answer." Sam whistled through his teeth.

"It didn't really work though, did it? They all ended up in Stammheim Prison."

"And Portugal became a democracy," Luisa said. "So they were both wrong."

"The campaign was premature," Dave said. "They didn't see thirty years of frenzied consumer credit coming down the pipe."

"So that was a bit of an oversight?"

"They were ahead of their time, that's all. You can't win this argument. Look around you, see what's happening. The global financial system delegates some of its functions to what you call the government. That's the reality."

"The front office of gangster-capitalism?" Sam said.

"That's right. We are now living in the exact political conditions that Andreas and Ulrike thought they were living in. Their time has come at last."

"I think we need more gin," Kate said. "This is getting a bit serious. I liked Mother Teresa's withered hand much better."

"Grasping Franco's mummified cock," Marley said. "Now you're talking."

Chapter Eighteen

. . .

"*The dead brood over Europe,*" Howard said. "You know that, Morgan. You've been there; all those lives that didn't get lived."

"Aren't you hot?" Morgan said. "Didn't you bring shorts or anything?" Howard sat on the edge of the sun-lounger, watching the brilliant facets of the swimming-pool dancing in points of light as the pump impelled the surface into restless motion. Arno's little dog appeared from the shadows of the arcade and tripped along the flagstones at the edge of the pool. It stopped opposite them, looking across the water, then stooped to drink, folds of hairless skin quivering around its neck. Howard stared at it.

"What is that?" he said.

"I know," Morgan said. "Don't ask; a counterfactual dog." He looked at his watch. "So Anne's having her first session," he said. "It's so good that she got here." One of the Barbies hurried across the terrace, heels clattering; she waved and smiled at Morgan. The little dog looked up from drinking and trotted after her.

"I need to find somewhere to run," Howard said.

"Wouldn't you rather swim? I can lend you some trunks."

"I was watching the trip-meter coming here in the car last night," Howard said. "I think it's five kilometres from the main road up to here, so there and back would be about right, given it's quite steep."

"I suppose you'll need a breeze-block," Morgan said. "Or is it two by now? I'm guessing you didn't bring any with you?"

"I calculated the excess baggage charges while I was on the website," Howard said, grinning. "Surprisingly high."

"Here's a challenge," Morgan said. "Swim twenty lengths of the pool with ten kilos on your back."

"You're on."

"Only kidding."

"Not at all," Howard said. "A bet's a bet." He stood up and started to walk along the edge of the pool, taking long, measuring strides. "So I finally got to Portugal," he said. "After all this time. How about giving me the guided tour?"

They crossed the terrace at the far end of the pool, turning through an archway into a cobbled alley between high walls.

"I don't know where I am half the time," Morgan said. Howard nodded.

"Now you know how it feels," he said. The alley led them under a trellis of vines into a small courtyard, lined with white-washed outbuildings. Two men in denim overalls were crouched round a man-hole in the centre of the yard. One of them was working a length of alkathene piping into the opening. There was a strong smell of drains. Howard walked over to them, looking down into the hole. "*There's Hell,*" he said. "*There is the sulphurous pit, burning, scalding, stench, consumption.*"

The man with the pipe looked up at him, nodding and grinning, holding his nose.

"*Merda!*" he said. "*Um rio de merda!*"

"When's Matty getting back?" Howard asked. "Where did you say she was? I thought she'd be here, I was really looking forward to seeing her."

"Let's go this way," Morgan said, turning through a gateway into the walled garden. "She's been on the coast, organising something for Arno. She'll be back this afternoon." They watched as Julietta hurried along a path at the far side of the garden, carrying a tray. She was wearing a maid's uniform, a black dress with a white apron.

"How do you fit in here, Morgan?" Howard said. Julietta saw them and waved. "How does Matty fit in? Does she work for Dr. Bendt? You never explain anything." A peacock was picking its way between the trees, pausing every few paces to scratch at the dusty earth.

"There are tennis courts down there," Morgan said, pointing down the sloping grounds towards the line of cypresses. "The kids have organised a tournament; I seem to have been roped in to that as well."

"How big is this place?" Howard said. "I tried to read one of his books; I

159

didn't get very far."

"Come up onto the top terrace," Morgan said. "You can see most of the compound from there." Howard shook his head.

"You don't explain anything," he said. "I have no idea where we are. Where's my room? I want to change, I need to go for a run." He watched the peacock for a moment, then turned away. "Compound," he said. "What a horrible word."

"I don't fit in," Morgan said. "I just happen to be here, that's all. And I wanted to be around when you and Anne arrived. Shall I help you find a boulder for your back-pack?"

He navigated them back to the main lobby, crossing from dazzling light into dim spaces of black marble and dark drapes; at the far end of the hall, shallow flights of stairs led off to the guest corridors. Howard glanced from side to side, watching their reflections recorded in dim mirrors as they passed. As they reached the foot of the stairs the lift arrived with a ping of its bell, the doors hissing open across a rectangular tank of bright light in which a male nurse and two old ladies hung suspended for a moment, like specimens in a jar.

In the car-port Howard bounced on his toes, shadow-boxing, his jogging-pants flapping; there was a smell of hot oil and wax-polish and leather as the sunlight struck fiercely off the lacquered bodywork of the red Mercedes.

"I'll go down to the main road and back," he said. He jogged across the yard, stopping at the steel bars of the front gates. "How do I get out of here?" he said. "Are we locked in?" As he spoke the gates shuddered and began to slide ponderously apart.

"Closed circuit TV," Morgan said, as Howard looked at him. "There must be a camera somewhere." He turned at the sound of voices, footsteps on the gravel behind them.

"*Olá Jorge!*" Luisa called out. "*Deixa o portão aberto se faz favor, a gente vai sair!* Do you want to drive, Sam?" Howard and Morgan stood aside as the kids bustled around the car, piling equipment into the boot, Marley vaulting into the back seats over the top of the door. He swung it open for Enid.

"Want to sit on my lap?" he said.

"I want to show you the rushes from the café scene," Luisa said to Morgan, raising her voice over the smooth breathing of the engine.

"You were brilliant," Enid said, wedged between Marley and Kate, turning and calling back to him as the car surged forward under the archway, a curtain of red dust closing after it.

"What was all that about?" Howard said. "Who's that girl?" He gripped the straps of his back-pack, settling the weight. Morgan walked with him through the gateway, watching as he set off down the track, following the long descending sweep of the curve as it cut through the trees across the slope of the hill, a tumbled scree of rocks and boulders on the upper side. Howard's trainers were raising little puffs of dust as he ran, momentary exchanges of energy between him and the dry earth, each footfall recalibrating his size, dropping him down through layers of heat and distance. Morgan turned back; the gates of the compound began to slide shut and he quickened his pace towards them. As he approached, the bars shuddered and stopped, then began to open again, letting him through with a faint rumble and grind of hidden mechanisms.

In the little courtyard, the workmen had started to excavate a trench leading away from the manhole, one of them prising up cobble-stones with an iron bar while the other followed, digging with a long-handled shovel. There was a dead rat stretched out on the ground beside them; blood had leaked out of its mouth, pooling into a bright red circle the size of a euro coin. Both men had tied rags over their mouths, stopping to slap away the flies that circled round their heads, blinking and grimacing as the insects settled on grime and sweat around their eyes. In the alley beyond, double doors stood open at the back of the kitchens; a woman in white overalls heaved the contents of a saucepan into the gutter in clouds of fishy steam.

***

"The system has its attack-dogs," Dave Leaper said. "The riot police, the snatch squads, the Tactical Support Groups. It's easy: recruit violent criminals into the police, how can you lose? But it's much better to spread inertia and despair." He put a hand on the dashboard, steadying himself as Luisa swung the Mercedes through a sharp left turn into the main square. "So you choke off access to the law, to higher education, to health-care. You leave people powerless, ignorant and sick; anyone over twenty five is too demoralised to come out on the streets."

"There's Manólo," Kate said, pointing across the square.

"I'm sitting on your lap on the way back," Marley said. "I've gone numb."

"You force-feed them garbage through the gutter press," Dave said. "They don't blame the system, they blame themselves. They collude in their own oppression."

"The poison-toads of the gutter press," Sam said. Enid glanced at him. "The Daily Mail," he said. "The Sun."

"The Mail did a piece on me last month," Enid said. "It was quite good as it happens."

Manólo saw them and waved, gesturing them down a side-street. As they waited to cross the square a black police van drew up alongside them, riot-mesh over the windscreen, the tinted windows darkly impenetrable.

"Public Security Police," Dave said. "The Portuguese heavy mob: counter-terrorism, armed robbery, hostage-taking." The driver lowered his window, turning his head to look at them, his face a blank mask behind mirror sunglasses. "I was looking at their website," Dave said. "They have a great motto: *While you sleep, we look after you.*"

"Strangely not-reassuring," Sam said.

"But a pretty good definition of banker-democracy, wouldn't you say?"

The lights changed and they drove slowly across the square, the police vehicle swinging away to the left. Luisa stopped the car in front of a modern concrete building, its flat roof untidy with TV aerials, solar panels, a satellite dish.

"I can't feel my legs," Marley said.

"The uniforms I have arranged," Manólo said. "For six soldiers." In the hallway he pushed open a pair of swing doors and led them into a long narrow room, a ping-pong table halfway down it, a low stage at the far end, curtained in dark red. The walls were lined with movie posters: Marlon Brando, Lisa Minelli, Marlene Dietrich. There were half a dozen men in the room.

"And guns?" Luisa said. "Did you manage to get some guns?" Manólo led them over to a bar set back in an alcove on their left.

"Please," he said. "You are my guests." A bearded man behind the bar nodded and smiled at them, and at tables set out further down the room three or four people raised their glasses. "We have German beer here, very good," Manólo said.

"And gin and tonic?" Marley asked him.

"Over there is my friend Felix," Manólo said. "Sitting with the young man there, do you see him? A very fine actor, he will be a soldier if you want, I have asked him." Felix raised his hand in a vaguely military gesture.

"There's going to be a general strike on Friday," Luisa said. "Did you know that?" She held a newspaper up, pointing out the headline: *Greve Geral!* Manólo shook his head.

"It's not so much," he said. "Only buses, trains, public workers. You can drive your car, you can go to a restaurant or a bank, it's the same as normal." They carried their drinks over to a table, pulling up extra chairs. A framed poster hung on the wall behind them: *Ernst sein ist Alles* in ornately decorated script. "Our last year production," Manólo said. "Felix plays Ernst, it was very fine. He will come and talk with you."

"It's the politics of nostalgia," Dave said. "Strikes and demonstrations, everyone marching up and down; it's play-acting." He swirled his drink, ice-cubes bobbing in the effervescence.

"It's Oscar Wilde," Manólo said. "*The Importance of Being Ernst.* But we play it in German."

"But people have to defend their jobs," Luisa said. Dave shook his head.

"Do you think the gangsters care?" he said. "Do you think the speculators travel by bus? What does it matter to them if the trains are running or not?" He got up and went to the bar, sliding his glass across the marble top. "*Noch eins,*" he said. "*Bitte.*"

"I still don't understand," Luisa said. "You were here in the revolution, you saw what happened."

"For the bus-drivers it's a day off," Manólo said. "Maybe they go to the beach. For me, every day it's a working day."

"Portugal was a prison before the revolution," Dave said.

"Exactly!"

"But when they opened the gates, they let the criminals in." He grinned, raising his glass. "Let's drink to the bankers," he said. "Let's drink to the dealers and the traders and the hedge-fund managers, to the spivs and the con-men, to the whole pack of plague-rats that swarmed in from Wall Street and Frankfurt and London and took this place over."

"What's gin in Portuguese?" Marley said. "And tonic?"

"*Genebra,*" Luisa said.

"I thought the revolution meant that political life started again," Sam said. "And *agua tónica.*"

"This is the new age," Dave said. "Politics belongs to the past. They won that: game, set and match." Manólo pushed his chair back and got to his feet.

"I must return to the clinic," he said. "I have two clients to attend. Stay here, talk to Felix. They deliver the soldiers' uniforms tomorrow. I'll see you at the evening meal later."

"So you sit back and do nothing?" Sam said.

"On the contrary."

"Damn!" Luisa said. "We never sorted out the guns."

"*Der Kampf geht weiter,*" Dave murmured, the glass hissing at his lips. "The struggle continues."

"One genebra," Marley said, holding up a forefinger. "And tonica. How about you, Dave? Anyone?"

"Was that German?" Enid said. "Do you speak German?"

"*Ein bisschen,*" Dave said. "A little. Enough to get by." He drank, emptying the glass, reaching it over to Marley.

"I wish I was good at languages," Enid said. "I really admire that." She turned, watching the tick-tock of a ping-pong ball as Felix and his friend flicked it back and forth across the table.

"Shall we give them a game?" Dave said. "You and me?" Luisa rustled through the newspaper, folding it into a manageable size.

"*No payment of the debt to the big capitalists,*" she read out, translating. "*Nationalize the banks and the other monopolies under the democratic control of the working class.*"

"Shoot a few bankers would be more to the point," Dave said. Luisa looked up, watching the table-tennis.

"Maybe Felix would know where we can get guns," she said.

"Come back with us tonight, Dave," Marley said. "Come and drink champagne at the Hotel California."

***

The evening meal had started. They waited in an archway of the arcade as Dr. Bendt finished his address. He noticed them and made a gesture towards the foot of the table, watching them as they sat down. Julietta set an extra place, bobbing and smiling as she came and went with glasses and cutlery and champagne.

"That's Dave Leaper," Matty said. "He's the author of the play." Arno nodded. "They must have been working late," she said. "They're so enthusiastic!" She raised her glass in a toast. "And it's all thanks to you, Howard," she said. "So clever of you to find it!" Across the table, Anne closed her eyes. Arno leaned towards her, whispering, and she nodded and smiled. He put his hand over hers.

"You are strong," he said.

Howard glanced down the table, identifying Dave, talking to the girl with the red hair.

"Why didn't I go to Lisbon with you and Morgan?" he said. "What happened to me? I like your music, by the way."

"Thank you darling," Matty said. "That's so sweet!" She leaned forward, looking down the length of the table. "It's wonderful to see them working so hard," she said. "They're all so talented, don't you think?" She watched the bright faces of her daughter's friends, lit by the soft radiance of the oil-lamps, the deepening twilight filling the arches of the arcade behind them with pools of darkness. Marley was clinking glasses with Steffi and Eva.

"Jürgen Ponto," she heard Dave say. "July seventy seven, just three months after old Buback." She was aware of a sudden stillness in Arno, an intense focus of concentration as he looked down the table. Julietta brushed against her shoulder as she served the next course.

"Crayfish!" Marley called out. "What did I tell you Dave? Look at those little claws!"

"They were at my club this evening," Manólo said. "I introduce them to some acting friends."

"Tomorrow we have hydrotherapy," Arno said to Anne. "But in the morning you and I will do a focusing. This will help you find your strength." Frau Wanner smiled at her from across the table.

"The hydro with Manólo is invigorating," she said, and a couple of places down a younger woman nodded emphatically:

"*Stärkend, wirkliche stärkend!*"

In silent, darting forays, bats were flickering in and out of the darkness surrounding them, hunting the little moths that danced in the lamplight.

"Morgan says you run every day," Matty said. "I wish I had your discipline."

"There must be owls here," Howard said. "All these bats, something must be eating them."

"Hanns-Martin Schleyer," Dave was saying, his words hanging in a momentary silence. "That really got their attention."

"Maybe you and I should go running with Howard," Matty said. "What do you think, Morgan?"

"The play-writer has a loud voice," Arno said. "Herr Schleyer was a friend of mine. I was invited to his house many times. He was a good man, a family man. This should not have happened." He shook his head. "And for what? For nothing; for anarchism."

"I need to go to my room," Anne said. "It's lovely here, Dr. Bendt, it's perfect, but I need to lie down." Arno bowed from the waist.

"*Schlaf gut,*" he said. "Be strong; remember that you are strong."

Howard leaned into the inertia of the wheelchair; the little wheels below Anne's sandals swivelled, knock-kneed, then straightened up as the thing began to move. He gripped the handles and lengthened his stride across the terrace.

"What a horrible idea," Anne said. "Why can't the bats just fly around? Why does something have to eat them? What made you say that?"

"I'm going to run on the road below the track tomorrow," Howard said. "It's dead straight for about five miles. There's a ruined tower on the horizon; it's something to aim for." He pressed the button for the lift and they waited in silence.

He helped Anne wash, and lifted her on to the bed.

"Open the shutters wide," she said. "Turn the lights off. I want to see the stars." He stood on the balcony, looking down over the roofs and terraces of the compound. On the western horizon, in the greenish afterglow of sunset, a flight of birds laboured across the sky on dark wings. A shooting-star flared and faded.

"Make a wish," he said.

"What is Morgan doing here?" Anne said, her voice discarnate in the darkness of the room behind him. "He seems to be besotted with that woman. What does he see in her? She's like something out of an opera."

"I think I just saw an owl," Howard said.

"He looks at her like she's the tragic heroine: the dying courtesan." Howard could hear the laughter in her voice as she coughed. "Stop singing! It's not *La Traviata!*" she said. "It's more like *Miss Triviality.* Poor Morgan; he's really deluded."

"I don't think Morgan is ever engaged enough to be deluded," Howard said. "He's just charmed by her, that's all; she makes him happy. He's drifting; that's what he does."

"It's worse than drifting," Anne said. "He's slipping away. Can't you feel it? He's becoming invisible."

"Not invisible," Howard said. "Transparent, maybe; or do I mean opaque? He's an actor, after all." He leaned out over the railings of the balcony. "It was an owl," he said. "There it is again."

"And what is she playing at?" Anne said. "Does she live with Dr. Bendt, or is she with Morgan?"

As Howard watched, the owl lifted off from a chimney-pot on the other side of the terrace, crossing the well of darkness below it on heavy and unhurried wings. He saw it jink and swerve, its talons outstretched, then lift away into the night.

"I think it just caught a bat," he said.

***

A corner of Luisa and Sam's room was lit by the pale radiance of the laptop screen. The doors onto the balcony stood open, the long drapes stirring.

"Come and see this, Enid," Luisa said, rotating the laptop on the desk. "Look how good this turned out."

On the screen, Morgan and Sam turned as the door behind them opened, spilling out bright light as they sat at a table littered with bottles and glasses, ashtrays overflowing with cigarette stubs. Enid stood silhouetted in the doorway for a moment in the incandescent lamp-light, flickering, transparent, swaying like a naked flame. In close-up her eyes were huge and dark, her face a dreaming mask, a little triangle of white in the flames of her hair. Stooping closer to the screen, Dave whistled through his teeth.

"I like that," Enid said. "I like the way you've got me looking. That's good, Luisa."

"Come and see this, Sam," Luisa called out.

"Something huge went by out there," Sam said from the balcony. "Some huge thing just flew by in the dark." He pushed through the drapes into the room. Luisa moved the slider and the door opened again, framing Enid in the light.

"What sort of a huge thing?" Marley said. "Do you mean like a bat?"

"Bats are tiny, pinhead. This was huge."

"That's beautiful," Dave said. He swayed against Enid, putting his hand on the desk to steady himself.

"I mean like a vampire," Marley said. "A vampire bat."

167

"That's a beautiful shot," Dave said. "You look beautiful."

"Thank you," Enid said. "It's a good scene, it was fun to do; the writing is really good." Luisa dragged the slider back. "This is what runs into it," she said. "This is the scene you watched us do." Dave glanced at Enid, then back at the screen.

"Can't you get rid of people like that?" Sam was saying, his face half-lit in the flickering shadows of an oil-lamp. *"Take direct action? Can't you just execute them? In the name of the people? Like the Baader-Meinhof?"* He turned as a door opened behind him, spilling light, Enid outlined against the brightness.

"Come here Marley, you little bat," Kate said. "I want to give you a cuddle, I want to suck your blood."

"Der kampf geht weiter," Dave said. "Mind if I show you something, talking of direct action?" He leaned over the laptop, propping himself against the desk, his fingers brushing over the track-pad. A search-page opened, and then a black-and-white photograph. A man stared back at them from the screen, middle-aged and heavy-set, a strong, scowling face, the mouth turned down, the eyes intent, as though memorizing the unseen photographer. A placard was hung round his neck: *SEIT 31 TAGEN GEFANGENER.* You couldn't see his arms, but something about the set of his shoulders made it plain that they were tied behind his back.

"What does that mean?" Enid said.

"Held captive for thirty one days," Dave said. "That's Hanns-Martin Schleyer: ex-Nazi, big-time capitalist, taken prisoner by the Siegfried Hausner Commando of the Red Army Faction." Behind the man's head a logo was painted on the wall: the letters *RAF* over a sub-machine gun in a five-pointed star. "And that's a Heckler & Koch MP5," he said, his finger tapping the gun. "A bullet in the back of the head: now that's what I call direct action."

"You guys have got a mini-bar," Marley said. "How come we don't have one in our room?" Dave was speaking softly, as though reciting a remembered text, his face lit by the screen.

"After forty three days we have put an end to the pitiful and corrupt existence of Hanns-Martin Schleyer," he said. "His death is meaningless to us; nothing can compensate for our pain and our rage. *Der kampf geht weiter.*" He put his lips to Enid's ear. "I wrote that," he whispered.

Chapter Nineteen

. . .

They drove down through the foot-hills to the city. Morgan waited in the car for her while she went to the bank. Through the glass front of the building he could see her talking to a cashier. A young man appeared, florid in a chalk-striped suit, waving his arms in silent gestures of delight, air-kissing; he led her away out of sight behind a screen of rubber plants. Morgan slid lower into the upholstery of the little BMW as the traffic boiled and idled around him, barely moving in the narrow streets of the Old Town. Level with his head a face appeared, inches away from his, peering at him over the top of the car door: a child, no more than five or six, shaven-headed, dark with grime. Morgan sat up, and the little boy backed away, holding out his hand.

"*Fome,*" he said. "*Tenh'fome.*" Morgan held out a euro coin; the little boy snatched at it in a clenching fist and dodged away into the traffic.

"This is such fun, sweetheart," Matty said, the car door thumping solidly behind her as she slid and wriggled herself into the seat, smoothing her dress over her knees. "Doing my little errands with you, it's so romantic! And I like it when you drive; it makes me feel safe." She leaned across and kissed him on the cheek. "Did I see you giving that little chap money?" she said. "You shouldn't do it, you know, it only encourages them."

"He looked like he could do with a little encouragement," Morgan said.

"You're such a sweetheart!" She took out a note-book from her hand-bag. "Next stop Rafaela's," she said. "My dress is ready. I can't wait to show you, it's the sexiest thing you've ever seen! I'll model it for you tonight."

Morgan jolted the Z4 out into the traffic with a brief shriek of rubber, setting off brassy fanfares of hooting. They turned down a side-street and found a space to park; he watched her cross the road to the boutique, a little glossy shop-front, chocolate and gold, as lacquered as a hat-box. She'd left a large envelope on the passenger seat, and he glanced at the printed address: *Senhora Matilda Gonçalves, aos cuidados da Clinica Bendt.* She pulled a face as she slid back into the car.

"They're shut," she said. "There's a card in the window: *'We support the workers of the public-sector unions.'* They could have let me know!" The envelope had slipped to the floor as she got in. Morgan reached down and handed it to her.

"Matilda Gonçalves," he said. "Is that you?"

"Of course it's me, darling. It's my married name. Mrs. Matilda Gonçalves!"

"It doesn't sound like you," he said. "It doesn't sound like someone I know."

"Darling, it's someone you know intimately." She lowered the sun-shield, checking her make-up in the mirror, touching up the glistening scarlet of her lips. "Don't you baby? You know her inside out." She flipped the sun-shield back up and dropped the lipstick into her bag. "Let's drive down to the harbour," she said. "I love it down there; we could have a drink at the Yacht Club."

There was a traffic jam in Largo do São Pedro, all the lights on red. On four sides of the square disordered lines of vehicles idled, stranded, motors drumming, the air torpid with fumes, a grumbling undertone pierced by the shrilling of mopeds and the bugle-calling of car horns. High above, swallows were circling the bell-towers of the Cathedral.

"I'm worried about Howard," Morgan said.

"Are you baby?" Matty put her sunglasses on, looking up into the blue dome of the sky.

"I'm worried about Anne, obviously," Morgan said. "But she knows why she's here; she wants to be here."

"I'm sure Arno will help her," Matty said.

"But Howard doesn't seem to know where he is, let alone why."

"I knew there was something wrong," Matty said. "I could feel it, but I didn't know what it was." Morgan looked at her. "There are no aeroplanes," she said. "Look up, there hasn't been a single flight, in or out all morning." She looked at her watch. "The Lisbon plane should have come in ten minutes ago."

Morgan levered himself up from behind the wheel and looked out over the cars around them, a blinding, undulating surface of roofs and windshields, a mirror-glare of chrome and metallic paint, pooling in mirages like a lake of mercury, the heated air thickening like blood in a pan.

"There are no buses either," he said. "Or lorries; it's all cars."

"Of course," Matty said. "How silly of me! It's the *Greve Geral*. There's a General Strike today; that's what the card in Rafaela's window was about. Is anything moving? Can we get out of here?" Morgan sat down, shaking his head. "Haute couture on the barricades," Matty said. "They could have waited for me to pick up my dress."

"You know he puts bricks in his back-pack?" Morgan said. "I don't know why but it didn't seem quite so weird in Wales. It was his routine; I took it for granted."

"We're starting to move," Matty said. "Take the next left, baby. He was always a little strange, wasn't he?"

"Anne thinks he's competing with her," he said. "Or punishing himself. Maybe it's the same thing."

"Look, Alberto's is open, we could have a drink there; but it's nicer on the harbour, don't you think, sweetheart? It's bound to be open. I can't see the Yacht Club showing too much solidarity with the public-sector workers, can you?" The cars ahead of them came to a halt. "That Rafaela!" she said, shaking her head. "Seventy years old and taking on the riot-police, can you imagine!"

A police helicopter passed low overhead, the clatter of its rotors reverberating in the narrow street. Matty looked up at it. "You see, they've had to send for reinforcements." She lit a cigarette, glancing at Morgan. "You're very quiet, baby," she said. "Is something wrong?" Morgan shook his head.

"Just thinking," he said.

"I've been thinking about Arno's idea for setting up a concert on the coast," Matty said.

"I thought you were dead against that."

"I've thought about it some more; and anyway he keeps going on at me. He can be very persuasive; and you never know darling, I think it could work. I could probably find some old radio-buddies of José, get them to take an interest, send some reviewers down. We might get some TV coverage. It's a question of putting the resources in, giving it plenty of time to build. I could do interviews with the hotel magazines and local papers. It could be fun!"

"I thought you wanted to make your mark as a jazz-singer," Morgan said. "Shouldn't you be singing in jazz clubs? In London, or Lisbon?"

"Of course, baby. But sometimes you have to take one a step at a time. The important thing is to be singing." The line of cars moved forward again.

The police were in grey fatigues and forage caps, not riot-gear, but there were a lot of them, and they were carrying batons on their belts. Morgan stopped behind the other cars at the intersection with the esplanade that ran the length of the harbour-front. The crowds had been penned back on the pavements behind striped tape; the centre of the esplanade was clear. On either side of the road dense masses of people were packed together, swaying, chanting, linking arms. Those at the front held long banners stretched between many hands: *Luta contra este sistema corrupta!* They had the look of people lining the route of a parade, waiting for the celebrities. A confused uproar of sound swelled out of them: laughter, shouting, singing, the braying of plastic trumpets.

A policeman waved the little motorcade on, and Morgan followed, the last in the line, turning right onto the esplanade, the crowd stretching ahead of them on either side. A group of demonstrators were trying to push out into the road-way, placards swaying above their heads, the police linking arms to pen them back.

"Do you think we should wave?" Morgan said. "Should you give a little royal wave?"

"My adoring fans," Matty said. "My public! How they love me!" An empty Coke can clattered off the bonnet of the BMW. Morgan watched the faces in the crowd, seeing himself through their eyes: a foreigner in an expensive sports car, complete with glamorous blonde. A firecracker went off, as sharp as a gun-shot.

Ahead of them, the police were directing the convoy of cars to take a left turn, forcing open a gap through the demonstrators, waving the drivers down a street that led off the esplanade towards the harbour. The crowd-noise was deeper and harsher, the line of police shoving and swaying; some of them had drawn their batons.

"This is all a bit Dealey Plaza," Morgan said. "Sunshine, crowds, an open car."

"Dealey Plaza?"

"The grassy knoll?" Morgan said. "The Book Depository?"

"Sorry darling, you've lost me."

They turned off the esplanade, following the other cars through the crowd, a heated mass, suddenly very close, arms raised and banners waving. A moment later they were on the harbour-front, shaded by palm-trees, the air cool and salty at the water's edge.

"The Kennedy assassination," Morgan said. "Lee Harvey Oswald?"

"The Yacht Club's over the far side," Matty said. "Do you see, with the flags? We can sit on the terrace."

The inner harbour was bright with boats, pennants flying in the rigging, the water chopping in the breeze and slapping at the shining hulls, speed-boats bobbing at their moorings. From the terrace, the demonstration was invisible behind the line of palm-trees; from time to time dissociated waves of crowd noise travelled across the water, the sound of spectators at a football match. "How gruesome!" Matty said. "What made you think of that? Poor Jackie, in her pink Chanel." She lit a cigarette, waving the smoke away from her face. "Get me a glass of champagne would you, sweetheart? They have a house-brand here, it's quite good."

Below them, a power-boat backed slowly out of its berth in the marina, twin outboards bubbling and grumbling at its stern. Matty settled the bottle in the ice-bucket, watching the boat as it swung through a half-turn in the crowded dock and gathered way, heading for the harbour-mouth and open water. A young man in a dazzlingly white shirt waved to her from the cockpit and she blew a kiss at him.

"I must be spending too much time with Dave Leaper," Morgan said. "Too many assassinations."

"Look at that thing," Matty said. "All that glass and chrome and plastic; it's not a proper boat at all." She sipped at her champagne. "Ours was wooden-built," she said. "A converted fishing-boat, the real thing." The driver of the power-boat opened the throttles in a gargling roar, throwing out a sheet of spray as he turned for the harbour entrance. "Here's to us, baby," Matty said, raising her glass. "And to Dave Leaper too, I suppose; after all, it's thanks to him we're sitting here now."

"It's strange to be on this side of the police-line," Morgan said. "The last time you and I were at a demo, we were the ones shouting the slogans. This feels a bit like being the enemy; I don't like it very much." Matty leaned back in her chair, turning her face to the sun; she closed her eyes.

173

"I've got quite used to this side of the barricades," she said. "This is the side the champagne is on."

The breeze freshened, stippling the surface of the water, and for a moment the noise of the crowd carried clearly to them: questions, called out high and clear, and deep surges of response from hundreds of voices, like waves running up the shingle. Matty turned, shading her eyes, watching the line of palm-trees as the wind moved through them. "It all seems so different now," she said. "I don't think those people over there are going to change the world, do you sweetheart? I didn't see much optimism in their faces."

"What are they shouting?" Morgan said. "What is that phrase they keep repeating?" Matty closed her eyes, listening.

"*Basta dos banqueiros criminais!*" she said. "An end to the criminal bankers!" She turned her head, listening again as the response rolled back. "I think that's what they're saying; it's something about bankers, anyway."

On the other side of the terrace the barman was polishing the chrome surface of the counter in short, vigorous circles, the damp cloth squeaking; he stopped in mid-swipe, turning to listen to the voices of the crowd across the water. "Pour us some more champagne, dearest Morgan," Matty said.

"Here come some of them now," Morgan said, looking across the terrace to where a party of elderly couples had gathered at the bar, sleek and affluent, the men in linen suits, the women thin and vividly tanned. "Criminal bankers, by the look of them." The barman was bowing and smiling, reaching down bottles, scooping crushed ice into tall glasses, rattling a cocktail-shaker. Matty smiled and waved.

"That's Lucinda de Gaia," she said. "In the green. She was at the clinic last year. I don't know the others."

"I'm going to Paris at the end of next week," Morgan said. "I told you, didn't I? With twenty five American teenagers. It's going to be a nightmare."

"I don't think that's her husband," Matty said.

"I'll be gone ten days, but maybe we could meet in London when I get back? You could stay at the flat, we could spend some real time together, just the two of us."

"That's such a sweet thought, baby," Matty said. "It's just I ought to be here while Luisa's filming, don't you think?" The barman juggled a couple of bottles, flipping them end over end, showboating.

"When she's finished shooting, then. Come and stay with me after that."

Matty got to her feet, waving at the people around the bar.

"I'll only be a moment, darling, Lucinda's calling me over; I better see what she wants." Morgan watched as the group crowded round her in a flutter of jazz-hands and trilling laughter, Matty up on tip-toes, pecking and air-kissing as she was handed from cheek to cheek. Several people were looking over at him; the woman in the green dress raised her glass towards him, and he lifted his in return.

She came back to the table flushed and smiling. "They all think you're terribly handsome, sweetheart," she said. "They were so intrigued!" Morgan poured more champagne and they touched glasses. "I told them all about Luisa's film, and what a brilliant actor you are!"

"What do you think about coming to London?" Morgan said.

"And they were so interested to hear about my concert. They all promised to be there, and bring lots of friends, and put the word out." The group were moving away from the bar, heading for the restaurant, blowing kisses. "I think I did myself some good there." Morgan nodded.

"I'm glad," he said. "And London? What about coming to London when Luisa's finished shooting?"

"Baby, that could be a little difficult right now," Matty said. "You know how much I'd love to, sweetheart, but just now I need to do some spadework for the concert. It's not for ever, but I need to be out there, I need to put the effort in. It's all about publicity, darling. You saw what happened with Lucinda and her friends just then, didn't you, sweetheart?" She put her hand over his. "It wouldn't be every day, baby," she said. "We could have a weekend or two in Lisbon, don't you think? Wouldn't that be nice?" She looked at her watch. "We should be going, darling," she said. "I promised Luisa we'd be on the set this afternoon. It's a big day today, they're filming the demonstration."

As they came around the corner of the club-house, the noise rolled over them as though a door had been opened into some enormous stadium. The gates at the far end of the car-park had been closed, and the archway was filled with a solid mass of people, packed tightly together. They were shouting and chanting, gripping the bars of the gates, shaking and rattling them on their hinges.

Morgan and Matty stopped, and at the same moment the club manager caught up with them; he took Matty's elbow and drew her back, his voice low and urgent. Morgan watched as the gates strained inward under the force of the crowd, held together by a padlocked chain.

"I like to explain, but my English is not so good," the manager said.

"He says we can't go out that way," Matty said. "He says we can get the car out at the back of the club, through the service bay."

"They are bad boys," the man said. "You can see, they are anarquista." He turned back to Matty, speaking rapidly in Portuguese. Nearly everyone in the crowd was young, Morgan noticed. A cobble-stone clattered through the bars of the gates, rattling across the tarmac.

"He says to give him the keys," Matty said. "He'll send one of the staff here to move the car. He doesn't think we should go over there to get it."

"There's no doubt which side of the barricades we're on now," Morgan said. He handed over the keys.

"These boys are anarquista," the manager said. "They want only trouble."

"They'll bring the car round the back," Matty said. "He says to close the roof before we leave. He doesn't think we should be driving around in an open car today."

***

The palace wobbled in the heat, a pink and ochre mirage framed in the vanishing point of a long avenue of plane-trees, details swimming into focus and solidifying as Morgan bumped the BMW down the rutted, pot-holed driveway - a flamboyant gateway opening onto a courtyard, and then the shambling, 19th Century facade, studded with ornate decorations: plaques, coats-of-arms, wrought-iron balconies and marble balustrades. A broad flight of steps led up to a colonnaded portico and massive, iron-bound front doors.

As they approached, the building seemed to sag and shrivel, falling in on itself, as though some withering disease was rushing through it, attacking every element of the structure, as though a hundred years of dereliction had swept through it in a single fetid breath. The stuccoed facade was pitted and crumbling; one of the front doors was hanging at an angle, half unhinged; the upper windows were boarded-up and sightless. Weeds had pushed through every crevice of stone-work on the steps and terraces and balconies, a desiccated web of growth as thin and grey as cobwebs. The red Mercedes was parked in the shade of an out-house at the side of the courtyard, Dave Leaper's hire-car tucked in behind it. Morgan parked beside them.

"Where is everyone?" Matty said.

"What is this place?"

176

"Isn't it fabulous?" Matty got out of the car, shading her eyes against the intense brightness, and walked across the courtyard towards the front of the house. At the foot of the steps she turned back. "Don't you love it?" she called out to him, her voice muffled, distant. "Isn't it perfect?" Behind her, the palace trembled in the heat. "Come over here sweetheart. Come out of the sun." She took his hand and led him up a few steps into the shade.

"How did they find this place?"

"Isn't it beautiful? Arno and the consortium have just bought it - *Palácio da Senhora das Sombras:* the Palace of the Lady of Shadows - such a strange name! He's got big plans for this place: a new clinic, *super-luxe,* the very best of everything!" She flinched as a pair of swallows flashed between the columns. "As soon as I saw it I couldn't wait to tell Luisa; it's the perfect place to film the demonstration, don't you think so baby?" With a faint crepitation, as though dislodged by the sound of her voice, a swallow's nest detached itself from the vaulted ceiling of the portico and fell to the ground in a soft explosion of powdery earth and fragments of eggshell. Matty got to her feet, brushing dust off her dress. "Where have those children got to?" she said.

"Tell me about Arno's consortium," Morgan said. "It sounds extremely sinister."

"He's been showing me some of the plans," Matty said. "There's going to be a spa, with a huge steam-room, like a Roman baths. Doesn't it sound fabulous? Imagine, baby, all that steamy heat, and perfumed oil, and naked flesh."

"And gold taps, presumably," Morgan said.

"Don't mock, sweetheart, you're such a cynic." She stepped down into the courtyard and turned to face him, looking up at the house. "It used to belong to a branch of the Royal Family," she said. "That's their coat-of-arms up there, the House of Bragança."

"A long way from the revolution," Morgan said.

Arno's extras arrived in a hired bus. They watched it draw a plume of red dust along the scar-line of the new road, appearing at the far end of the driveway, blurring in the heat. They counted thirty five of them as the men stepped down from the coach, mostly middle-aged, a few teenagers and younger men among them.

"Their hair's too short," Luisa said. The men pooled into little groups, talking in low voices, keeping close to the bus. "And there aren't any women."

"This is a bonus, though," Kate said. She looked up into the cloudless, empty dome of the sky. "No aeroplanes messing up the sound-track. There's something to be said for filming through a general strike." Luisa shook her head.

"There should be more moustaches," she said. "They don't have that 70s look." She sighed, turning away.

"You're right, they need tank-tops and flares," Kate said. "Except they're supposed to be farm-workers of course."

"Still, there's plenty of them," Luisa said. "Try the light-levels in front of the house, Marley. Where's Enid?"

"Getting the party line from Dave," Sam said. "He's taking a keen interest in her political education."

Disembodied, Dave Leaper's voice floated across the courtyard, and a moment later he appeared, following Enid round the corner of the outbuildings beyond the parked cars.

"Just wait and see," he was saying. "Portugal will be cut up into bonus-sized chunks and fed to the bankers." Enid nodded, turning away.

"They look terribly nervous, poor darlings," Matty said. She took a few steps across the courtyard towards the bus. "*Boa tarde!*" she called out. "*Bem-vindos ao Palácio da Senhora das Sombras!*" The men turned towards her, responding gratefully, straightening up, returning her greetings. An older man at the front of the group bowed, taking off his cap with a slow smile.

"*Boa tarde, Senhora Matty!*" he said.

"I think he's one of the gardeners," Matty said. "I know him from somewhere."

"I'll need you to keep well back once we start filming, Mum," Luisa said. "The camera's going to be very fluid; we don't want you coming in on the edge of the shot."

"There's something you have to understand," Dave Leaper said. "Nothing will change until we start killing bankers."

"Absolutely," Enid said. "Can we do my make-up now Kate? Can we do that waif-look? I really liked the way you did that."

Luisa spoke to the bus-driver and the man nodded and reached for the ignition, the motor grinding, shuddering out gouts of black exhaust; he backed the bus away behind the out-buildings.

"I wish you'd think about coming to London," Morgan said, aware of

Dave glancing at him as he spoke. "When this is all finished; even if it was just for a week or two."

"You're so sweet, baby," Matty said. She brushed her finger-tips across his cheek.

"*Vamos andando!*" Luisa called out, shepherding the extras towards the Palace. "Bring the banners from the car, Sam. Let's get to work."

They watched her as she hustled the men into loose groups around the flight of steps at the front of the building, her voice clear and bright across the courtyard, arranging them with large and vivid gestures, like a conductor. Matty lit a cigarette.

"I love to see her like this," she said, letting her breath out in a long, exhaling sigh. "It makes it all worthwhile, every bit of it."

Luisa was standing halfway up the steps, counting down in vigorous sweeping movements of her arms, marking the cue with a final, crashing gesture. There was a moment of silence, and then a timid chorus of chanting drifted back to them from the extras, hesitant, apologetic. Marley and Kate joined her on the steps, the three of them framed under the portico as though on stage, dancing and waving above the dark sea of upturned heads.

"*Outra vez!*" Luisa called out to them. "*Mais força!*" All three were conducting with outstretched arms: "*O povo... unido...jamais sera vencido!*"

"What are they saying?" Morgan asked.

"Don't you remember that, sweetheart?" Matty said. "The people… united… will never be defeated! How many times did we hear that!" The extras murmured and groaned, a few voices beginning to rise melodically above the droning undertone.

Kate and Marley had linked arms and were cake-walking up and down the flight of steps, prancing like models on a catwalk, punching the air, swinging their hips. Ripples of laughter began to run through the men, drawing them together into a single audience, leaning in to each other, shoulder to shoulder.

"*Viva a revolução!*" Luisa called out, raising a clenched fist. "*A luta continua! Viva a revolução!*" She stepped down into the crowd, pushing through the front ranks, and a moment later a banner was lifted above their heads, stretched between reaching hands: "*A terra à quem a trabalha!*"

"The land to those who work it," Dave Leaper said. "Remember that one?" He shook his head, smiling. "The land to those who own golf-courses more like," he said. "And five-star hotels, and luxury villas. The land to the bankers."

"We'd better find some shade," Matty said. "We're going to get awfully hot out here." She crossed the courtyard, vanishing into deep shadow in the lee of an outbuilding; Morgan and Dave followed, walking into darkness as though a door had closed behind them. They turned at the sound of a vehicle in the driveway, a German SUV, dark and bulbous, its baleful gaze impenetrable behind tinted glass, silent but for the discreet crackle of tyres on dirt. Five men got out, bulky in army uniforms, Manólo among them, doors thumping heavily shut behind them. One of them said something in German, setting the others off into shouts of laughter.

"It's my friend Felix," Manólo, said, shaking hands with Morgan and Dave, brushing his cheek against Matty's, left and right. "He says you must not start the revolution without him!" He pulled at his combat jacket, straightening out the creases. "We are very smart, don't you think?" The other men were clowning about - setting their forage-caps at jaunty angles, stamping their feet, standing to attention puff-chested, saluting.

Luisa jogged across the yard towards them. Behind her the crowd subsided, dispersing into groups, smoking cigarettes. Manólo's friends saluted again as she approached.

"No guns?" she said. Manólo shrugged.

"I tried," he said. "We can have shotguns, hunting-rifles, but they don't look right. It's better they have nothing."

"They didn't need guns, baby," Matty said. "They were on our side. *Sempre com o povo!*" She turned to Morgan. "Do you remember, sweetheart? Always with the people!"

"The Army and the People are One," Dave said.

"We're nearly ready to start rolling," Luisa said. "You guys come with me. You need to be out of sight behind the Palace, then you appear when things start to get out of hand. We'll add in the sound of your jeep in the edit."

She led the way across the yard, very straight-backed, the Germans following, their boots raising puffs of dust. Matty shuddered.

"She looks like she's under arrest," she said. "Like she's being taken away. Sometimes you forget how lucky we were, how different it might have been." She sighed. "We're never really safe, are we?"

Across the courtyard, Luisa and Sam had gathered the Germans around them in a semi-circle; Kate was working on Enid's make up, fretting her fingers through her hair, tilting her face into the light, touching colour into

180

her lips, the look of someone arranging flowers in a vase.

"I'm going to get a bit closer," Dave said. "I can't hear anything from here. Don't worry, I won't get in the frame; I'm quite good at being invisible." They watched him slip away, keeping to the strip of shadow at the foot of the wall, walking quickly out of sight around the corner of the building.

"I still don't know why you changed your mind about Arno's concert," Morgan said. "About letting him organise it all for you."

"Don't go on, sweetheart," Matty said. "Don't start that again. I told you, he can be very persuasive."

"When you first talked about it, you said it made you feel like your career was over."

"Did I, baby?" She turned as a whistle blew a shrill signal, watching as the figures across the courtyard shuffled onto their marks, the Germans trotting out of sight around the side of the Palace, the extras assembling at the foot of the steps, Sam and Enid near the back of the crowd. Luisa and Kate stood to one side, the boom of the mic swaying above their heads; beyond them Marley waited, the camera slung on his shoulder like a rocket-launcher. Luisa blew the whistle again. A banner rose above the crowd as the chanting began, ragged at first, gathering power and rhythm. "Listen to that," Matty said.

"What is it? What are they saying?"

"Death to capitalism," she said softly, her voice evaporating into heat and silence.

"What is it really?" Morgan said again. "Tell me."

"José would have loved all this," she said. She gestured towards the crumbling palace swimming in the heat, the voices rolling across the open space towards them as Arno's extras swayed and shouted; the busy, intent figures of her daughter and her friends. "He'd have been so happy to see this."

They watched as Luisa stopped the action, sending Marley in among the crowd, crouching and dodging through the pack of bodies, Kate following him with the boom. The whistle blew again and the chanting picked up quickly and confidently, banners waving, fists punching the air. "He'd have been up at the head of the march," Matty said.

"I know," Morgan said. "I was there."

"He had so much passion," she said. "I can see him now." She turned to Morgan. "I need a hug, baby," she said. "Give me a hug. Where did it all go?"

"You should be proud," Morgan said. "Luisa's doing a great job. Listen to them, she's really got them going; you'd swear it was the real thing." The extras had found a rhythm in the chanting, a thudding pulse like blood roaring in the ears, like the stamping of heavy feet. "Listen to them," Morgan said again. "They really sound like they mean it. That girl knows how to work a crowd."

"She makes it all worthwhile," Matty said.

They watched her setting up a new scene: a man had slipped into view through the half open doors of the palace and stood at the top of the steps, a small, shabby figure in a dark suit. He unfolded a sheet of paper and began to read, his words blown away in the uproar.

"It's the land-agent," Morgan said. "The bailiff for the big estate. Do you remember this scene? They accuse him of working for the secret police; the soldiers have to rescue him. Manólo and his troops should be along any minute now." The chanting intensified, the pitch rising. Morgan tilted his head, listening. "What is that they're saying," he said. "I'm hearing *banqueiros criminais* - is that right? Isn't that what they were shouting at the Yacht Club: the criminal bankers?"

Faint and thin, Luisa's whistle was shrilling above the noise of the crowd; she ran up the steps, waving her arms, shouting wordlessly. The chanting faltered, breaking up into individual voices, into isolated slogans, falling silent. The Germans appeared from behind the palace and pushed their way through the crowd; the extras shuffled and stared, letting them through.

Luisa re-set the scene, whistling up Arno's men. The soldiers pushed through to the steps again, raising clenched fists and V-for-victory signs; Manólo was standing off to one side, smiling nervously, shifting from foot to foot. One of his friends started to address the crowd, his voice high and sharp:

"*Viva o 25 d'Abril!*" he called out. "*Viva a revolução! Viva as Forças Armadas! Sempre com o povo!*"

"I remember that one," Morgan said. "*Sempre com o povo!* Always with the people!" Matty pulled a face.

"Oh dear," she said. "His accent isn't awfully good. They're going to have to over-dub him. Too Bavarian!"

"The Army and the people are one," Morgan said softly. "Do you remember that bar in Lisbon, across the street from the barracks? Do you remember those soldiers buying us brandy all night? What was that stuff called? *Medronho!*" He shuddered. "I can still taste it. That was the best, the time we spent in

Lisbon. Why did we leave?" Matty looked at him.

"It was your idea to come south," she said. "Don't you remember?"

"I do," Morgan said. "It's not a very happy memory."

Across the courtyard, under Luisa's direction, the demonstration was beginning to break up, the mood relaxing, the force that had pulled the crowd together releasing them into little groups and individuals, the soldiers genial and relaxed, the camera following them as they dispersed. Luisa gathered the Germans and a dozen of the extras for the final scene, arranging them in a loose semi-circle around Sam and Enid. Marley tracked round the edge of the group, the camera on his shoulder, taking long, hesitating strides like a wading bird. Enid was surrounded by men in bulging uniforms, bulky bodies pinched in by straps and belts and heavy boots, crowding round her, ponderous, fascinated. One of them lifted her hand and kissed the tips of her fingers, bowing. In a white vest and denim shorts she was naked, sacrificial.

"She's so pretty," Matty said. "Like a china doll."

"We should have stayed in Lisbon," Morgan said. "I wonder if it would have made a difference." Matty stroked his cheek.

"Don't be sad sweetheart," she said. "We'll be there again."

"But I don't know where, or when," Morgan said.

"I sang that at Jimmy's Place!" Matty said, her eyes shining. "Peggy Lee! You remembered! That's so sweet!"

They looked up as a sudden outburst of shouting rolled across the yard towards them. A scuffle had broken out between two of the soldiers and some of the demonstrators: a clumsy, bullish tussle, dark faces thrusting forward at each other, someone shoving, jolting flat hands against a uniformed chest. Sam and Manólo were caught up in it, pushed about as they tried to separate the blundering opponents.

"Something seems to have come between the Army and the people," Morgan said. "I don't remember this bit. She's getting some amazing performances out of them, though. She really is good."

"I don't think they're acting, darling. I don't think that's in the script. Shouldn't you go over there?"

As Morgan approached, the huddle loosened, the men backing away red-faced, pointing stiff, accusing fingers at each other. Arno's Portuguese gathered themselves together and set off towards the bus, one or two of them turning back and calling out as they walked away. He watched as Matty met them halfway across the courtyard; they gathered round her, talking in low voices, glancing back at the Germans, shaking their heads.

"I got all of that, Luisa," Marley said. He tilted the display out of the sunlight, peering into it. "At first I thought you must have rehearsed them, then I just kept rolling anyway."

Kate put her arm round Enid's shoulders. Manólo stepped away from his friends to meet Morgan; he was shaking his head and blinking, squinting away tears.

"I am ashamed," Manólo said. He took Morgan's hand in both of his, pumping and squeezing. "I am ashamed." He pulled out a handkerchief and blew his nose. "And Sam was wonderful," he said. "Have you seen how he was helping me? He is a true friend."

"Sweetheart, are you alright?" Matty said, pushing past them. She took Luisa's hands in hers, looking into her eyes. "How terrible! What happened?"

Luisa shrugged.

"We'd finished," she said. "It was a wrap anyway. Don't fuss, mother."

"I wouldn't call it fussing, sweetheart. Sam, talk to me, what happened?"

"Actually, we finished earlier than I expected," Luisa said. "I wanted the light to be a little deeper, a little more saturated. I wanted the chanting to fade out, like an echo from far away, as the light turns golden. I don't think we'll get them back to do it again though, somehow."

"We can do all that in Final Cut," Kate said.

"Manólo, then," Matty said. "You must be able to tell me what happened."

"Some of the men that Doctor Bendt has paid," Manólo said, shaking his head. "They call my friends parasites, they say they are capitalists, blood-suckers."

"Also homosexual," Felix called out. "They call us cock-suckers."

"I apologise, Senhora Matty, he should not say that."

"Maybe they are drunk," Felix said. "Too much *aguardiente de medronho.*"

"Please do not listen," Manólo said. He turned towards Felix, speaking rapidly in German. "My friend is upset," he said to Matty. "He exaggerate. It's politics; some of the men don't like that we wear Portuguese army uniform. They say it dishonours the revolution. I didn't understand everything they say. They start talking about the crisis here in Portugal, the unemployment. They say it is our fault. They say we are bankers."

"That's a lot ruder than cock-suckers," Kate said.

"Where's Dave?" Sam said. "He'd so have a theory about this."

"He's a perve," Enid said.

"That's a bit harsh."

"I'm very unhappy this happens," Manólo said. "I am very ashamed, I do not know what to say to Dr. Bendt."

Behind him, Marley was sneezing with laughter; he held the camera up for Luisa, turning the viewfinder towards her.

"There has to be a way to use this," he said, lowering his voice as Manólo glanced at him. "It's so cool! It'll get us a million hits on YouTube!"

Chapter Twenty

. . .

The air was cold but the earth still radiated the heat it had breathed in the day before, made visible in exhalations of rising mist, the world-cow breathing out, warm brown mother. Howard ran with the full moon staring over his right shoulder and the apricot and green of sunrise coming up behind him. Far ahead the stump of the ruined watch-tower rose and fell with the rhythm of his footsteps on the powdery roadside, the back-pack bumping him forward with every stride.

He passed an abandoned vine-yard, choked with weeds, and a rubbish dump full of shattered bricks and gutted sofas, overlooked by brooding cypress trees. The light strengthened and filled, the stars going out. He picked up the pace, keeping his eyes on the Moorish tower on the horizon. Layers of colour were washing into the low hills on either side of the valley: umber and red, the dark green of cork-oak, the silvery sheen of olive trees.

He passed a farm, a little shanty-town of dilapidated huts and hovels, leaning against each other around a scratched and littered yard, the peevish early-morning conversation of chickens carrying to him from their hutch. A tethered goat lifted its head and looked at him with yellow eyes. The tower seemed to be drawing away from him as he ran towards it, and he lengthened his stride, tasting blood. A lorry blew past him in a hot rush of rubber and oil. After another half an hour he turned, jogged on the spot for a moment and then set off again, running back into the rising sun.

Anne was sitting in her wheelchair at the pool-side.

"We must be the first ones up," she said. "The first guests, I mean. Steffi got me dressed, and Julietta brought me a delicious cup of coffee. No sign of anyone else." She sighed, leaning back into the chair, her face turned towards the sun. "This is that moment," she said. "The one I told you about: the cool of the morning. Did you find your ruined tower?" Howard shook his head. "It's further than I thought," he said.

"So cool and still," Anne said. "No loud voices, no Hollywood Princess and her film-crew. Do you know what she reminds me of? Marie-Antoinette, with her little flock of sheep at the Petit Trianon; playing at life." She put her hand to her mouth. "My god," she said. "I'm sorry; that wasn't me. It's this damned illness, this fucking Neutered Moron Disease: disinhibition, it's a classic symptom. It's like being possessed." She sat forward in the chair, her eyes suddenly bright. "But you know what, Running Man? I've just realised Arno warned me about this. He said the first sign of getting better, that I was beginning to respond, would be that I would feel like I was getting worse." Howard looked at her, nodding. The sun cleared the compound wall, and behind her the murmuring water of the swimming pool burst into blue fire, dancing with light. "What is it?" Anne said. "You look like you've seen a ghost."

"I have," Howard said, looking at something over her shoulder. Frowning with effort, Anne worked the wheelchair slowly round to face the pool. She raised her hand, shading her eyes against the glare.

"What is that?" she said. "What is that thing?"

Arno's little dog was floating on its back, legs splayed, its head underwater. The filtration system was propelling it gently down the length of the pool towards them, bobbing in the ripples; one of its front paws was bent over in a gesture of languid greeting, waving at them as it passed.

"Is it me?" Howard said. "Am I making this stuff happen?"

"Shouldn't you get it out of the water?" Anne said. Howard shuddered.

"I'd rather go and find somebody," he said. "Look at it, I really don't want to touch it." Anne swung the wheelchair round again.

"Don't leave me here," she said. "Take me up to the room first."

"How am I going to explain?" Howard said. "Did you bring a phrase-book? What's *dog* in Portuguese? What's *dead*?"

In their room he opened the drapes and stepped out on to the balcony. From the second floor, the little dog was an indeterminate object, bumping and nudging against the chrome grab-rail at the far end of the pool.

"*Piscina*," Anne said from the bedroom. "A swimming-pool is a *piscina*. That's straight from Latin."

"And dead dog?" Howard said. A young man appeared on the terrace at the side of the pool. "Isn't he the chap that collected us from the airport?" Howard asked. "Hello!" he called down. The man looked up, shading his eyes. Howard pointed at the pool. The man smiled and waved.

"Bom dia!" he said. *"Um lindo dia pra' nadar!"* He mimed swimming movements with his arms.

"Morto," Anne said. "Dead is *morto*. I can't find dog."

"Morto!" Howard called out, pointing urgently at the far end of the pool. "There's a dead dog down there." The man looked up at him again, shading his eyes with his forearm. He turned towards the pool; Howard saw a stillness fall over him, like a shadow.

"I'm feeling very odd," Anne said. "Will you get me a sip of water?"

"I don't feel that was the right way to do it," Howard said. "I don't think I handled that very well. I should have gone down and talked to him." He watched as the young man hurried out of sight through the arcade of the cloisters. He heard him call out, and a woman's voice answering, rising in a sudden shriek. "Not just shout at him from up here."

"Would you fetch me my beaker," Anne said. "My mouth is so dry."

The man reappeared with a net on a long pole, a woman in white kitchen overalls following him. The two of them looked up at the balcony as they crossed the terrace to the poolside. Howard stepped back into the room.

"I should have gone down and told him," he said again. "Standing up here shouting like a maniac; I'm embarrassed."

"Let the water run a bit," Anne said. "Let it get cold." There was a knock on the door. "That'll be Manólo," she said. "It's time for my session, I have to go. Will you be alright?"

***

Morgan didn't answer his phone all morning. Howard lay on the bed, watching the light intensify through the long drapes, listening to the sounds of the clinic running through its functions: footsteps in the corridor and the ping of the lift-bell, the rumble of a vacuum-cleaner and somewhere a telephone ringing; the rasp of a stiff broom on paving stones, someone calling out a name, and a girl's voice, singing. He took the lift to the ground floor, through the dim foyer and out into the brightness. He walked quickly past the swimming-pool, where the young man was back again, fishing for something in the water with the long net. In the walled garden a girl in a black dress hurried towards him carrying a tray; he stood aside to let her pass. He followed the path at the far end of the garden, where it sloped away towards the tennis courts.

By the time he reached the line of cypress trees he could hear the sounds of a game, feet scuffing on the clay, the hollow smack of the rackets, someone calling out a score. At the top of the flight of steps he stood and watched for a minute or two. Luisa and her boyfriend were playing the skinny kid and the big Australian girl. The actress with the red hair was sitting in a deck-chair on the veranda; Dave Leaper was standing behind her, leaning over her, talking. Howard turned away and walked back up the path, patting his pockets for his phone.

"I need to know if it's me that's doing this," he said. "It's as though I'm triggering these things off."

"I can give you fifteen minutes," Dr. Walters said. "I have someone coming in at midday. Slow down a little; start at the beginning."

Howard had turned through an archway into a courtyard he didn't recognise. One of the blonde girls hurried past him in her white uniform, her heels clattering on the cobbles.

"It's as though everything is radiating out from that event," Howard said. "Like cracks in a broken mirror." He watched as the girl answered her phone, breaking into a skipping run. "Or maybe ripples in a swimming pool," he said.

"Tell me why it makes you think of the owl," Dr. Walters said. "You said it was like the owl in the lecture theatre."

"They aren't supposed to be there," Howard said. "They're counterfactuals, but it's as though I'm bringing them into existence, like I'm a conduit." The courtyard led into a covered alley, narrow, with a vaulted brick ceiling, a dark tunnel. As Howard turned in, the figure of the blonde girl was silhouetted for a moment in the bright opening at the far end. A rat hurried past him coming the other way, round-shouldered, keeping to the wall. "Can you hear me?" Howard said. "I think I've lost the signal."

"Are you still running, by the way?" Dr. Walters was saying. "Is that still helping?"

"It's like the dead cow," Howard said. "It suddenly comes to the surface, it breaks through; it's an eruption."

"Go on," Dr. Walters said. "Develop that thought."

"It's an eruption of anxiety, isn't it?" Howard said. "The return of the repressed?" The tunnel released him into an open space, blindingly white. Howard stood still, blinking in the glare for a moment.

"What was that noise?" Dr. Walters said. Howard looked around, recognising the car-port and the main vehicle-entrance.

"A peacock," he said, watching the creature pick its way delicately along the top of the wall.

"Are you alright?" Dr. Walters asked him. On the far side of the courtyard glass doors slid apart, letting Matty and Morgan out into the car-port. Howard watched them as they crossed the yard towards him. Matty was wearing a white dress, splashed with red flowers. She was carrying a wicker box, like a hamper.

"You still walk like a dancer," he said as she approached. She turned her face to him to be kissed.

"Are you alright, Howard?" his phone said in a tiny voice. Howard held it to his ear. "I think we should go on with this," Dr. Walters was saying. "I have an hour free at four o'clock, can you do that? We should try and get further with this." Howard nodded, ending the call.

"What's in the basket?" he said to Matty. "Are you going on a picnic?"

"I just don't see why you should have to do it," Morgan was saying. "Why didn't he ask Jorge, or somebody?" Matty looked at Howard.

"It's Fritzli," she said. "Arno's little dog. The poor little thing drowned in the pool, they found it this morning."

"I found it this morning," Howard said. "That was me."

"He wants Matty to take it to the vet," Morgan said. "For a post-mortem. Can you fucking imagine?"

"I don't mind," Matty said. "It's important to him."

"It's a power thing," Morgan said. "He just wants to control you. Why doesn't he get Jorge to do it?"

"It's not like that sweetheart, it's something I can do for him. I've never seen him like this before."

"And it's pointless," Morgan said. "What's the vet going to say? The fucker drowned, what more does he want to know?"

"Don't be like that, darling," Matty said. "I won't be long." She put the wicker box on the back seat of the red Mercedes, settling herself behind the wheel as the roof folded itself away in a series of fastidious movements.

"Why don't I come with you, at least?" Morgan said above the soft roar of the motor.

"It's better not, baby," Matty said. "I'd rather just do what he wants me to do." Morgan and Howard watched as the steel gates drew ponderously apart and the Mercedes swept under the arch and away down the curve of the track.

"I couldn't believe it," Howard said. "It was like the dead cow all over again." Morgan looked at him. "It was me that found the damn thing. I came back from my run and there it was, upside down in the pool, waving at me."

"It's grotesque," Morgan said. "This place is crawling with people on his payroll, why should Matty do his dirty business for him?"

"That was Dr. Walters on the phone," Howard said. "I think he's worried about me."

"It's some sort of ritual humiliation, how can she not see that?"

"But of course the cow was huge," Howard said. "And the dog was tiny. So maybe I'm improving; maybe there's less repressed material to break out, what do you think?"

"What are you talking about, Howard?" Morgan asked him, shaking his head.

"On the other hand, maybe I'm repressing the same stuff, but more vehemently," Howard said. "So less gets through."

"Vehemently?" Morgan said. He began to laugh. "More vehemently?" He put his arm round Howard's shoulders, turning away as the gates closed behind them with a kiss of steel on steel. "What time is it? Why don't we go and drink some of Dr. Bendt's champagne?"

***

Crouching, knees locked, Marley slid the last two or three metres to the net and flicked the ball over. He straightened up and threw the racket high in the air, watching it turn over and over against the deepening blue of the afternoon.

"So this young superstar puts the tournament beyond reach," he said. He fumbled the catch, dodging and wincing as the racket bounced and clattered at his feet. Across the net, Dave put his arm round Enid's shoulders; she ducked and twisted away.

"I need to cool down," she said. "You played really well, Kate."

"Thank you. Let's break out the gin." Dave stood at the net, watching the two girls walk across the court to the veranda.

"Did you hear about the dog-thing?" Marley said. Dave turned to look at him. "Dr. Bendt's dog, the little weird thing?" Dave shook his head. "Bald?" Marley said. "Wrinkled? It drowned in the pool; they found it this morning." He shuddered. "I'm so glad I've never gone swimming here. I always thought it probably pissed in the water anyway." He looked up at the sound of voices.

Steffi and Eva were standing at the top of the flight of steps above the tennis courts. They waved and called out again, stepping into a little cabaret-routine, arm in arm, swinging their hips and pointing their toes as they sashayed down towards them.

"*Hallo Leute!*" Steffi called out. "Hello boys!"

"They're still in their uniforms," Marley said. "They're not wearing tennis shorts; I don't think I can stand the pain."

"*Ciao-ciao* baby!" Eva said. "Kiss-kiss, Marley!" The two girls trotted across the court, holding out slim, tanned hands to be shaken or kissed.

"I thought you'd be wearing shorts," Marley said. "Do you know how much you're hurting me?"

"We don't have so much time today, boys," Steffi said. "Maybe we play the match tomorrow?"

"Did you win, Marley?" Eva said. "I like to play with you if you're the winner!"

Steffi's phone was trilling; she wriggled it out of her hip pocket and held it to her ear, listening, nodding.

"*Ja, gut,*" she said finally. "*Kein Problem, alles klar; danke Herr Doktor.*"

"*Was bedeutet das?*" Eva asked. Steffi snapped the phone shut.

"*Er meint wir sollten alles überwachen heute Nacht.*" She turned to Dave and Marley. "We have to go," she said. "We play the match tomorrow maybe, or the next? Kiss-kiss!"

"*Tschüss,* Marley!" Eva said. She kissed him quickly on the lips. "Ciao, baby, I like to play with you soon!" They turned, waving and blowing kisses as they crossed the court and trotted back up the steps.

"What was that about?" Marley said. "Why did they have to rush off? What did Steffi say?" Dave looked at him.

"She said: *We have to monitor everything tonight.*"

"What does that mean?"

"Good question."

"I saw that, Marley!" Kate called over from behind the bar. "I've got my eye on you, you horny little weasel!"

Dave took his sunglasses off and polished them on his shirt.

"What does it mean?" he said.

"Come here, dick-on-a-stick!" Kate called out again. "Get over here!"

"I'm going into town," Dave said. "There's something I need to check out. Do you want to come for the ride? I'll buy you a beer, celebrate your victory."

"I'll see if Sam wants to come," Marley said. Kate caught Luisa's eye, shrugging.

"It's a boy thing," she said. They watched as the three of them climbed the steps at the far end of the courts, Marley bunny-jumping ahead of the other two, Dave chopping the air with his hands as he spoke to Sam.

"And a middle-aged guy thing," Enid said. "It never stops."

"You never saw the pony-tail," Luisa said. "You got off lightly."

On the motorway, Dave pulled the hire-car out into the fast lane, buffeting through the slipstream of an articulated truck, giant chrome wheels filling the passenger windows as they passed.

"This is the smallest car I've been in since we got here," Marley said. "I miss my red Mercedes."

"I need an electronics shop," Dave said. "We'll go downtown, there's bound to be somewhere in a place this big."

"Somewhere with a nice long bar," Sam said. "I'm picturing stainless steel, and cocktail waitresses."

"Somewhere selling security equipment," Dave said. "There's a lot of money salted away down here." They were passing the yacht-harbour: white, swan-like boats that barely seemed to touch the surface of the water, glittering with chrome and tinted glass; the ice-cube tinkle of rigging in the breeze.

"Cocktails on the poop-deck," Marley said. "Now you're talking."

"A million euros a pop," Dave said. "That kind of gear takes a lot of protecting." He fitted the little car into a parking slot, pointing up at the steel and marble facade of a big hotel. "There's a bar on the top floor," he said. "I'll meet you up there. You get a good view of all the money from that height."

In the foyer, a boy in a page's uniform waved them over towards the lifts, his eyes flicking over their T-shirts and baggy shorts. The bar was stainless steel and mirrors, floating like a silver balloon above the city. They sat on tall bar-stools and drank icy blonde beer in glasses as delicate as champagne flutes. On the other side of the room a couple leaned towards each other across a low table, heads close, whispering.

"You know when he said 'salted away'?" Marley said. "He was talking about money, but I immediately thought: pistachios, peanuts, cashews. And here they are: the power of magical thinking!" He scraped a handful out of the bowl. "Wasabi peas! Have you noticed, when you pick up nuts, you never use your thumbs?" he said. "Is that some kind of monkey-thing?" The barman gestured at their empty glasses, and they nodded.

"Who's paying for them, though?" Sam said. "Where is he?"

"I don't have any money salted away," Marley said. "Just nuts. I'm hungry, now you mention it."

They were on their fourth beer when Dave joined them, hefting himself up onto a stool beside them. He had a carrier bag with him; he took out a glossy cardboard box and laid it on the bar.

"What do you think Steffi meant?" he said. "*He says to monitor everything tonight* - what do you think that meant?"

"Heart monitors?" Marley said. "Blood pressure, that kind of thing?" He sipped at his beer, closing his eyes. "There you'd be, all tucked up in bed," he said. "And she'd be leaning over you in that tight white uniform, and she'd say something like: *Just pop this in your mouth, Marley.*" He looked up at them. "Taking your temperature, obviously."

Sam turned the box towards him; there was a photograph on the front, a device like a mobile phone: a hand-held with a screen, two stubby aerials, a row of buttons.

"*It's off the chart,*" Marley said. "*Fever pitch! We have to find a way to cool you down, it's an emergency!*"

"It doesn't look like a heart monitor," Sam said. Dave reached for the box. "It isn't," he said, turning it over in his hands.

"Do we need another beer?" Sam said. "To celebrate Marley's victory?"

"I'll show you tonight," Dave said. "I think you'll find it interesting."

"Only I don't actually have any money with me," Sam said.

They waited for him in the foyer.

"He didn't look very happy about paying," Marley said. "Did you see his wallet?" Sam said. "He must have had twenty credit cards in there; I've never seen anything like it. What's he doing, anyway?"

"He said he had phone-calls to make. I don't want to miss dinner, I'm starving."

Arno's address was shorter than usual. There were three or four new guests, and he introduced them briefly.

"We greet our new arrivals," he said. "And we make our farewells." He spent much of the meal talking to Matty, his head close to hers. Morgan had been placed halfway down the table with Howard and Anne.

"How was your trip to town?" Luisa said.

"Dave's got something he wants to show us after dinner," Sam said. "Haven't you, Dave? He's being very mysterious." Kate leaned over to Enid, whispering in her ear.

"I think he's got something he particularly wants to show you?" she said.

"Please," Enid said. "I'm trying to eat."

"The demonstration footage is brilliant," Luisa said. "I'm really happy with it. It's a mess at the moment of course, but we've got everything we need in the can; now it's all down to the edit. That palace was the perfect location. Thank you everybody!"

She looked up towards the head of the table, watching Arno talking intently to her mother. Matty was nodding, her hair a halo of flame in the lamplight, her expression abstracted, unreadable.

In Sam and Luisa's room, Dave picked up the clinic phone on the bedside table; he held it to his ear for a moment, nodding, then replaced the receiver.

"When you pick it up, do you hear that little squeak before you get the dial-tone?" he asked. Luisa shrugged.

"I've never used that phone," she said.

"It's bugged," Dave said. "That's the sound of a slave device; that's the infinity transmitter kicking in."

"Cool name," Sam said.

"So, if I call room service?" Kate said. "You're telling me somebody is listening to every word I say?"

"You can laugh," Dave said. Marley picked up the phone.

"There is a little squeak," he said. "Like a tiny dog or something." He pulled a face. "I wish I hadn't said that. Maybe like a bat."

"I'm off to bed," Enid said. "Goodnight, everybody."

"Wait," Dave said. "There's something else I want to show you."

"What did I tell you?" Kate said.

Dave took something out of his pocket, holding it up for them to see: a clunky handset, like an old-fashioned mobile phone. A light started blinking on the display, and the thing vibrated briefly. He nodded, moving it round in a slow arc.

"What would they focus on?" he said. "The desk? The bed?" There was a flat-screen TV mounted on the wall; as Dave moved towards it the handset started to vibrate in a continuous drone. "Bingo!" he said. "The lens aperture is less than a millimetre across on modern kit; it'll be behind the speaker-grille." He dropped the handset into his pocket and crossed the room. "I'll leave you to it," he said, turning in the doorway. "Smile, kids, you're on camera. Big Brother is watching."

"He's such a perve," Enid said as the door closed behind him. "It's not just me, is it? Don't you think he's weird?" Marley peered into the TV screen.

"Steffi?" he said. "Eva? Are you back there somewhere? Can you see me?"

"Do you think any of it's true?" Luisa said. "Do you think maybe he's just a fantasist?"

"Dave Leaper: international man of mystery," Kate said.

"He's creepy," Enid said. "Don't you think?"

"Tell me exactly what you're wearing," Marley said. "You first, Eva."

***

"This is such fun, baby!" Matty said. "It's ages since we've done anything together, just the two of us." Luisa leaned across the front seats and kissed her mother on the cheek.

"There's a space," she said. "Park there."

Across the road, the Moorish arcades of the market were crowded with shoppers and stall-holders, bright with trays of iridescent fish in beds of ice: the gleaming sheaths of eels and scabbard-fish, dark baskets of clams and mussels, translucent coils of squid; boxes of whitebait as bright as silver coins.

"I'm going to cook lunch for us today," Matty said. "I'm going to grill sardines the way we used to."

"You didn't answer my question, Mother," Luisa said as they dodged through the traffic and into the teeming alleys of the market-place.

"What question was that, sweetheart? We remembered to put the ice-box in the car, didn't we? We'll need to keep the fish cold; I thought we could have a drink at Alberto's when we've finished shopping; or the Yacht Club?" Luisa watched her mother pushing through the crowds, chatting with the fish-sellers.

"You look so at home here, Mother," she said, catching her up.

"I feel like a house-wife again," Matty said, smiling. "The way it used to be, years ago. We'll need tomatoes, and bread, and olives and red wine. We'll do everything the traditional way, the way the three of us used to do it."

"Is Morgan alright?" Luisa said. Matty glanced at her.

"Of course, darling. Why wouldn't he be? He's catching up with emails, or paperwork or something. He's fine." Matty watched the stall-keeper fill a plastic bag with gleaming sardines. "Tomatoes next!" she said, linking arms with Luisa as they made their way through the market.

At Alberto's the waiter led them to a table in the courtyard, the sunlight dappling through a trellis of vines, the air cooled by the splash of fountains.

"Why are the rooms bugged, Mother? Don't you think that's horrible? Why would Arno do that?"

"I wouldn't call it bugging, sweetheart," Matty said. "It's a clinic, after all. The staff need to keep an eye on people; someone could be ill in the night, the nurses would need to know. It's like the baby-alarm you had in your room when you were tiny - we didn't call that bugging!"

The waiter brought their drinks, setting out glasses and dishes of nuts and olives, stepping back from the table with a bow. Matty smiled at him. She raised her glass to Luisa. "I'm going to miss you so much, baby!" she said.

"Don't miss me, Mother. Don't stay here; come back to London with us when we go."

"I haven't told you, have I?" Matty said. "Arno heard you talking about your wrap-party, and he's booked you all rooms in Lisbon, at the Avenida Palace - the best hotel in town! A couple of nights of luxury to celebrate finishing the filming, and then flights back to London, all laid on." She stirred her drink, spearing out a piece of fruit. "Isn't that fabulous? What a place for a party! Isn't he a sweetie!"

"I don't think that's the word I'd choose," Luisa said. "I'm worried about you, Mother. Come back to London when we leave. Why stay here?"

"I know what I'm doing, baby," Matty said. "I'm a grown woman, after all. Arno's a friend; I need you to believe that." Luisa bit into an olive, blowing the pit into the hollow of her fist.

"You know that story he always tells?" she said. "The one about the pig and the melon? The sturdy farmers, the circle of life?"

"Of course I do," Matty said. "That story has a lot of meaning for him; it's important to him."

"Julietta told me the sequel the other day," Luisa said. "Do you want to hear it?"

"What are you trying to tell me, baby?"

"That farm he visited when he was first here, where they offered him the watermelon? That was the compound, that was Arno's clinic; he bought the place."

"I don't understand, sweetheart."

"The pig got the melon," Luisa said. "But Arno bought the farm. He bulldozed everything down and built the clinic. The old farmer took the money and bought a little house in São Miguel. He drank himself to death in less than two years. So much for the circle of life."

"That's horrid, baby. Julietta's got no business telling you horrid stories like that. I don't believe a word of it." Luisa shrugged.

"He wants to own people," she said. "He wants to control them. Doesn't it make you feel weird that there's a hidden camera in your room? How would Morgan feel about that?"

"I don't know that there is one, dearest; I'm sure Arno wouldn't do that to me. So there's no need to tell Morgan."

"Dave showed us where it was."

"That was your room, sweetheart, not mine. And I told you, it's for the nurses. I really don't want to talk about it any more."

"Everybody's leaving, Mother," Luisa said. "I don't mind taking him up on the hotel in Lisbon if that's how he wants to spend his money, but we'll be straight back to London after that. Morgan's off to Paris. Don't stay here by yourself. Come to London."

"I won't be by myself," Matty said. "And you're forgetting my show. A lot of effort is going into that concert, not to mention money. If I want to make it a real success I have to be here flat out, baby, talking to my contacts, networking. I'm seeing the hotel people tomorrow morning."

"It feels all wrong," Luisa said. "Let him help you if you want, but you have to keep your independence, can't you see that? He doesn't own you. What are you doing about getting another flat in Lisbon, by the way? We talked about it in London, do you remember? You haven't mentioned it since."

"Finish your drink, sweetheart. Let's drive down to the beach; I'd like a bit of sea-air before we go back up to the compound."

The wind was coming off the sea, combing plumes of spray off the breakers as they ran up the sugary sand; crowds of children were leaping and shrieking in the surf. Music and charcoal smoke, and the smell of grilling meat, drifted across from the beach-cafés in the dunes. Brightly coloured wind-breaks were snapping in the breeze. Far out in the bay, the white sails of a big yacht dipped and stiffened in the wind like the wings of a gull. They took their sandals off, wriggling lacquered toenails into the sand.

"Listen to me, Mother," Luisa said. "Please think about what I'm saying."

"Arno wants to help," Matty said. "I wish you could accept that. He does a lot for us, you know."

"I'm an artist," Luisa said. "I'll take whatever funding I can get. But I'm not dependent on his money; it doesn't buy him anything beyond a line in the credits."

"I'm the same, sweetheart," Matty said. "I can be paid for, but I can't be bought." She sighed. "But if I did come to London? Say, after the concert? What would I do? Where would I stay?"

"With Morgan," Luisa said. "Obviously! The two of you have got a good thing going, anyone can see that. Leave here, Mother. Go to London; be happy with Morgan."

"You're sweet, baby," Matty said. She stroked her daughter's cheek. "Morgan is precious; I love him dearly." She jumped back with a little shriek as a wave ran up at their feet, subsiding into creamy foam in the glistening sand.

"You could get your career going again," Luisa said. "They loved you in those London jazz-clubs."

"They did, baby, didn't they? Well, who knows? Who knows what the future holds?"

"You're right for each other," Luisa said. "You're both free; you deserve to be happy." Matty looked at her watch.

"Only the rich are free, baby," she said. "Only the very rich. We should be getting back."

Chapter Twenty One

. . .

"Is that a snake?" Howard said. "Over there by the wall?" He stooped to pick up a pebble from the path and skipped it across the dusty ground. The creature stirred, power running through it like a blade in a sheath, and flowed away through a gap in the rocks, sliding like mercury. "At least it's not dead," he said.

They sat in the shade of the cypress trees above the tennis courts. Below them, the German girls were playing Marley and Kate. The bright voices of the kids and the slap and scuff of feet on clay drifted up to them. Luisa and Sam and Enid were leaning on the railings of the veranda at the far end of the courts.

"I think this must be the finals," Morgan said. He watched as Steffi raced back towards the base-line, turning and reaching, floating weightlessly for a moment above the surface of the court.

"There seems to be a sequence: dead animals followed by live ones," Howard said. "The finals of what?" Shouts of laughter rose up towards them from the courts.

"But at least they're getting smaller," Morgan said. "You were right about that." Steffi was crouching at the net, Eva serving from the base-line; she threw the ball high into the air and rose up after it, the elastic smack of the racket following the sweep of her arm a heartbeat later.

"He was big, that snake," Howard said. "One of the lords of life. He could have swallowed the little dog whole." He shaded his eyes, watching the tennis for a moment. "And I have something to expiate," he said. "A pettiness. I must tell Dr. Walters about it."

"Anne is looking so much brighter," Morgan said. "Don't you think? She really seems happy to be here." Howard nodded, watching the players, Marley flailing across the court, his racket wind-milling above his head.

"When she talks about the treatment she's getting, it sounds like CBT," he said. "Dr. Bendt's own version of course, mediated through his guru-stuff: *Regret vanishes! Radiance pours down on us!*" He looked up, squinting into the intense blue of the sky. "Which it does, in fact. Anyway, it's giving her something she didn't have before; she really believes he can work miracles; and maybe he can." He caught Morgan's eye, looking quickly back at the tennis. "I think the nurses are going to win," he said. "Where's Matty this morning? I thought you two were supposed to be playing." Morgan shook his head.

"She's busy with this concert Arno's organising for her," he said. "She's talking to people from the hotels on the coast; I'd have been a real spare prick at that wedding." On the court, the players changed ends, high-fiving. Morgan got to his feet. "I'm going to drive into São Miguel," he said. "Come with me. I feel like having a drink that I've actually paid for myself." As they walked up the hill the kids' voices followed them, rising in whoops and yells as high and clear as play-time in a school-yard.

In São Miguel they sat under the awning at Café Central, opposite the bus-station. Pigeons picked and strutted through the dusty shrubs and flower-beds in the centre of the little square. A group of ex-pats were sitting at a nearby table: elderly British, defeated by heat and alcohol, nursing their beers as their savings melted away.

"What will Matty do?" Howard said. "Will she come to London with you?" A bus was pulling out of the station, shuddering and rattling, the driver gunning the motor and letting out a blast on the air-horn as it crossed the square and set off down the road to the coast.

"I hope so," Morgan said. "I've asked her."

"She won't want to stay here without you once her daughter leaves, will she?" The waiter brought them tall beers, beaded with icy dew, glittering with effervescence.

"No," Morgan said. "I'm sure she won't. It's only this concert."

"I'll come and see her the next time she sings in London," Howard said. "You never know, she might come to Cardiff."

"I wish I knew more people in the music-business," Morgan said. "Any people at all would be a start." Howard set his glass down with a click on the zinc table.

"Look," he said. "That's Dave Leaper, isn't it?" Morgan looked over to where a figure was walking towards the hotel on the right-hand side of the square.

"I don't really feel like talking to him," he said. "I don't think he's seen us." They watched as Dave stopped at the corner of a side-street, answering his phone.

"This is so unreal," Howard said. "How did we all fetch up in this little town in Portugal together?" Dave had his phone crooked into his shoulder and was writing in a notebook. "You walk into a second-hand bookshop in Llanfrychan and pick a book off the shelf," Howard said. He shook his head. "That's all it takes; you fall through a hole. We are on such thin ice."

Dave snapped the note-book shut and crossed the alley, still talking into his phone.

"This is a bit embarrassing," Morgan said. "If he looks over here now, he'll see us."

With a shriek of tyres, a black police-van surged out of the side-street behind Dave and pulled up just ahead of him in front of the hotel. They saw his head flick left and right; he flattened himself against the wall. The rear doors of the van flung open and four riot-police jumped to the ground. They were wearing black fatigues and body armour, helmets and face-masks. Two of them rushed at Dave, swivelling him round and pushing him against the wall; the other two stood back facing out into the square, the muzzles of their sub-machine guns swinging in short arcs.

As Howard and Morgan watched, they wrenched Dave's arms behind his back, shackling him with handcuffs. His face was turned sideways, rasped against the hotel wall. They took him by the shoulders and ran him to the back of the van, lifting him up and scrambling in after him. The two policemen with the guns slammed the back doors shut and ran round to the front of the vehicle. The klaxon came on, whooping and shrieking as the van accelerated away out of the square down the road to the coast.

Howard and Morgan looked at each other. Behind them, in the café entrance, the waiter let his breath out between his teeth in a thin, sustained whistle. On their left, the British couples slowly lowered their glasses of beer. Into the silence, the sounds of the day, suspended in latency, returned to the square like liquid poured back into a jug. From the bell-tower of the church, electronic chimes sounded the unresolved half hour.

"I have to get back to Anne," Howard said. "She'll be finishing the morning session; she'll be wondering where I am."

***

"Baby, I'm distraught!" Matty said. "I thought you were staying over the weekend."

"No, Mum," Luisa said. "I told you, Arno booked us on the evening flight to Lisbon; Jorge is driving us to the airport after lunch. We're checking into the hotel tonight."

"I must have misunderstood, baby," Matty said. She sat down on the edge of the bed. "So this is our last meal together."

"Don't make that tragic face, mother," Luisa said, laughing. "I can't bear it! It's our last meal together here in the clinic, that's all!" She walked to the balcony, brushing through the drapes, looking out at the swimming-pool. Beyond the compound walls the hills ranged away towards Alentejo. "Your room has got the best view," she said, turning back into the bedroom. "I'll miss this place, in a funny sort of way." She sat on the bed beside her mother and put her arm around her shoulders.

"Go on down, darling," Matty said. "I'll catch you up. As it's a special occasion I'd better make myself beautiful."

She walked slowly down the flight of steps to the terrace, conscious of people turning to look up at her. Gusts of fragrant smoke from the charcoal grills were blowing about in the warm breeze. She saw Luisa on the far side of the terrace in a little group with Sam and Enid and Morgan, their heads close together, talking animatedly. Arno took his place at the head of the table, gesturing to Matty to join him. Manólo, Steffi and Eva moved about the terrace, seating the guests. Julietta and Maria were standing back, waiting to serve the wine.

Most of the recent arrivals were up at the top end of the table, and Matty smiled and nodded, introducing herself. She waved to Morgan, further down the table with Howard and Anne; below them, Steffi and Eva were sitting with Luisa and the rest of the kids, flushed and giggling.

"Our artists are leaving us!" Arno said at the end of his address. "They will be missed." He raised his glass towards Luisa and the young people.

"You've been so kind to them," Matty said, looking down the table at her

203

daughter. "They all look so excited today."

"The young are optimistic," Arno said.

"I'll miss them," Matty said. "I must have got in a muddle about the dates. I thought they were staying until Monday. I'm not quite ready for them to go."

"They will have some days in Lisbon," Arno said. "That seemed best to me. And you and I have work to do, in any case." He turned to the woman on his left, making introductions. "My friend Miss James lived in Lisbon until recently," he told her. "Perhaps you have acquaintances in common."

"I'll take my coffee and sit with Luisa if you don't mind, dear," Matty said at the end of the meal. "We have so little time left." Sam moved down the table, making room for her. "Tell me who won the tennis, sweetheart," she said. "I'm so sorry I missed it! I can't believe you're leaving today."

"Have you heard about Dave?" Luisa said.

"What about him, baby? Have you packed? Shall I help you?"

"The bogeymen got him," Sam said. "Just now, in the village. Morgan saw the whole thing." Across the table, Enid wrinkled her nose, sipping champagne.

"What happened?" Matty said. "What did Morgan see?"

"He shouldn't have gone around boasting about kidnapping that German," Enid said. "What did he expect?"

"He was only trying to impress you," Sam said.

"The police arrested him in São Miguel this morning," Luisa said. "Morgan said it was a snatch squad; they jumped on him and bundled him into a van."

"He was wasting his time," Enid said. "I was not impressed."

"I don't understand," Matty said. "What German?"

"I can't remember his name," Enid said. "There was a picture of him with a placard round his neck."

"The Baader-Meinhof gang abducted him," Sam said.

Steffi and Eva got to their feet, bobbing at Matty, turning and beaming at the others.

"We have to work now," Steffi said. "Bye-bye Sam, goodbye Luisa, we enjoy the tennis. Bye-bye Kate! *Ciao-ciao* Enid!"

"We will be sad without you," Eva said. "Kiss-kiss, Marley, goodbye, baby! *Tschüss* everybody! Come back and see us soon! Make another film here, we can be in it for you, we can wear bikinis, Marley!" Blowing kisses, they turned and trotted away on clattering heels. Manólo stood up, facing them with a short bow.

"I also must work," he said. "I say goodbye." He shook hands with Sam, his eyes glistening. Matty took his chair, sitting down opposite Morgan. "What happened, sweetheart?" she said. "What happened to Dave? What is all this?" The guests were starting to leave the table; Manólo was helping an old lady across the terrace. A male nurse appeared in a white tunic, pushing a wheel-chair.

"It was so fast," Howard said. "It was like a trap-door spider, leaping out of its hole. They were so black, it was like they had claws."

"I never really took him in," Anne said. "I never spoke to him. You spent quite a bit of time with him, didn't you?" She looked across at Matty. Arno backed his wheelchair out from the head of the table and appeared beside them.

"Shall we continue?" he said to Anne. "Would you bring your wife to the annexe with me, Dr. Lockhart? Manólo will return her to you later." He set his wheelchair in motion with a faint hiss and whine, then stopped, swivelling to face them. "I have been informed about your friend," he said to Morgan.

"How can we find out what's happening?" Morgan said. "Where's the nearest British Consulate?" Arno shook his head.

"They may not wish to become involved," he said. "I shall make my own enquiries." He turned away. Matty looked across the table at Morgan.

"I don't understand any of this, sweetheart," she said. "It's a mad-house. Who is this German that Enid keeps talking about?"

"The kids think the rooms here are bugged," Morgan said. "Did Luisa tell you that?"

"I wish they weren't going," Matty said. "I wish you weren't going either. Do you really have to leave tomorrow? Couldn't you stay a bit longer, baby?"

"Come with me."

"You know I can't, sweetheart. I have to do the concert."

"I'll have to try and find out where they've taken Dave," Morgan said. "We can't just let him be dragged off like that. I'll find out where the nearest Consulate is and go and talk to them this afternoon."

"Jorge is bringing the car round to the car-port at four," Luisa said. "We need to be packed up and ready to go by then."

"Let me help you pack, baby," Matty said. "We can check you've got everything."

"Safe journey, you lot," Morgan said. "It's been fun. Invite me to the screening; I want my moment on the red carpet." As he walked across the terrace, Luisa caught up with him and gave him a hug, her cheek brushing against his.

"Don't leave Mum here," she said. "Persuade her to come to London with you."

In the car-port, Jorge loaded their suitcases into the boot of the red Mercedes. He was wearing his chauffeur's cap, tipped back on his head.

"So much style, Jorge," Sam said. "Effortless."

"I need a lot of hugs," Matty said. "I'm going to miss you all so much."

"I'm going to get crushed again," Marley said. "Can't I sit in the front?"

"We'll come and listen to you sing in London," Kate said. "Won't we, Marley?"

"Do a jazz-version of *Hotel California*," Marley said. "I'll never hear that song again without thinking of this place. I'm going to miss those lobsters so much."

"Say goodbye to Morgan for me," Enid said. "I hope they don't lock him up too. You're better off without Dave, though, trust me."

"Seems like the bankers got him in the end," Kate said.

"I'll let you know when they give me a date for the screening," Luisa said. "I want you and Morgan to be there." She drew her mother away a few paces as the others got into the car. "Listen Mum, as soon as your concert is over, come to London, leave this place." Jorge started the motor.

"Don't worry about me baby, I'll get along just fine. Don't miss your flight now."

"You can check out any time you want," Marley said. "But you can never leave." Matty stepped back as the car began to move, tyres creaking. Luisa turned and called back to her as they swept under the arch and away down the curve of the track.

"Mum!" she called out. "Mum!" The steel bars of the gates shuddered and began to grind across the entrance. A plume of red dust rolled back towards her on the breeze.

At dinner, Arno gestured towards the seat beside him, but she shook her head.

"I'd like to sit with Morgan if you don't mind, dear," she said. "It's his last evening here, after all." The old man nodded, watching her as she made her way down the table.

"Hopeless," Morgan said. "The bloke here is just the Honorary Consul; the actual Consulate is down the coast in Portimão, but I wouldn't have made it there in office hours." He shifted in his seat as Julietta poured champagne for him. "There's nothing this guy can do on his own authority, but he's going to pass the information on to the Consulate. He said from my description they sounded like *GOE* - Special Operations Group; he thought the local police wouldn't know anything about it. He seemed very nervous about getting involved."

"You tried, sweetheart," Matty said. "That's all you can do."

"I didn't get very far," Morgan said. "I might try and ring the Consulate from Paris."

"How strange to think of you going to Paris," Matty said. "I haven't been there for years." She ran her fingertip around the rim of her glass, watching the effervescence winking in the evening light. "We filmed a TV special there; I sang a number on the deck of a *bateau-mouche,* can you imagine - *under the bridges of Paris with you* - too ridiculous!"

"I can't get it out of my mind," Howard said. "It was like he fell down a black hole. He just disappeared."

"It's so quiet without the kids," Matty said. "It feels so different."

"They told me Dave had shown them where the camera was hidden," Morgan said. Matty looked along the table, catching Arno's eye for a moment. She sipped at her wine.

"It seems a bit far-fetched," she said. "Don't you think so, darling? All a bit cloak-and-dagger?"

"No more than what happened to Dave," Morgan said.

"They were like black spiders," Howard said. "They just swarmed over him."

"You do know how to come up with the most horrible images," Anne said.

"He does, doesn't he?" Morgan said, smiling across the table at her. "How do you put up with it?"

Julietta moved down the table lighting the oil-lamps, brimming pools of yellow light, lemon-scented.

"I'm going to reach the ruined tower tomorrow," Howard said. "If it kills me." Morgan put his lips close to Matty's ear.

"Come for a walk," he said. "Walk down the track with me, just to be

207

outside the compound for a little while." She nodded.

"Later," she said. "I should sit with Arno for a minute; I can't neglect him all evening."

The sky was still pale in the west, but on either side of the valley the hills were dissolving into the night. The track was a ribbon of moonlight, dropping down into the darkness of the trees. She slipped her arm through his. "Send me a post-card from Paris," she said. "Do you know, I'd forgotten all about that show? It was the silliest thing - *Primavera em Paris!* They had me riding a bicycle in the shortest skirt you've ever seen. I can't remember what song I was singing, something saucy, no doubt." She gripped his arm. "I'm sorry baby, I'm babbling, it's just that I don't want you to go." Above them, a shooting-star flared and faded. "Make a wish, darling," she said.

"Your concert is nearly two months away," Morgan said. "I don't understand why you need to be here all that time."

"I have to give it my best shot, darling. I owe myself that much. I have to put myself about."

"And I still don't understand why you're doing it," Morgan said. "I thought you wanted to sing jazz. This is just cabaret, isn't it?"

"It gets me out there," Matty said. "It puts me in front of an audience. I have to make the best of things, baby, tell me you understand! And anyway, I'm committed now. I couldn't back out even if I wanted to."

"When it's over, then. Come to London when it's done. We've been given a second chance, Matty, a chance to start all over again; we shouldn't let it go."

Matty stopped suddenly, clutching his arm with a little shriek. Below the track, something large was moving about in the darkness between the cork-oaks, crunching through the debris of dead wood and dry leaves; there was a sharp crack as it snapped a low branch. They could hear the steady, bubbling rumble of its breath. Morgan peered into the darkness. "I think it's a wild boar," he said quietly. "I was reading about them. They were almost extinct but they've made a huge come-back. There are hundreds of them; every year they move further down out of the hills towards the coast."

"How absolutely horrid," Matty said. "Can we go back to the compound please? I've just realised I'm really not a country girl at all."

"Another counterfactual creature for Howard's collection," Morgan said. "A really big one!"

The clinic was silent and dimly-lit; the girl on the desk buzzed them in, murmuring a greeting, watching them as they crossed the lobby to the lifts. She clicked through a sequence on her keyboard, re-arming the system.

"Come to my room," Matty said. "Just for a little while let's be together."

The long drapes stirred faintly in the night breeze, translucent in the moonlight. She stood on tip-toes to kiss him, her arms around his neck. He buried his face in the hollow of her shoulder, breathing in the scent of her skin. "Look at me, baby," she said, lifting his head towards hers. "Look at me."

Looking over her shoulder, Morgan saw that she had draped a towel over the TV, masking the screen. He sighed, drawing away.

"This doesn't feel right," he said. "And anyway, I've got to make an early start."

"How can you say that to me?" Matty said. "How can you stand there and say *I've got to make an early start*? How can you do that? I deserve better than that, sweetheart, that was cruel." Morgan nodded.

"You're right," he said. "I'm sorry. That doesn't make it right though, being here." He nodded at the shrouded screen. "It doesn't really matter whether there's a camera in there or not. I want to be with you, Matty. We should be together; but not here, not like this."

"I wish you didn't feel like that."

"Do the concert, I hope it's a brilliant success. Then come to London and be with me."

"Don't sound so final, sweetheart," Matty said. "This isn't the last word. Let's take it a step at a time. Maybe we'll meet in Lisbon, don't you think? And anyway, we'll talk, we'll text."

"Of course," Morgan said. She kicked her shoes off and stood on his feet, holding on to his shirt-collar, drawing his face down to hers, whispering into his lips as they moved slowly across the floor in a shuffling waltz-time.

"Whatever happens, remember this," she said. "You're part of my life, Morgan, you're in my heart. You glow in my heart like a jewel. You're like a piece of amber; I'm trapped in there, in the golden light. That will never change."

Chapter Twenty Two

. . .

Manólo crossed the terrace towards her, carrying a cup of coffee. Matty looked up, shading her eyes against the glare as he approached. "With your permission?" he said, and she nodded. He drew a chair up to the table and sat down beside her. Behind him, the water of the swimming pool danced in points of light. He sighed. "I'm a little sad today," he said. "I must work as usual, of course, but my heart is a little heavy." He sipped his coffee, looking at her over the rim of the cup. "The young people, so talented, so full of joy! And Morgan is a fine man, of course. It is very silent without them."

"I know," Matty said. "They took the colour with them."

Julietta appeared through the arcade of the cloisters, breaking into a skipping run as she crossed the terrace towards them. She was carrying a radio, holding it up to her ear, turning it to get a better reception. Tinny music was crackling in the speaker.

"*Escuta-lá, Senhora Matty!*" she said, breathless, beaming. "*Escuta-lá!*" She turned the volume up, setting the radio down on the table. Thin, distorted, Matty heard herself singing *Flirting at the Funeral: Am I still in you, are you still in me?* "*É Kiss FM!*" Julietta said, spreading her arms wide in a gesture of triumph. "*Senhora Matty esta cantanda no Radio Kiss FM Algarve!*"

"It's the original version!" Matty said, smiling. She shook her head, listening to the brassy, Europop arrangement, the bouncing, mindless optimism of the bass-line, the trilling of the backing-trio. Manólo was playing air-bongos on the table top.

"*I'm looking through your eyes at me,*" Matty sang brightly through the little

210

radio, and the backing singers followed her with shrill enthusiasm: *"Deeby deeby deeby dee!"*

"I have heard this was to be organised," Manólo said. "This station has very big listeners in Algarve. It's very good for the concert."

"This is the version from *Reasons not to Kill Yourself,"* Matty said. "I do it a little differently now."

"I myself have bought tickets," Manólo said. "And many of my friends at the club." The backing trio twittered through the final chorus, and the song came to an end in a flourish of trumpets.

"They were so funny, those three girls," Matty said. "They came to Paris with us for *Primavera.* Happy days!" She looked round at the scuff of footsteps on the brick paving.

"Have I missed Morgan?" Howard said. He was dressed for running, a black nylon pack slung over his shoulder.

"He had to make an early start," Matty said. Howard nodded. He slipped his arms through the straps of the pack and settled it on his back, bouncing on his toes. He seemed about to say something, then shook his head and jogged away towards the car-port. Matty watched him until he disappeared through the arch at the far end of the terrace. "Damn!" she said. "I should have warned him about the wild boar."

"I think Dr. Lockhart is a good runner," Manólo said. He started laughing. "I think he run too fast for the pig!"

At lunch she sat beside Arno, chatting to the woman on her right; Mrs Honderich lived in New York, but she knew Lisbon well, and they compared boutiques and favourite restaurants.

"It's a fine city," Arno said. "But here in Algarve we have simplicity, we have balance; we live within the circle." He leaned towards Matty. "Come to the top terrace after lunch," he said. "There are things we should discuss."

She watched the Lisbon flight touch down, a point of light like a star on the hazy margin between sky and sea. Somewhere beyond the compound walls a flock of milking sheep were moving through the cork groves, bells clanking as they grazed the thorny scrub. She listened to the thin shriek of a moped racing along the São Miguel road. Across the terrace, the doors of the lift hissed open and she woke with a start as Arno rolled silently towards her.

"Luisa and the kids will be having a wonderful time in Lisbon," she said, smiling at him. "I was thinking of them when we were talking at lunch. You're very kind, dear Arno!"

"It's my pleasure," Arno said. "Your daughter has a gift, and I am happy to help her." Matty nodded.

"You know how grateful I am," she said softly. She leaned forward and touched his hand. "And they've had such fun filming here," she said. "It all worked out so well, you're such a darling!"

"She should be thinking how to merchandise this film," he said. "She must present it to a bigger audience; we will see how we can help her."

"That would be wonderful," she said. "What would I do without you, dear Arno!"

"Luisa is talented," Arno said. "As you are; I like to make an investment in her. She should come to me with her next film project, I can be her producer." He took her hand in his, turning it over and drawing a circle on her palm with the tip of his finger. "How white you are," he said. "Be careful of the sun."

"Have you heard anything more about Dave Leaper?" Matty said. "Isn't it strange to think that all this started with him?"

"The playwright with a loud voice!" Arno said. His eyes flashed, the blue of the pool. "His name must not be on the film. This man sat under my roof and ate food at my table, and boasted about the death of my friend. I don't wish to speak of him. We will hear nothing more of him; he is gone. I am very disappointed with your friend Morgan that he should bring him here."

"I'm sorry," Matty said. She watched a flight take off, the turning curve of the sand-bar falling away behind it. The dull roar of the jet-engines rolled up the valley towards them.

"Forget him," Arno said. He took her hand again, looking into her eyes. The plane banked away, climbing steeply, following the silver path of the sun across the ocean to America.

"They played *Flirting* on the radio this morning," Matty said. "Such a nice surprise. It's been a long time."

"I know," Arno said. "It's publicity for the concert; we will do much more. There will be posters all over town, in all the hotels. We'll take more radio-time, of course, and space in the newspaper, and I have been talking to RTV Algarve: we can do a little TV slot."

"My goodness," Matty said. "All this for me? Darling, you're like a whirlwind, you sweep me off my feet!"

"I am involved now," Arno said. "There is much to prepare. We need to think immediately about the kind of music you will do. This is urgent; we must not make the same mistakes we made at Flor do Mar. We must find the songs the audience want to hear."

"And the songs that I want to sing," Matty said.

"Hopefully," he said. "But we must start with the audience." He smiled at her. "However, first of all, we need your dress. For this concert we need the most beautiful dress in the world."

Matty found a space directly opposite Rafaela's; the grandson hurried across the road to greet them, fussing round the red Mercedes, setting up the folding wheelchair, stepping back as Arno levered himself lightly out of the car. Rafaela held open the doors of the boutique for them.

"How are you, darling?" she said. "More beautiful than ever! And Arno, my dearest!"

"This afternoon is all for you," Arno said to Matty. "The shop is closed to anyone but us."

"Such luxury!" Matty said. "I adore it! You're spoiling me so much, baby!"

Rafaela and the two girls brought swathes and bolts of silk and shimmering satin, armfuls of creamy lace, plumes of feathers, ropes and chains of jewellery. Half-naked, Matty was lifted on tip-toe and turned and posed, her arms raised and lowered, sheathed and unsheathed in iridescent rainbows of cloth. Rafaela gathered folds and pleats and pinned them up, and stood back, and rearranged and pinned again. From time to time she added detail to the sketch-pad she was working on, taking it across the room to show to Arno. He nodded, glancing at it, watching Matty as she twirled and pirouetted in front of the mirrors. "I'm glad I'm wearing my best knickers!" she said, blowing kisses at him.

"Beautiful," Arno said. "Bravo! We come back for the first fitting next week."

They drove to the Yacht Club. "This afternoon I'm seeing no patients," Arno said. "It's just for you and me." The manager led them to the Members' balcony at the top of the Club House, looking down on the main terrace. "Jorge will come down and drive us back," Arno said. "I would like us to drink some champagne together."

"I'd like that too," Matty said. "You're very good to me, dear Arno. The dress is going to be beautiful."

"And you will be beautiful in it."

"Darling, you have a way with words."

Someone called up to them from the lower terrace, and Matty looked down, recognising Lucinda de Gaia in a group at the bar. "*Ciao* Lucinda, darling!" she called out, turning to Arno. "Do you remember Lucinda? She was at the clinic last year?" He nodded.

"Of course. And I have seen her more recently," he said.

"Where is the handsome Morgan?" Lucinda called up. Matty glanced at Arno.

"He's gone home, of course," she called back. "He has his own life to lead. *Ciao-ciao,* sweetie!" She turned to Arno, leaning back in her chair. "Such a gossip, that woman," she said. "Always trying to make trouble." The waiter brought champagne, the silver bucket beaded with icy dew.

"Morgan is not good for you," Arno said. "You don't see him any more. He has no passion in him; can you not see that? He is inert. Also he has no power, he has no standing in the world. He cannot protect you. Forget him."

"Sweetheart, I don't need protection," Matty said. "Not while I have you." She raised her glass. "Chin-chin, baby, here's looking at you!" Arno touched his glass to hers.

"To us," he said. "We can do great things, you and I. We should be together."

"Of course, darling, always!"

"You will see, Matty, next year, when we open the new clinic at *Palacio das Sombras:* such opportunities!" He leaned back in his chair, looking up into the deepening blue of the sky. "Our world is so rich," he said. "So radiant, so full of joy."

Matty's phone trilled an alert.

"*Off to Paris first thing tomorrow,*" Morgan had written. "*I walked through the Park this afternoon, along the Serpentine. London is empty without you!*" She deleted the text, glancing at Arno.

"That was Luisa," she said. "They're having a wonderful time, they love the hotel." She put her hand over his. "You're so generous, darling," she said.

"Let's go back," he said. "There is something I want to show you." He spoke into his phone. "*Esta-lá com o Mercedes? Alles gut.*"

At the compound, they took the elevator up to Arno's private apartments at the very top of the main block. "I have been making changes," he said.

The lift doors opened directly into the dazzling space of the penthouse. On two sides, north and west, the walls were armoured glass; Arno touched a recessed screen, and muslin drapes floated down, like clouds rolling down the blue of the sky. He touched it again, and a section of glass wall slid silently aside, opening onto a balcony. Matty stepped out into the sunlight. Far below, in the golden light of early evening, in the lengthening shadows, the compound lay spread out in all its intricate geometry of roofs and terraces and trellised vines, shaded courtyards and walled gardens; the vivid acrylic of the pool, bright splashes of scarlet and purple bougainvillea, the dark crowns of palm trees nodding in the heat, the slim rise of cypresses. A tiny, foreshortened figure in a black dress, Julietta or Maria, she couldn't tell which, hurried across the pool terrace and through the arcade of the cloisters.

Arno rolled out onto the balcony beside her. "There is more," he said, smiling. "Come with me, I will show you everything." She followed him across the blond oak floor to a heavy door, set in an ornate frame of carved stone. Arno motioned her forward and she walked through into the master bedroom, cool and white, further doors opening off it.

"This is beautiful," Matty said. "What a lovely place you've made here."

"I am glad you like it," Arno said. He moved past the double bed to a door on the far side of the room. "Look," he said, opening it. "Come and see, here is a dressing room, a little bathroom, everything you need! We should be together, Matty."

A grab-handle was set into the wall at Arno's bedside, a heavy rod of brushed steel. Matty ran her fingers along it.

"Why, Dr. Bendt," she said. "This is all so very unexpected!"

"Is it?" he said. "Surely not." Her smile deepened, and she leaned over him, stroking his cheek.

"You're such a sweetheart," she said. "But you're rushing me off my feet! A girl needs a little time to think about these things. And that champagne has gone to my head. You wouldn't want to take advantage of me, would you, baby?"

In her room she showered and did her hair, moving about in a mist of Chanel. She picked out a new dress: Egyptian cotton, dazzlingly white, cut so that it clung and floated, trailing after her. At the big mirror she did her lips, glistening, crimson. She dimmed the lights and stepped back to assess the effect, smiling at her reflection.

She sat at the top end of the table on Arno's right, aware of the attention she was getting from the other guests.

"Regret vanishes!" Arno said, looking at her. "Radiance pours down on us!" Julietta and Maria moved down the table, pouring wine, serving the entrées. Opposite her, Mrs Honderich cut curling tendrils of baby octopus into tiny pieces, feeding them to her mother on the end of a fork. From a couple of places further down, Howard raised his glass to Matty.

"Have you heard from Morgan?" he asked.

"Yes," Matty said. She cleared her throat. "No, I haven't. Have you?" Mrs Honderich's mother stopped chewing, the tip of a tentacle clinging to the corner of her mouth.

"Just a text to say he was back in London," Howard said. "He says he's missing everybody. You're looking fabulous, by the way."

Anne trailed her fork across the plate, watching the beads of golden oil that followed it.

"Morgan doesn't stay anywhere for very long," she said.

The hills were dissolving into the night sky, the first stars beginning to flicker. The chorus of cicadas modulated, the singing becoming hesitant, softer and sweeter. Julietta and Maria lit the lamps. Arno put his hand over Matty's, looking into her eyes. She touched his cheek, leaning forward and whispering into his ear.

"Give me a little time, sweetheart," she said. "You move so fast! I need to let it all sink in. I won't keep you waiting forever." Arno nodded.

"I know how to wait," he said.

***

Julietta brought breakfast to her room, drawing open the drapes and setting a tray down on the bedside table: cherries, figs and sweet rolls, dark coffee in white porcelain. Matty sat up and the girl plumped up the pillows behind her head.

"You're spoiling me, sweetheart," she said, half-asleep, sipping her coffee. Her phone was vibrating on the desk; Julietta handed it to her.

"*I didn't wake you, did I?*" Morgan said. "*We're an hour ahead here. We've just got off the Eurostar.*" Matty blew a kiss at Julietta as the girl left the room.

"No, baby, I've just been brought a delicious cup of coffee. It's a beautiful day here. Are you surrounded by American teenagers?"

"*A bus-load of them. Do you miss me?*"

"Of course, baby, how can you ask?"

"What are you doing today? What are your plans?"

"You know, sweetheart, the usual sort of thing." She set her cup down on the bedside table and lay back into the pillows. Through the phone she could hear the whooping siren of a police car. "That sounds so French," she said.

"I didn't get that," Morgan said.

"You sound so far away," she said.

"I don't have to be. You could come to London when I get back. The concert's a long way off."

"Did I tell you, they're playing *Flirting* on the radio here?" Matty said. "Isn't that fun? Just like the old days."

"Don't let yourself get taken over, Matty. This isn't the old days."

"I didn't catch that, baby. What did you say?"

"Don't let him try to own you," Morgan said. *"I want you to be free."*

"We're breaking up, darling," Matty said. "I'm losing you."

"Don't say that," Morgan said.

"I can't hear you baby; let's talk later." She heard the sound of a police siren again for a moment before the connection dropped. "Nobody's free," she said.

Arno sent for her to meet him by the pool at the end of the first morning session. Matty watched as Manólo led the group away for hydrotherapy. The old man was signing papers on a clipboard; he handed them back to Steffi and rolled across the terrace.

"I have good news," he said. "We have a TV slot, two minutes. If we can complete it quickly, they'll show it four or five times before the concert."

"Darling, you're a genius!" Matty said. "That's wonderful news! I can't believe it, am I really back on TV?"

"It's a big step," he said. "But it's not all. I have hired a director. He was in retirement, but I persuaded him to come back to work the final time." He watched her for a moment, smiling as she fidgeted.

"Who is it, Arno?" Matty said. "Don't torture me! Who have you got?"

"Vasco Monteiro," Arno said. In the silence, Matty's eyes filled with tears.

"Vasco!" she said. "He directed my first TV Special! How did you even know that? He directed *Viva Bimbo-Boumbo!* How did you find him?" She put her arms around his neck, sitting awkwardly on the frame of the wheelchair. "Arno, sweetheart, you are the loveliest man! I can't believe it, I'm working with Vasco again!" She pressed her lips against his cheek. "*Bimbo-Boumbo* is back!" she said, pecking kisses at him. "Matty James is back on TV! Darling Arno, you have no idea how much this means to me!"

She slipped off the wheelchair, straightening her dress as Julietta approached them. The girl handed an envelope to Arno; he slit it open, scanned quickly through the letter and handed it back.

"*Tudo bem,*" he said. Julietta bobbed and hurried away.

"We did *Viva Bé-Bé!* in 1987," Matty said. "And six months later *Flirting* was at Number One: such a good year! I can't believe I'm going to be working with Vasco again! It's like a dream, it's like getting a chance to start all over again."

"That's exactly what it is," Arno said. He looked at his watch. "Now I have a focusing with Anne Lockhart. I'll see you at lunch. Please sit beside me."

"Of course, darling."

Her phone vibrated in the pocket of her dress as they were finishing the meal. Julietta began clearing away the plates. Across the table, Mrs. Honderich's mother had fallen asleep. Matty held the phone on her lap, shielding the screen from the sunlight. Morgan had sent her a photo: he was standing on the deck of a *bateau-parisien,* surrounded by students. Behind him, a section of Notre Dame was sliding by: a rose window, flying buttresses. Looking up, she caught Arno's eye.

"Something important?" he said. She shook her head.

"My agent, Isabella," she said. "Nothing interesting." She touched his hand. "Sweetheart, can I take the Mercedes out this afternoon? I want to go for a little drive up into the hills. It'll help me to collect my thoughts."

"Please," he said. "Of course."

"After all, there's a lot to think about."

"Do all the thinking you need, dear Matty," Arno said.

***

At the bottom of the track she stopped the car. To her right the two-lane country road tunnelled away into the heat, straight and dusty-white on a rising incline until it puddled into mirages in the middle distance, pools and eddies of tormented air.

Matty opened Morgan's text and enlarged the image: a row of excited faces, students linking arms and waving, Morgan in the centre smiling for the camera. Zooming in closer, she looked into his eyes; they were dark, unfocused, dissociated from the busy scene around him. She called his phone, going through to voicemail.

"Darling Morgan," she said after the tone. "You look so handsome on that boat, I wish I was there: *under the bridges of Paris with you, I'll make your dreams come true!*" She paused, wondering if he would hear the cicadas singing in the dry scrub when he listened to the message. "I'm getting very excited about the concert," she said. "I'm doing a promo on TV, can you imagine! Couldn't you come to the concert? It would be so lovely to see you in the audience, like I did that first time, at Jimmy's Place." With the air-conditioning off, the heat of the afternoon was pressing her down into the hot leather of the seats. "It seems so long ago already," she said. "Bye bye, baby."

She started the car and the cooling came back on in a soft roar. Swinging right, she drove slowly through the heavy, scented afternoon. The low hills were breathing softly, warm gusts of wild thyme drifting across the road. At the vanishing point, where the road disappeared into the foothills, something was solidifying in the vortices of rising air, a dark shape beginning to organise itself out of formlessness, a compact column, rhythm flicking through it like a flashing light.

Matty accelerated, dust rising behind her, and a moment later recognised Howard, pounding along the road, head down, his back-pack bumping and shoving at every footfall. He didn't hear the car until she slowed up alongside him. He broke his stride, jolting into a walk, tripping over his feet. His face was white with dust, scored by pink trails of sweat, his eyes red-rimmed and streaming.

"Sod it," he said. "Give us a lift, will you? If you drive me to the tower I'll run back. It might be a bit cooler by then." He threw his pack into the back of the car and climbed in beside her. "Where are you off to?" he said.

"Nowhere in particular," Matty said. "Where's this tower of yours?"

They parked in the shade of a battlemented wall, blocks of dressed sandstone crumbling back into the red earth, and walked through a horse-shoe arch under the vaulted brick ceiling of the gate-house. On the far side of the open space beyond, the broken shaft of the watch-tower rose into the blue of the afternoon, untidily thatched by an abandoned stork's nest.

"Look out for snakes," Howard said. "This place is crawling with them." Matty took a few tripping paces through the thorny scrub under their feet and scrambled up onto a square block of stone.

"I'm not really dressed for snakes," she said, looking down at her bare legs and open sandals. A lizard flickered across the face of the stone and she jumped, going up on tiptoes. Howard stepped up onto the block and sat down, drumming his heels on the edge of the stone. He brushed down the dusty surface with the flat of his hand and gestured for Matty to sit beside him.

"This place was built during the Almoravid Caliphate, in the 11th Century," he said. "It took me two attempts to get here; it's bigger and further away than I thought. That must be a metaphor for something." He unhitched the back-pack, stretching and rolling his shoulders. "Anne's very happy here," he said. "She thinks Dr. Bendt is doing wonderful things for her."

"I'm glad," Matty said. "I'm sure he is. He has a gift; everybody feels it."

"Do you think he arranged for Dave Leaper to be picked up?"

"That's a strange question, sweetheart," Matty said, looking at him. "Why would you think that?" Howard shrugged.

"Something Morgan was saying," he said. "How's he getting on in Paris, have you heard?"

"What did Morgan say?" Howard shook his head again.

"Things he talked about with Dave," he said. "Terrorism, revolution, assassination, that kind of thing."

"As you do, of course!" Matty said.

"It's just that Arno seems like the kind of man who gets what he wants."

"What does that mean, darling?"

"That he can make things happen," Howard said. He looked up into the bowl of sky above them, shading his eyes. "Is that an eagle?"

"Isn't that why you and Anne are here, because he can make things happen?" Matty said.

"Dave Leaper had something to do with it too," Howard said. "He made a bridge between two worlds; maybe he fell into the gap between them." He narrowed his eyes, squinting into the glare. "It is an eagle," he said. "But it's you and Morgan, all those years ago; we're all here because of you two."

"He just sent this from Paris," she said, showing him her phone.

"Enigmatic as always," Howard said. "Or do I mean opaque?"

"Lean in," Matty said, shifting herself across the stone until they were touching, hip to hip. She put her head on his shoulder and held the phone out at arm's length. "There," she said, straightening up. "That's on its way to him now."

"I wonder what would have happened if I'd come to Lisbon with you," Howard said. "There'd be old photos of the three of us, smiling into the camera; train tickets, city maps with favourite cafés marked on them; addresses of people we never met again, relentlessly cheerful postcards: a whole counterfactual past."

"Surely life isn't that random?" Matty said. "People make choices, don't they? I choose what happens to me." Howard looked at her. She shrugged. "Or maybe I have no choice," she said. "I suppose it comes to the same thing in the end."

"I think you should choose Morgan," Howard said. "Choose Morgan over Dr. Bendt."

"I know we go back a long way, darling," Matty said. "But don't you think that's a teeny bit personal?" She got to her feet. "I'm too hot," she said. "I need to get into the shade." She looked down at the tangle of undergrowth around the stone. "Oh God," she said. "I'd forgotten the snakes, how horrible." Howard shouldered his pack and dropped to the ground.

"Follow me," he said. "Walk in my footsteps; I'll clear the way." She held on to the strap of his pack as they crossed the yard into the shade of the gate-house.

"Thank you, darling," she said. "That was sweet of you, you're such a gentleman!" She kissed him on the cheek. "I didn't mean to sound cross. Morgan is precious; I love him dearly." She slipped her arm through Howard's, patting his hand. "But I have to think about my career too," she said. "You can see that, can't you? I have to follow my star." She took a breath. "At any rate, I have to make the best of it. I have to keep on flirting at the funeral, like the song says."

"People slip away," Howard said. "You have to hold on to them, or they slip away." He walked through the vaulted archway of the gate-house into the dazzling afternoon light.

"You can't hold on to them," Matty said, hanging back inside the key-hole of the arch. "They slip away anyway." There was a slight resonance in her voice, a hollow echo. Howard turned, looking back into the darkness.

"Don't say that," he said. "Sometimes you get a second chance; you can choose a different path through the woods." Matty touched the side wall of

221

the vault; the brickwork was cool and smooth. Howard was framed in the archway, as brilliantly lit as on a stage.

"Morgan said you were like Aladdin," she said. "You found the magic lamp, and all of this appeared." She gestured invisibly in the dark. "The gorgeous palaces, the princes and princesses, the caverns full of treasure. But none of it's real. It all melts into air, into thin air."

"The cloud-capped towers," Howard said, looking up to where the watch-tower rose above the battlements. "Not for Dave Leaper, though. He's in an antechamber of Hell; it's real enough for him." He drew a breath, shifting the weight of his pack. "Anyway, Morgan is real; in Paris, admittedly, but real all the same."

"He said we could start all over again," Matty said. "But that's just what you can't do. You can adjust, you can change direction, but you can't get the past back."

"Not the same past," Howard said. "A different one." He waited, the cicadas counting time around him. "Are you still there?" he said.

"You can't repeat the past," Matty said. "Look at Dave Leaper, trying to re-play the revolution. Look what happened to him." Her voice was faint and hollow, as though she had stepped further back into the vault. "I'm living my life for the last time," she said.

"Then keep Morgan in it," Howard said. "Even if I am being too personal." He watched as Matty appeared from out of the darkness, squinting in the light. She put on her sunglasses. Howard watched his reflection in the lenses.

"I need to get away from here, sweetheart," she said. "This place is making me far too serious, just listen to me!" She shuddered, a theatrical wiggle of her shoulders. "Do you think it's haunted?" She touched his cheek. "You're sweet, Howard," she said. "Don't worry about me. Did I tell you, I'm doing a TV promo for the concert: imagine, Matty James is back on TV! So maybe you can repeat the past!" She walked over to the Mercedes. "Let me drive you back," she said. Howard shook his head.

She watched him in the rear-view mirror as she drove away from the fort, bobbing in the heat as though running on the spot, dropping down through the narrowing aperture of the road, a figure seen through the wrong end of a telescope until he was lost in the rolling dust.

At dinner, Matty was aware of Anne watching her from where she was sitting with Howard, a few places down the table. Several times she looked up to find the other woman's eyes on her.

"Howard says you've heard from Morgan, in Paris," Anne said.

"Just a quick text," Matty said. "He's busy with his students, going up and down the Eiffel Tower, I expect." She could feel her phone vibrating in the pocket of her dress. She turned to Arno, patting his hand. "I'm so excited about the dress that Rafaela is making," she said. "I was thinking about it this afternoon. It's going to be beautiful!"

"I think so, *liebchen,*" Arno said. "I think it will be."

"*Liebchen!*" Matty said. "What a pretty word! What does it mean?"

"It means sweetheart," Arno said softly. "It means darling."

"What a lovely word," Matty said.

"I didn't tell you," Arno said. "I had an email from Vasco Monteiro this evening. He flies in on Tuesday, we'll meet him at the RTV studios Tuesday afternoon."

"Oh baby!" Matty said. "Do you have any idea how excited that makes me feel?" Her phone was vibrating again.

In her room, she showered and put on a cream silk robe. She walked out onto the balcony, into the cool silence of the night. Very faintly, the electronic chimes of São Miguel carried to her on the breeze, sounding midnight. She turned back into the room, switching her phone off and dropping it into the drawer of the desk. The corridor was dim and silent, dark mirrors recording her briefly as she passed, the robe flowing around her. She took the elevator to the penthouse floor.

"What was that word?" she said. "The one that means sweetheart?"

"*Liebchen,*" Arno said. Matty opened the robe, slipping it off her shoulders and letting it fall to the floor.

"*Liebchen,*" she said, laying herself down beside him on the bed, looking down the length of their bodies, his dark angularity, his parched dryness, feeling it suck at her.

"You are sweet milk," Arno said. "And cream." He touched her, sending a shiver running through her; he drew his hand down over the soft rise of her stomach. "And strawberries; you are wild strawberries, you are sharp and sweet."

***

She had a missed call from Luisa, and three from Morgan. She took her phone out on to the balcony and called her daughter. Across the compound, at the top of the highest building, the armoured glass of the penthouse windows was catching the sun.

"*We're leaving this afternoon, Mum,*" Luisa said. "*We have to be at the airport at one thirty. I wanted to say goodbye.*"

"Did you have a good time, sweetheart?"

"*It was fun,*" Luisa said. "*Thank Arno for us. When are you coming to London?*"

"I will, baby, of course. He'll be so pleased."

"*We'll be about a month editing,*" Luisa said. "*They may give me a screening quite soon after that. I want you and Morgan to be there.*"

"Guess what, baby, I'm going to be on TV! Isn't that exciting?"

"*Did Morgan get away OK? Where is he now? Tell him about the screening. Will he be in London next month?*"

"He's in Paris, baby. I'm doing a promo for the concert, can you imagine? I'm so thrilled about it!"

"*I hate to think of you there on your own. Come to London.*"

"I'm not alone, sweetheart."

"*It was different when we were all there, but it's a creepy place, Mum, you know it is. Is there any more news of Dave?*"

"Listen to me baby," Matty said. "I'm being given a second chance. Music was given to me, it's a gift. And now I'm being given my audience back. I can't turn that down, you can see that, can't you?"

"*Jazz was given to you,*" Luisa said. "*Not cabaret in cheesy golf hotels. You should be singing in London and Paris.*"

"One step at a time, sweetheart. And it's a theatre, not a hotel."

"*I have to go, Mum,*" Luisa said. "*I'll call you from London. Don't forget to tell Morgan about the screening.*"

Morgan hadn't left a message; his last call was timed at quarter to two in the morning.

"*I keep missing you, baby,*" Matty texted. "*I must have been fast asleep when you called last night. Let's catch up soon.*"

Arno had sessions back-to-back all morning and she didn't see him until the midday meal. She sat on his right, at the head of the table. As Julietta cleared the plates, he stroked Matty's hand, running his fingers up the inside of her arm, resting them lightly in the hollow of her elbow.

"My mother is much stronger today, Dr. Bendt," Mrs Honderich said from across the table. "Almost her old self." Arno nodded.

"I see it," he said. "I see the woman that she was; she is coming back to us."
The old lady opened her eyes, turning her head slowly towards the sound of
his voice. A few places down the table Anne put her hand over Howard's; she
looked across at Matty, catching her eye for a moment before turning away.

They took coffee in the walled garden; Arno sat with Matty in an arbour
shaded by jacaranda trees, a little apart from the rest of the group.

"Luisa called this morning," Matty said. "They had a wonderful time in
Lisbon, they're so grateful to you, sweetheart! She sends you lots of love!"
She looked up, watching an aeroplane draw a razor-cut of silver across the
blue. "She'll be back in London by now," she said. "Perhaps I'll call her this
evening." Arno put his hand over hers.

"You should move your things to the apartment," he said. "You have
everything you need there."

"But I love my little room, darling!" Matty said. "I couldn't bear to leave
it!" She leaned towards him, lowering her voice. "And I love padding about
in the corridors in the dead of night, so romantic, taking the lift to the top
floor, it makes me feel like a teenager!" Arno shook his head.

"You should be in the apartment," he said. Julietta set the coffee out on
the table, glancing at Matty with a quick smile.

"*Obrigada, menina,*" Matty said. She turned to Arno. "I've had a wonderful
idea," she said. "We can hire Gil and Ernesto!"

"Gil and Ernesto?" Arno said. "Who are Gil and Ernesto?"

"You remember, darling, the musicians at the Flor do Mar. They were the
only good thing about that ghastly evening! Gil especially, we were so good
together!"

"I don't think so," Arno said.

"We could really read each other," Matty said. "We didn't need explana-
tions, we just got each other. That's the most important thing in jazz." She
looked at him. "Sorry, darling, what do you mean: *you don't think so?*" Arno
lifted the tiny cup of coffee to his lips.

"I told you we must learn from our mistakes," he said.

"But sweetheart, the band was the only thing that wasn't a mistake. And
little me, of course! The audience were just frightful, what can you do with
people like that?"

"We must find the common ground," he said. "You are not there to sing
to other musicians. I've been thinking about your career, you need a new

approach. You need to make a big impact. You need colour, and light! No more singing in little clubs; no more singing to twenty people in London. Put that behind you, finished!"

"You have to be true to yourself," Matty said. "You have to follow your star. That's the only thing that matters." Arno shrugged.

"I have a group session now," he said. "We'll discuss all this again."

Chapter Twenty Three

...

"Finally!" Matty said. "We keep missing each other! Is this a good time?" She settled herself in the lounger, the phone tucked into the hollow of her shoulder as she sipped her drink. Below her in the marina, yachts and power-boats stirred at their moorings. "Guess where I am!" she said.

"Yes, it is," Morgan said. *"The students are running around the Louvre, they're on an unguided visit. Unless they get themselves into trouble I've got a free hour. I'm off for a beer."*

"I'm at the Yacht Club," Matty said. "On the terrace; I'm sitting at the same table we sat at. I miss chatting with you."

"That's easily fixed."

"So where are you, sweetheart? Tell me exactly where you are. I want to picture you there. Is the sun shining?"

"I've just walked through the Tuileries," Morgan said. *"And right now I'm crossing rue de Rivoli. "What are you doing at the Yacht Club?"*

"The Tuileries!" Matty said. "That's where we filmed the bicycle song in *Primavera*! I was telling you about it, do you remember? The short, short skirt! What did you just say, baby?"

"What are you doing at the Yacht Club?"

"Thinking of you, sweetheart! No, seriously, I've got a fitting in half an hour; Rafaela is making me this fabulous outfit for the concert, it's the most beautiful dress you've ever seen!"

"How's that all going, the concert?"

"I've got to tell you about Tuesday, baby, too bizarre for words!" In the marina an out-board motor started up, someone gunning the engine in shrill bursts. "Did I tell you, Arno hired Vasco Monteiro to do the TV slot, the promo for the concert? I was so thrilled! He directed *Viva Bé-Bé*, my first TV special! I couldn't believe it! So on Tuesday Arno and I drove down to meet him at the studio." In her phone, disembodied traffic surged through Paris. "I hadn't really thought about it," she said. "But of course, we did *Bé-Bé* in 1987, how many years ago is that? It's too awful, isn't it? The years flick by like a calendar in the wind, like one of those weepie old movies!"

"Just a second," Morgan said. *"I nearly lost an argument with a bus then. Go on."*

"Anyway, dear Vasco was such a handsome man, I never forgot him, a real silver fox! But he was in his late fifties or early sixties when we did *Bé-Bé,* so you can imagine! He must be eighty something, he's been retired for years, he walks with a stick, two sticks, actually! So there I was, in the RTV studios, with these two ancient men, combined age pushing two hundred!" She paused, listening to Morgan's laughter. "He isn't senile or anything," Matty said. "He was on the ball, and he could remember the old days as if they were yesterday." She sighed.

"What is it?" Morgan said. *"Go on, I like it."*

"That's just it," Matty said. "He's stuck in the old days, he hasn't moved forward a single day since the eighties. His mind is full of sequins and mirror-balls and feathers. And his taste in music, oh baby! Drum-machines! Synthesisers! The whole electro-pop thing, too awful! So here I am, stuck with these two old men, one on wheels and the other on sticks; one of them knows nothing about music and the other is in a time-warp where it's always 1987, and they both think they know what's best for me!" She started laughing. "It's not funny though, sweetheart!" she said. "They both want to manage my career. Stop laughing, Morgan, I'm in despair, if you really want to know!" She waited for him to say something. "Where are you now?" she said. "Is the sun shining?"

"Just walking into Place de l'Opéra," Morgan said. *"And it's a beautiful day. Go on with your story."*

"The two of them got on like a house on fire," Matty said. "They're talking about making Vasco artistic director for the whole concert. Can you imagine? Arno thinks you can solve any problem just by throwing money at it, and Vasco has the most awful taste; what a lethal combination! No doubt what they'd really like is a line of chorus-girls behind me, in silver spandex, robot-dancing."

"With fixed, expressionless faces," Morgan said. *"And German accents."*

"Exactly, baby! I knew you'd understand! Can't you just see it, too awful!" She heard him say something away from the phone, and a voice murmuring a reply, the clack of footsteps on the pavement, the scrape of a chair being pulled up. *"I'm just getting a beer,"* he said. *"I've earned it this week. Nice kids, but I've been having big problems with the senior teacher."*

"Did you, baby? Anyway, we've hardly discussed the playlist," Matty said. "We're going to argue about everything, it's a nightmare! We talk in a mixture of English and Portuguese; Vasco's English isn't very good, and nor is Arno's Portuguese; but Vasco speaks German, which I don't, of course, so there's always someone feeling left out of the conversation, and a lot of the time the two of them switch into German and ignore me altogether. Don't laugh, Morgan, it's a nightmare!" The Yacht Club waiter paused at her table; she shook her head, holding her hand over her glass. "It's nice to hear you laugh, though," she said.

"Me too," Morgan said. She heard the faint click of a glass being set down; from further away, the two-tone whooping of a police siren. *"Merci,"* Morgan said. *"Listen, Matty, give it up, this isn't doing you any good. This isn't what you should be doing."*

"I can handle it, darling; I need to assert some control, that's all."

"How will you do that?"

"It isn't perfect, but it's a platform," Matty said. "A launch-pad. I have to work with what I've got, and anyway I couldn't possibly back out now."

"Why not?" Morgan said.

"Perhaps this concert will be a teeny bit cheesy, but it'll get a lot of attention," she said. "It'll lead to better things. Arno's been talking about organising something in Lisbon, playing to a more sophisticated audience." She waited for him to answer. "And I'll insist we hire a younger director next time," she said. "Say something, sweetheart. I'm committed to this, I can't get out of it. Too late to stop now."

"You're compromising yourself," Morgan said. *"You're going in the wrong direction. Believe in yourself; you'll get gigs, they don't have to be massive. Play the 909 again, and Jimmy's Place."*

"I'm taking the only way forward that I can see," Matty said. "I don't have a choice, I have to be realistic. I have people who depend on me. I don't have your freedom, Morgan."

"You know, for a moment," Morgan said, *"when you were laughing then, you sounded as if you'd got free."*

"When I'm talking to you I feel free, sweetheart," Matty said.

"And for one moment," Morgan said, *"I thought you were about to tell me that you'd changed your mind, that you were coming to London."*

"You know I'd love to baby. You know you're in my heart, I meant every word of that. But this is my career, I have to go where it takes me." She waited as the Lisbon flight passed overhead, hanging low in the sky, obliterating every other sound. "Another thing Arno and I have been talking about is a new DVD," she said finally. "Professionally produced: a top studio, the best musicians, I'd have complete control of the material. I can't let a chance like that go by," she said. "You can see that, baby, can't you? I have to follow my star." The aeroplane was crossing the sand-bar, banking steeply over the sea as it gained height. "Can you hear me, sweetheart?"

"You're not planning to come to London at all, are you?" Morgan said. *"That isn't where your star is leading you, is it? Are you sleeping with him yet? Or are you holding out for a better deal?"*

"What did you say? What a horrid question. Why do you ask me that?" Matty shook a cigarette out of the packet, clicking the lighter half a dozen times before it caught.

"Something Anne was saying," Morgan said. *"You don't have to answer."*

"I should think I don't!" Matty said. She took a long pull on the cigarette. "What exactly has Anne been saying? How dare she? I knew she didn't like me, but this is really too much! I'm sorry she's so ill, but it's no excuse!"

"I mean, there's no need to answer," Morgan said. *"I already know the answer. In any case, they're leaving, did you know that?"*

"Who's leaving? Howard and Anne? I had a long chat with Howard on the weekend, he never said anything. I thought they liked it here. He said Anne was happy here. That spiteful creature!"

"They did," Morgan said. *"They did like it. You changed it for them; can you really not see that?"*

"Baby, please, don't leave it like this," Matty said. "I can't bear it!"

"It's you that's leaving," Morgan said. *"All over again. You're making choices you won't be able to come back from."*

"Don't say that, baby! Please don't say that! Everything will work out fine, you'll see, I promise you it will!" She stubbed the cigarette out. "I have to get to my fitting," she said. "Please don't let's end on such a bad note, sweetheart. We'll talk soon, won't we? Everything will come right in the end, I know it will. Is that accordion music I can hear? How romantic! Darling Morgan,

230

I'm sending you a thousand kisses! Can you feel them, baby?"

A couple of Romanians had stopped by Morgan's table and were grinding out a wobbly version of an Edith Piaf song on squeeze-box and violin. A little girl held out a tin cup, and Morgan dropped a coin into it. He got up and went to the bar to pay for his beer.

***

He bumped his suitcase up the steps of the Underground and out into Praed Street, joining the crowds of displaced travellers, journeys beginning or coming to an end, converging and dispersing around Paddington. His phone picked up a signal again, beeping a voicemail alert at him.

"Welcome back, Morgan," Angie's voice said in his ear. *"How was Paris? When are you bringing your paperwork in?"*

In Star Street, at the traffic lights, music was thumping out of an open sports-car, a grey z4, Aretha doing *Dark End of the Street: They'll never find us! They'll never find us!* The lights changed, and the car accelerated away with a brief shriek of tyres. The wheels of Morgan's suitcase clicked and rumbled in the narrow street.

There was an empty vodka bottle on his front doorstep. He picked it up and dropped it into the bin in the lobby. As he let himself into his flat his suitcase caught the edge of the kilim, dragging it across the parquet floor. He pushed his case through the bedroom door and straightened out the rug. The original copy of *Red Hammer* was where he had left it on the kitchen table; the cover soft and scuffed with age, the lettering of the title still an intense crimson, as bright as lipstick, as vivid as if it had been printed yesterday. He opened the book.

"As the lights come up on a stretch of dusty road," he read, *"we hear the sounds of a bus pulling away from a stop - the roar of the motor shifting up through the gears, quickly fading. Loud buzzing of cicadas."*

There was a stale smell in the kitchen, which he tracked to something wrapped in tin-foil, rotting in the bin. He leaned over the sink and raised the window a couple of inches, where it jammed, as always.

☙

A NOTE ON THE AUTHOR:

Chris Keil is the author of two acclaimed novels: *The French Thing* (Carreg Gwalch, 2002) and *Liminal* (Alcemi, 2007). He has held literary residencies, workshops and masterclasses in Europe and the United States, and as a university lecturer has taught courses on memory, identity and representations of the past. *Flirting at the Funeral* is his third novel.
www.chriskeil.eu

Lightning Source UK Ltd.
Milton Keynes UK
UKOW050754060812

197107UK00002B/7/P